THE JUMP

ALSO BY BRITTNEY MORRIS

SLAY

The Cost of Knowing

Marvel's Spider-Man: Miles Morales — Wings of Fury

THE JUMP

BRITTNEY MORRIS

SIMON & SCHUSTER BFYR

NEW YORK | LONDON | TORONTO | SYDNEY | NEW DELHI

SIMON & SCHUSTER BFYR

An imprint of Simon & Schuster Children's Publishing Division
1230 Avenue of the Americas, New York, New York 10020

Text © 2023 by Brittney Morris
Jacket illustration © 2023 by Kingsley Nebechi
Jacket design by Laura Eckes © 2023 by Simon & Schuster, Inc.

SIMON & SCHUSTER BOOKS FOR YOUNG READERS
and related marks are trademarks of Simon & Schuster, Inc.
For information about special discounts for bulk purchases, please contact Simon & Schuster Special Sales at 1-866-506-1949 or business@simonandschuster.com.
The Simon & Schuster Speakers Bureau can bring authors to your live event. For more information or to book an event, contact the Simon & Schuster Speakers Bureau at 1-866-248-3049 or visit our website at www.simonspeakers.com.
Interior design by Hilary Zarycky
The text for this book was set in Adobe Garamond Pro.
Manufactured in the United States of America
First Edition
2 4 6 8 10 9 7 5 3 1
Library of Congress Cataloging-in-Publication Data
Names: Morris, Brittney, author.
Title: The jump / Brittney Morris.
Description: First edition. | New York : Simon & Schuster Books for Young Readers, [2023] | Audience: Ages 12 up. | Audience: Grades 7–9. |
Summary: The stress of an oil refinery being built in their backyard, threatening their families' livelihood, prompts four working-class teens to join a dangerous scavenger hunt where the reward of power could change their families' fates and save the city they love so much.
Identifiers: LCCN 2022037718 (print) | LCCN 2022037719 (ebook) | ISBN 9781665903981 (hardcover) | ISBN 9781665904001 (ebook)
Subjects: CYAC: Treasure hunt (Game)—Fiction. | Power (Social sciences)—Fiction. | Seattle—Fiction.
Classification: LCC PZ7.1.M6727 Ju 2023 (print) | LCC PZ7.1.M6727 (ebook) | DDC [Fic]—dc23
LC record available at https://lccn.loc.gov/2022037718
LC ebook record available at https://lccn.loc.gov/2022037719

To everyone who's sick and tired.
We're going to make it.

Jax

I t's a regular Tuesday morning.

My mama is crocheting, my zaza is washing zucchini from the garden, my sister, Ava, is writing in her journal, and I'm trying to figure out where this QR code clue leads so my team can win this week's cryptology puzzle and stay at the top of the Vault leaderboard.

My fingers fly across my phone keyboard under the table as I stare absentmindedly into my almond-milk oatmeal with raisins and pepitas.

ME: I've looked at everything. Code might be a dead end.

At least I *hope* that's what I typed. Autocorrect gods, take pity on me. Phones aren't allowed at the table, or in the morning before school, but I have a clue to find.

Just as I'm about to let go of my phone, I feel four distinct buzzes in my hand. My phone only buzzes when I get a text in all caps, and the team only texts me in all caps when they've got a lead.

I *have* to look.

"So, Ava-bear," says Mama, setting her crochet project down and leaning her elbows on the table. "How's journaling going?"

Ava sighs and runs a hand through her long dark hair, pulling it all to one side and twisting it around itself. She's only older than me by a couple of years, but she has the cynicism of someone twice her age.

"I mean, it's going," she says, her voice a low early-morning croak. "I'm doing affirmations right now. None have come true, but they're making me more optimistic, I think."

"Good." Mama smiles, tucking a loose strand of hair behind Ava's ear. Mama reaches into the tiny satchel at her hip, and I wonder if I have time to glance at my phone, but she's too fast. She pulls a roller ball out of her bag, takes Ava's wrist in her hand, and rolls the oil gently over her veins.

"Lavender for calm," Mama says, still smiling, "and . . ." She pulls a crystal on a string out of her bag and slips it over Ava's head. "Blue tourmaline for tranquility."

The concentration grooves between Ava's eyebrows melt away, and a smile spreads across her face. "Thanks, Mama," she says.

"I know you don't think they work," says Mama, pulling out another crystal on a string and turning to me, "and you probably won't until you really need it. But even if it only works as a visual reminder of what it represents, it works."

The string goes over my head, and I look down at the pointy purple crystal sitting in the middle of my chest.

"Amethyst today," says Mama, "for protection."

That's a new one.

"Why do you think I'll need protection today?" I ask. She shrugs and scratches around a bandage taped to the inside of her forearm, covering a new tattoo.

"Just a feeling," she says, leaning in and kissing my forehead. "There are a lot of protests going on downtown today—okay, Jujubean? Be careful."

My phone buzzes again.

My heart skips.

I glance at the clock.

7:47 a.m.

Too early to leave for school.

I open my mouth to make an excuse to leave the table besides the fact that I want to go look at my phone. Maybe I forgot my backpack upstairs. Shit, it's on the floor next to me. My phone? Nah. As soon as I stand up, everyone will be able to see its imprint through my sweat-shirt pocket. Maybe I need to pee? Nah, Mama knows that one well.

Before I can think of an excuse that *will* work, the conversation continues.

"She's right," says Zaza, glancing over at all of us at the table and setting a colander full of zucchini on the kitchen counter. "Lots of protests. Everyone's angry right now."

"People are always angry," Ava mutters, shutting her journal and taking a sip of her breakfast tea. "If it's not one thing, it's another."

"Well, today the protests involve the garden," says Mama, "so even *I'm* a little angry. We've had refineries in Puget Sound, but never one smack dab in the middle of a residential neighborhood. And cer-tainly never one that's wiped out a community garden."

Never mind. The puzzle can wait.

Mama's forehead is furrowed, and her fingers whip the yarn around the needle lightning-fast. I clutch the crystal around my neck and wish there was something I could give her to make her feel better through all of this. But all I have are my words.

"I don't think it'll go through, Mama," I say.

"It *is* going through, Jax," Ava insists with a finality that sours my stomach. "The city has officially submitted a notice of intention to repurpose the land."

"But we're in the middle of Beacon Hill," I argue, as if fighting Ava is fighting what's inevitably going to happen to our garden. "Why would they put an oil refinery *here*?"

"Likely because we're by an airport," she grumbles. "How much do you wanna bet Roundworld has a deal with King County Inter-national to supply their fuel?"

"We're also in the not-so-expensive part of Beacon Hill, Jax," says Zaza, carrying the colander to the kitchen table. Before they sit, they lean down and give Mama's lips a quick kiss good morning. Zaza pulls out a kitchen chair and settles into it, peeler in hand, and soon peels begin falling into a bowl in their lap as they continue, "And the garden is a community space. State-provided. Land isn't cheap in Puget Sound like it used to be, so it's fair game for them to take back and repurpose whenever they want."

I can feel my blood warming with rage. How the hell is this legal? Matter of fact, how the hell hasn't someone stepped in to stop this? Some rich company must have a bunch of money to throw at this for environmentalism clout. Maybe one will buy Roundworld out of the land? Protests are great and all, but how has no one from the bottom tunneled in from the inside? Actually, why hasn't the Order gotten wind of this shit? They were there to rat out social media accounts after the Capitol invasion, and after the Taliban took over Afghanistan. Not that Mama's garden is anywhere near the same scale of importance in the world, but . . .

It is in *my* world.

I remember when I was little—maybe seven or eight—walking down the rows with Zaza's hand in mine, planting little yellow and red corn kernels. It was freezing cold that day, and Mama had a big batch of her coconut-milk hot chocolate waiting for us when we finished. We've been to the garden every weekend ever since. Ava will sit with a book among the flowers or do yoga in the community yard. I usually sit at the picnic table with my phone and piece together cryptography clues.

My phone buzzes again, four times. But now I'm distracted. And pissed.

How can the state just take back the garden whenever they want?

We've been using it for years to feed our community in ways the state only *wishes* their public service programs could, and they haven't been interested in it this whole time. Why now? I know why now.

Because now, money is talking.

"I don't see why they don't start taxing these corporations for more money," I say, anger boiling up in me at the idea of losing Mama's garden. Well, it's not really her garden. It's all of ours—the Rainiers', the Browns', the Hansens', and dozens more. We all plant. We all grow. We all harvest. But Mama started it. Before Ava and I were born. When she and Zaza had only just met. I guess that makes the garden kind of like her first baby.

It's where we get most of our food. I look up at our counter, stacked cabinet-high with fresh cucumbers, zucchini, butternut squash, and miniature pumpkins. I can't imagine living without it. We'd have to go to the grocery store instead, where the produce is *way* smaller and *way* more expensive, especially for the organic stuff, and where families like the Rainiers, the Browns, and the Hansens aren't there.

I look at Mama, who's turned her focus back to her crocheting, her fingers whipping the yarn around the needle faster and faster, doing a shoddy job at masking her distress.

I swallow the lump in my throat and rest my hand on the table in front of her.

"I want to protest, Mama," I say.

Zaza puts down the peeler. Ava looks up at me across the table. Mama sets her needle down.

I do. I want to march out there, bandana over my face, holding a sign up that says *Keep your oil out of our gardens*, defending everything my family holds dear, with my middle finger waving in the establishment's face.

"No," she says. "Absolutely not."

"Come on," I argue. "I've got my amethyst on and everything."

"Amethyst isn't a bulletproof vest," says Zaza, soft even though their words are sharp. "It's too dangerous."

"Besides, you're needed here," Mama says with a smile, running her fingers gently along my chin where there's the faintest bit of stubble growing in, not nearly fast enough. "The best way you can help is by voting when you turn eighteen, and by 'being the change' in the meantime."

"I hate that phrase," mutters Ava. "It doesn't mean anything."

"Ava," grunts Zaza.

"It's true!" she snaps. "Nobody knows what 'be the change' means. It's just a platitude beloved by people who don't want *actual* systemic change enacted. Prove me wrong."

"You can only be proven wrong if you believe you can ever be wrong," says Zaza in the brightest, airiest voice possible. I can't help but grin.

"Zaza has a point," I say. Ava rolls her eyes and scrapes the last of her oatmeal from the sides of her bowl. Once the spoon's in her mouth, she's out of her chair with her backpack on her shoulder and headed for the door.

"Well, on that note," Ava says, "you're all coming tonight, right?"

"Wouldn't miss it," says Mama.

Ava's captain of her debate team, and we always go, but I secretly hate it. It's the most boring shit ever. Nobody really wins in the end anyway. Everyone just argues about abstract political and philosophical topics that have no real answer. What's the point?

Bzzzzt. Bzzzzt. Bzzzzt. Bzzzzt.

All right, I can't take this anticipation anymore.

I *have* to know what's up.

Mama gets up to join Zaza in giving Ava a hug goodbye, and I sneak a peek at my phone.

SPIDER: IT'S A 12-DIGIT NUMBER.

My eyes light up, and my heart starts to race. Twelve digits . . . Phone numbers are only nine digits here in the US, but . . . could it be an international one? That would explain it! The QR code embedded in the image we found pulled up a phone number!

ME: TRY CALLING IT. SPIDER, YOU HAVE AN INTERNATIONAL PLAN, RIGHT?

Bzzzzt. Bzzzzt. Bzzzzt. Bzzzzt.

SPIDER: YOU MIND CALLING? BAD WIFI, NO DATA.

Shit.

I'm outta data too, but I can call from my laptop via email for free. I look at the clock. 8:01.

My bus arrives at the corner at 8:10 sharp. If I'm not on it, I'll automatically be twenty minutes late waiting for the next one, and since I'll already be late picking up this clue downtown, I don't have another minute to spare.

I glance up and find Mama standing at the window to watch Ava walk down the front steps, and Zaza shutting the front door after her. I shovel the last bit of oatmeal into my mouth, snatch my bowl off the table, run some water over it in the sink, nestle it in the dishwasher, and dart for the stairs, wiping my hands off on my shirt as I bound all the way up, two at a time.

I dive for my computer, almost falling off the stool that doubles as my computer chair, and scribble my fingers desperately over the trackpad.

The screen finally flashes to life, and I mess up my own password twice trying to log in too fast. Finally I'm in. I click to open the browser. That spinning icon rotates in the middle of my screen. And rotates. And rotates. And spins. And spins. And freezes. And spins some more.

Come on, come on!

While I wait, I look at my desktop, with the black wallpaper behind the icons, and that single white eye in the center, a cat eye–shaped pupil in the middle, and three eyelashes fanning out from the top. The symbol of the Order.

Someone has to tell them what's happening here. They have to know. But how would one even reach them? It's not like they have a "Contact us" page or even a website. Their whole deal is "If you need us, we'll find you."

I sigh, and then I notice that stupid icon is still spinning.

Damn this slow Wi-Fi! Who else is using it right now anyway? Ava just left, Zaza is peeling zucchini, and Mama is probably still crocheting. I growl and jump out of my seat, realizing I'm going to have to reset the modem downstairs. I race for the stairs and fly down to the kitchen again, where Mama and Zaza are waiting for me with confusion written all over their faces.

"Jax, you okay?" asks Mama.

"Yeah! I just forgot something—be right back!" I say, whipping around the corner so fast, I almost forget about the glass cabinet in the hallway—the antique that came from my granny's house across town "before I was even a thought," as Mama says. I dodge the cabinet and make for Zaza's office, where I find the modem. I flick off the switch and count—probably too fast—to thirty, while the internet resets itself. I can't wait to go to college. Even community colleges probably have Wi-Fi more reliable than this.

Thirty!

The switch is back on, and I'm back in the kitchen, rushing past Zaza and hurling myself around the corner and back up the stairs.

"Jax, is this about a puzzle?" hollers Zaza. Well, they don't really holler. I can't imagine Zaza raising their voice to anyone. Wouldn't hurt a fly. Literally. We had one trapped under a jar in the kitchen once, and they actually slipped a piece of paper underneath it and took it outside. But they do call after me, and I feel bad slamming my door with such a short answer.

"Yup!"

But I have a case to solve and a number to dial.

I race to my laptop and sit down a little too hard on the step stool, wincing as I feel the sudden pinch between my legs. If I sit on my own balls one more time on this goddamn stool, I'm going to huck it out the window and sit on the floor.

I open the chat window and find Spider's messages, and type furiously.

ME: AYO IM ON, WHAT'S THE NUMBER?

SPIDER: 1239-7657-29 AND THE NUMBER OF PEOPLE WHO HAVE ASKED TO JOIN JERICHO.

I smirk. He's speaking in code, in case anyone's "supervising" our texts.

So, 1239-7657-29-57.

Yup. Fifty-seven people have asked to join our team. Only the original four have stayed in. Me, Spider, Yas, and Han. The fabulous four. The quintessential quad. Whenever a new person asks to join, we ask what skills they bring, and if they can't offer something we don't already have, it's a no. Not their fault, though. We're already unstoppable. Don't really need any new skills. Spider's our tech wiz with mad connections, Yas is the parkour master who can climb up anything and into anything, Han has a map of Puget Sound locked in his head and knowledge of its history and evolution, and me? I'm the cryptologist— my expertise is piecing clues together. Dialing phone numbers, scanning QR codes, flipping photos upside down to see things from a different angle, unscrambling letters and untangling riddles.

I *live* for that shit.

Now, if my slow-ass tech would just cooperate and let me be great . . .

I open my email and dial, and in the other window, I notice I have a few missed texts from the master group chat. I open it and read while the call rings.

SPIDER: Can anyone dial?

YAS: I'm outta data and the Wi-Fi at the store is too slow for calls. You?

SPIDER: Nah, I'm already downtown with no data. Han?

HAN: Just hung up. Phone number has voicemail message that says "PAC north side, chromedome. Clean up them thoughts."

I hang up my own call, which is still ringing, lean back in my chair, and rest my hands behind my head. I shut my eyes. I think. PAC, huh? Like a political PAC? What does that mean? This is supposed to take us to the final answer—the endgame of this week's puzzle. If we win, we'll have kept up our streak, maintaining our #1 spot on the leaderboard.

HAN: Give up?

My fingers fly back to the keyboard, and my heart thunders. How the hell did Han figure it out first? I'm the cryptologist! Must be a physical location. That's Han's forte—geography.

ME: Wait, you know?? Tell me!

YAS: I've got the first part, headed there now. Over and out.

I'm getting mad now. It's already a given that Team JERICHO is in the lead. We're *so* good, we compete against each other to get to clues first. Our only competition now is each other, and they're about to leave me in the dust.

Because of this slow-ass Wi-Fi.

SPIDER: Nah-uh, Jax—what ya payin?

ME: Spider, so help me, what do you want?

That's how it goes here. You want a clue from the team? You gotta haggle a bit.

SPIDER: Download Pokémon Go and play with me?

I suck my teeth and roll my eyes.

ME: You know you're the only person under 40 who plays that shit anymore, right?

SPIDER: You speak lies! And you better stop insulting the person you need something from.

ME: Fine. Name another price.

SPIDER: I'll settle for summa that sweet garden bounty.

A laugh bursts out of me. Mama's garden is famous around Beacon Hill for being full of fresh produce all year round—produce and nuts and mushrooms. It's kinda cool. People can just go in and grab what they need, free of charge, as long as they're on the email list.

ME: You want some zucchini?

SPIDER: 5 of 'em

ME: They're huge! I can barely carry 3!

SPIDER: Fine, 3. Ok—answer to the first part is this: I think PAC stands for Post Alley Court.

I suck my teeth again. Of course it does. Obvious answer, if I hadn't been so distracted. Post Alley Court is in Pike Place Market, so I'm out of my seat, backpack slung over my shoulder, feet hopping chaotically into my slip-on shoes, and out the window to the roof—the quickest way out of here—before I take a minute to reply via text.

ME: Thanks!

I jump and I'm off, sprinting around the side of the house to the front.

"Bye, Mama!" I holler to the front door.

"Jax, did you go out the window again?" asks Zaza, who surprises me by walking out from the other side of the house straining under the weight of a basket full of something else heavy, which reminds me about my deal.

"Hey, Zaza, can I bring three zucchinis to school?"

"Only if you promise you'll remember the plural of zucchini is zucchini," they say, grinning. They wink a brown eye at me and pull a folded reusable grocery bag from their pocket. "Go grab 'em off the counter."

"Thanks." I grin, bolting back through the front door to find Mama sitting at the table, crocheting again.

"Jax!" she says, jumping at my sudden burst into the room.

"Sorry, Mama," I say, darting to the kitchen counter and stuffing three zucchini into my canvas bag. "Gotta bring these to Spider for a clue trade."

Mama stands and folds her arms, which are covered from wrist to elbow in tattoo sleeves, and smiles at me.

"Tell Spider hi for me. You sure you don't want to take some cucumbers, too? We just picked some out back—"

"You're really bad at negotiating, Mama."

She shakes her head and steps forward, resting a hand gently at the back of my head and pulling me into a warm embrace.

"Negotiation isn't everything, Juju," she says. "Life isn't give and take. It's give and give."

"Yeah, you right," I say with a nod. "Can I go to school now?"

She smirks.

"Sure, school, right. You're *this* excited for 'school,'" she chuckles. "Just make sure wherever you're headed this morning, you make it to class on *time*, okay?"

"Okay," I say, a little pang of guilt finding its way into my throat, knowing I'm lying to Mama's face. I'm already guaranteed to be late, whether I make this bus or not. The question is, *how* late. I turn back to the door.

"And say goodbye to your zaza before you go, okay? They missed your goodbye yesterday and it ruined their whole day."

"Not my fault they were taking a piss when I left!" I laugh.

"Juju!" she says, throwing a nearby dish towel at me.

"Fine." I grin and toss it back. "But I gotta go!"

"All right," she says, and once I've darted back out onto the porch: "I love you!"

"Love you too, Mama! Bye! Bye, Zaza!"

Zaza is bending down to water the herb pots on the porch, but extends a hand up to wave goodbye.

"Love you, Juju!" they say, wiping their beard with the scarf around their neck.

I turn and focus on trying to run with this zucchini bouncing at my hip. The E bus to school comes every ten minutes, but the C bus, which drops off right around the corner from Post Alley Court, comes every twenty, and it's parked at the corner. I hear the hiss of it kneeling as a passenger in a wheelchair rolls through the back door, and the hiss of it standing again.

"Hold the bus!" I holler. I have to make it to Post Alley first. If Han figured out the abbreviation from the voicemail—as much of a genius as he is—others may have found it too, and how am I supposed to let a bunch of people beat me—Jax Michael—captain of Team JERICHO—lead admin of the Vault Cryptology Forum—in an amateur puzzle like this one?

The bus's hazard lights shut off just as I reach the door. I grab the handrail and swing myself up through the door and it slams closed behind me.

My lungs are on fire, and I lean against the wall to catch my breath for a minute.

"You got two twenty-five?" demands the driver. I open my eyes and look at her. Her eyes are flashing at me like I definitely don't have it, and that I'm trying to ride the bus for free, and that I'm costing them tax dollars. I roll my eyes.

"Yeah, I got it," I say, feeling around in my pockets for my wallet, and then gasp as I realize I left it at my desk. I can picture it, next to my mouse.

We're stopped at the light.

"I, uh . . . ," I say, "I swear I have an ORCA card in my wallet at home with thirty dollars on it, I just—"

"You know the rules, son, g'on."

The doors hiss open. I glance over my shoulder at the passengers. The bus is mostly empty except for three: a tired-looking mom in a beanie, breastfeeding a baby and keeping her eyes on the window to avoid conversation, and two men sitting in the front rows across the aisle from each other, both typing away furiously on laptops. All refuse to look at me, so I look back at the driver.

"Please, ma'am, can I pay twice next time? I swear—"

"Off!" she snaps. "Light's green, I gotta go!"

"Hey!" hollers a familiar voice from behind me, and a figure bursts through the door, caramel-colored arm outstretched holding . . . my wallet!

I grab it before I notice who's on the other end, and I'm suddenly staring into the warm eyes of my zaza.

"That makes twice this month, Jax. Keep it up and I won't need a gym membership," they say, giving me another wink and stepping off the bottom step onto the sidewalk again.

"Thanks, Zaza," I say, breathing a sigh of relief. What would I do without them? Without Mama loading my card before I even remember I'm about to run out? "Thanks a million."

Zaza is too out of breath to reply, but their smile says enough as they wave and the doors close. The bus hisses as it moves, back on the road to downtown. I swipe my ORCA card and find a seat toward the front, in the row behind one of the businessmen—techies. They've each got a blue badge dangling at their hip, so they probably work in South Lake Union. They're both so glued to their laptop screens—working before they get to work—they didn't even look at me when I walked past them. Probably thought I'd ask them for a handout or something.

I roll my eyes, slide my wallet into my pocket, and lean my head against the window.

And then I notice it.

A sticker clinging to the top left corner of the window with a picture of an eye. Not just any eye. I'd know that eye anywhere. It's the same symbol as the one on my desktop. It's the symbol of the Order.

My heart flutters, and I can't help but smile. Anytime I see that eye, it reminds me that justice exists. That equity is possible. Why? Because the Order has power. No one knows who they are, or why they do what they do. But they first appeared several years ago, just a few years before I started the Vault.

Everything the Vault is, everything the Vault stands for, is modeled after the Order.

The rules of the Vault? Exactly the rules of the Order.

The law must be obeyed, especially by those in power.

Rules must be followed, especially by those in power.

Fellow humans must be respected, especially by those in power.

The Order are the OG cryptologists. They'll hack into anything for any cause they deem worthy. My little corner of the internet could only dream of measuring up.

My phone buzzes in my pocket.

YAS: Race ya

Dammit. Of course, the parkour master herself is going to race me to this last clue.

ME: You're on

I try to be a good sport when I'm about to lose, especially when it's to a friend, especially Yas.

YAS: Too easy. You on the E line? I'll meet you downtown after I win.

ME: Nah, I'll meet you at school after I win.

I lean my head against the seat and sigh, staring at the ceiling the whole way there, willing this bus to move faster.

Yas

'm about to jump off a building.

Literally.

Why? Because it's fun.

But first, I say a quick bismillah and sprint down Pine Street toward the market, past Westlake Park, which isn't really a park at all. It's an empty stretch of concrete at 4th and Pine with a fountain through the middle. It's beautiful, yes, but calling it a park just feels wrong. There's not a blade of grass to be seen, not that one could tell today. I can't see the ground, because it's covered inch-to-inch in shoes—shoes that belong to protesters holding signs and hollering into the cold Seattle air.

"Renewables! Now! Renewables! Now! Renewables! Now!"

I know better than to run while distracted, but I can't help it. I glance at a few signs when I can as I dodge pedestrians.

KEEP SEATTLE CLEAN!

NO REFINERIES!

NOT IN OUR NEIGHBORHOOD!

And one sign with a giant planet Earth being impaled by a fracking derrick, with a red circle and a slash through it and a caption underneath that reads, "Humanity is a plague."

That doesn't sit well with me. Sure, most of us use way too much plastic and don't conserve water as much as we should, but there are people whose cultures are directly tied to protecting the earth. Like the

Duwamish tribe. If it weren't for them, ecosystems across Puget Sound would be in major jeopardy.

Into Pike Place Market I fly, weaving between clusters of tourists—people pushing strollers and holding hands with their sweethearts, clutching bouquets bursting with red and pink, and cups of coffee from the very first Starbucks.

I don't run into a single one of them.

I'm on a mission, and I've done this too many times to make a mistake.

I dart into an alley and leap up onto a dumpster. From here, I jump and grab the lowest bar of a metal staircase, swing my feet up, and launch my body up over the bar onto the platform. I bolt up the stairs, my soft-bottomed shoes making so little noise, I'm not even concerned that I'm trespassing. I leap up onto the roof and sprint the length of the building, flying past all the tourists below. My white hijab and gray sweater camouflage me against the cloudy sky, and besides, everyone's too busy shopping to notice me.

I race to the end of the building and hurl myself across the gap to the next roof.

Don't think.

Just make the jump.

My feet find the wall on the other side, my hands find the very edge of the roof, and I bounce myself up and over and take off running again.

I count the alleys.

Just now, I ran up the staircase in the first alley, leapt over the second, and I slip down into the third via another staircase. I feel my phone in my pocket, which is why I wear semi-tight but extremely stretchy pants. I need ultimate flexibility, but I also need to be able to feel texts against my thigh.

PAC North Side, the voicemail said.

The staircase I'm standing on descends into Post Alley Court—a long strip of alleyway through the middle of Pike Place Market, the spot with the fresh produce, and the brewery that leads through to Third Street. Just out of smell-shot from the infamously minty, sickeningly sweet gum wall. My feet hit the ground, and I take a deep breath so I don't look or sound like I've been sprinting across rooftops for the last two minutes. I step out into the crowds, and my eyes scan.

I'm looking for the mark.

The Vault—the cryptology forum I head up with Jax, Han, and Spider—bears a symbol that we all know well. A round vault door with a plus-shaped handle and a cobra wrapped around it.

It's usually on a lamppost or a mailbox or some other piece of public property—always someplace that corresponds to the host team's name. The DUCKLORDS team is hosting this week's puzzle, so the sticker should be on something related to water.

Every team has its signature. JERICHO's is—predictably—walls. Or rather, any surface derived from earth. Stone. Concrete. Brick. Clay. Soil.

That's us. Naturally strong together.

My mind turns the next part of the clue over and over.

Chromedome.

Chromedome.

Chromedome.

Something related to R2-D2? Nah, too easy.

And then there's the next part.

Clean up them thoughts.

CUTT.

Cutters? Like the expensive crab place down the street? Nope, that's like ten minutes away, from even the northernmost part of Post

Alley. It's probably not an acronym, then. I sigh in frustration. I'm good at what I do—sprinting like a jungle cat through the city with ease—though I'm no cryptologist. But I glance around and see no sign of Jax anywhere.

Which is great, because now I stand a chance at beating him to the answer.

I navigate the crowds and keep my eyes moving for anything related to the terms "chromedome" or "Clean up them thoughts," turning sideways to slide past tourists. Since so many Seattle residents are new arrivals, it's getting harder and harder to tell the difference between them and the tourists. But there are some dead giveaways. Protest getup, for one. Tourists don't usually protest unless they've specifically traveled to Seattle *to* protest, in which case, I wouldn't lump them in with everyone here to visit the Space Needle and hike Rainier. Two people my age walk past me with what looks like makeshift blue warpaint, with sleeveless white shirts that read "Fuck your refinery" in what looks like hot pink Sharpie.

Residents, pretty sure.

I smile at them, but I can't see their eyes behind their sunglasses.

They seem distracted too—they ignore me. Maybe they just didn't see me. In any case, I'm on their side. Abba's store in South Lake Union is already suffering from rent hikes. The industrial truck delivery route included in the refinery proposal would jam up Westlake Avenue with traffic even worse than it is now, which would spell trouble for letting Abba's customers through.

Two more protesters walk past me, one wearing a Guy Fawkes mask and a shirt that says "The Order sees."

Okay, so this person *clearly* isn't a member of the Order, the extremely secretive, exclusive group bent on bringing to justice the untouchable elite. The group that's *never* been identified. They wouldn't be caught in public with a T-shirt like that, even with a mask. What if they're arrested or something? Mask confiscated. Cover blown.

Still, I wish the protesters success. I'm counting on them, since Abba would verbally tear me apart if he found out I was out there with signs, throwing tear-gas canisters back at law enforcement and dodging sprays of mace. Which I'm not. But he'd probably freak out if he knew I was out here climbing fire escapes and clearing gaps between buildings on foot too. So would Mama and Ranya.

Of course, we're *all* scared of this refinery going up. We know what it would mean for the store. But then why am I the only one in my family out here wanting to *do* something about it?

I try to focus again. I *have* to if JERICHO is going to win this puzzle. It takes all of us. *Chromedome. Clean up them thoughts.*

I reach Pine Street, pull off to the corner, and stop.

As much as I'm used to sprinting across buildings, I've been doing this cryptology thing long enough to know that sometimes when you're out of ideas, you need to just stop, breathe, and observe, and the ideas will come to you. What do I see?

I see brick and stucco buildings all around me and cobblestone on the ground. The Pike Place Market sign is far behind me, the open-air market tents and tables lined with fresh produce and flower bouquets bursting with reds and pinks and purples, and to my right, a place called Rachel's Ginger Beer that I've never been to but seen a million times. I see a restaurant above it called Steelhead Diner, and I see the big blue Post Alley sign above my head, signaling that I'm at the northernmost point.

Chromedome, I think quietly, inviting an answer to come to me.

I see nothing chrome around here. In fact, the only metal in the area is this railing blocking off steps down to someone's basement, and the little blue newspaper box next to me with nothing in it. A quick walk around them yields no Vault sticker.

Chromedome. Clean up them thoughts.

I feel a hand on my shoulder, and I look over to see glistening brown eyes looking back at me.

"Sup, Yas," says Jax, stepping past me and keeping his gaze moving, which tells me he's no further along in this puzzle than I am, despite how calm and collected he tries to seem.

"Nice of you to join us elites, Jax," I tease.

"Couldn't let you have all the fun. Now, where were we with this 'chromedome' stuff? This mailbox looks *kinda* like R2, I guess," he says, looking around it.

"I checked. Dead end."

"Dammit. By the way, I could've been ahead of you guys if it weren't for the bus hitting every light on the way here."

I roll my eyes, even though I know he's right. Jax pulls his sweatshirt sleeves down over his hands and sticks his tongue against the inside of his cheek, like he always does when he's thinking.

"Maybe we need to get creative with this," he says to himself. I realize with each word he says next that I'm in for a *long* Jax-brand soliloquy. "What else could 'chromedome' mean? 'Chromedome,' assuming it's all one word, has ten letters. Does that mean anything? Probably not. Backward, it's 'emodemorhc.' Nonsense. Maybe it's a euphemism? Chromedome? Metalhead? Is there a concert venue around here? All I know of is the Crocodile, but that's well into Belltown, about a twenty-minute walk from here by sidewalk, or ten minutes by rooftop . . ."

Hearing the word "rooftop," I look up and stare at the Steelhead Diner sign absentmindedly, letting my eyes glaze over as I dissect the word.

And then it clicks.

Chromedome.

Metalhead.

Or . . . Steelhead?

My heart thunders. *This* is why I do this. *This* feeling I get, once I've locked in on something.

Progress.

"Maybe it's an acronym?" continues Jax. "Calling Home, Reeling Over Medical Emergencies—"

"Nope," I say. "I've got the chromedome part."

"You what?" he snaps. "How?"

Looks like the puzzle master has been out-puzzled. I know I got lucky his bus took forever, and that he was thinking out loud so I could follow along; otherwise this situation would likely be reversed.

"You wanna trade something for that intel?" I grin.

"Uh," he says, flashing the most charming smile, "I've got this award-winning grin of mine."

"Cute," I say. "I'm sure that'll work on someone interested in guys."

I move on and try to focus on the last part.

Clean up them thoughts.

This is my problem. I see things head-on. Jax is the expert puzzler because he flips things totally around. He can see several dimensions of a clue when we get one. He can weave his way around plays on words and implications, technicalities and not-necessarilies. He puzzles like I parkour.

We both use what we've got.

"What's bakin', biscuit bitches?" comes a familiar, raspy voice from behind me. I feel a hand clap me on the shoulder, and Spider hops between Jax and me with his messenger bag, which is almost as big as he is, and always stuffed with way too much junk, and those signature aviator goggles resting against his forehead.

"I see you're both stuck at the 'chromedome' part of this race," he says, eyes darting around from possible clue to possible clue.

"Yas has the 'chromedome' bit!"

Spider looks up at me in equal parts disgust and awe.

"How?"

"That's what *I* want to know!" exclaims Jax, arms flying up in the air for effect. "Coming for my gig, the nerve."

"Listen, Yas," says Spider. "You can't be a genius, parkour master, *and* server of iconic makeup looks. Leave some talent in the pool for the rest of us, eh?"

I have to smile at that. If there's one thing I know, it's parkour. If there's another thing I know, it's my way around an eye-shadow palette. The genius part? Who knows. But my phone buzzes, indicating it's already 8:15 and we're going to miss the bus to class if we don't hurry. I'm instantly yanked back into reality.

"Yas, what do you want in exchange for a hint?" asks Spider. "Want me to jailbreak your phone for you like you asked?"

"Did it myself last week," I say. "You were too slow."

"Oof, she's coming for your gig too!" says Jax with a chuckle. "*Cold*, Yas."

"Okay, okay," Spider concedes. "How about a bowl of hot ramen?" Tonight at my place? You can all come over so we can write the next JERICHO puzzle together, and Yas, you can have a nice hot bowl of noodles."

Now, *that* catches my attention.

Spider lives with his mom in a modest apartment above their restaurant named Seoul Food, in the International District. Abba always warns me not to fall in love with earthly things, but their ramen is a thing I would gladly lie down and die for. All of their broths simmer for days before being served, and the black garlic oil they use turns the noodles into something straight from heaven.

"Veggie broth?" I ask.

"Only the best."

I narrow my eyes and prepare to raise the stakes.

"Tell your mom to throw in two extra marinated eggs, and we have a deal."

Jax whistles, knowing those eggs cost two dollars extra each in the restaurant, even though he's never eaten one. Spider's eyes get huge.

"How about an extra ramen egg, and a bottle of black garlic oil to take home?"

Jax looks back at me, waiting for my response.

"You know I can barely make a PB&J," I argue, "let alone something involving black garlic oil. Two eggs, or no deal."

Spider sighs.

"Fine. All yours. Now, what's the clue?"

I pull out my phone and text Spider, and *only* Spider.

ME: I think chromedome means Steelhead, as in the diner right next to us.

Spider, not being the most savvy in the stealth department, turns his gaze up to the Steelhead Diner sign and doesn't look away. I look at Jax, who's clearly locked it in as a clue and starts hopping around in place as he tries to piece together the last part of the last clue. I roll my eyes and try to focus again.

Clean up them thoughts.

Then I notice the pipe trailing up the side of the building, and it all clicks into place.

Clean up them thoughts, or *get your mind out of the gutter.*

I walk up to the pipe, check the back, snap a picture of the Vault sticker, and upload it in a comment on the forum in less than five seconds.

"Ah, dammit," spits Spider, kicking his shoe against a loose cobblestone brick and pulling a vape pen out of his pocket.

Jax sighs and walks up behind me to take his own photo. Second place. Spider takes third, because if he can't make first place, he doesn't care what place he comes in after that.

"Anyone check on Han lately? Where is he?" asks Jax.

I realize I haven't gotten a text from Han in a while—not since yesterday—but he was active in the forum thread just before I got here, so he should be okay . . . right?

I feel my phone buzz in my pocket just as Spider's pings in his bag and Jax pulls his own phone out. My new text reads:

HAN: SO YOU FINALLY MADE IT.

Wait, he's here already?

I lock eyes with Jax, then Spider, and when I see the same shock and confusion on their faces that I'm probably wearing, I look around. I hear the sound of metal sliding slowly against metal, and out from a hellishly dark space behind an alleyway door easing open, steps Han. Brown sweatshirt, shaggy brown hair, twinkles in his eyes like always.

"Oh, don't mind me," says Spider. "I'm just gonna lurk in the Post Alley Court shadows until my friends get here and then send them cryptic-ass texts from a nearby hidden door to hell."

Han smiles knowingly and shrugs.

Jax steps forward with a smile in return.

"Wassup, Han," he says with a fist bump.

Han daps all three of us in turn and then holds up his phone with a nod.

"Wait," I think out loud. "If you got here first, why didn't you solve the puzzle first?"

He holds up his phone again for emphasis, and we all take to the forum. I scroll up to several posts before Spider's, Jax's, and even mine, where I see another almost identical one, posted from Han, and I sigh.

"The human mole wins again," says Spider. "Well done, bro."

"No fair, Han—you know every tunnel and doorway in this city," Jax says, smiling.

"And under it," adds Spider with a grin.

"And *you* know the whole transit system by heart, Jax. What's your point?" I tease.

"Hey, hey, let's fight on the way to class, shall we?" asks Spider, slinging his messenger bag more comfortably over his shoulder and beginning the trek up the steepest part of Pine Street to our E-line bus stop.

Jax turns to me with a challenging wink and then takes off sprinting.

"Race ya," he yells, returning my earlier challenge. He darts up Pine Street, past a few tourists on their way down to watch the cheese curds churn in the vat behind the window at Beecher's.

"Hardly a race!" I shout back, feeling a smirk spread across my face as I bolt after him. My legs begin to burn, matching my lungs, but I live for the competition. The blood racing through my veins. The fear of losing, and by extension, the raging need to win.

"Such confidence for one in second place!" he hollers.

"Loser pays for the other's ramen!" I propose, looking up at the jungle gym of metal bars, platforms, and metal steps erected all along this street. He should know better than to challenge me to an uphill race when there's conveniently placed scaffolding nearby.

I dart forward, leap, grip the lowest bar, and up I go.

Han

I follow Yas, Jax, and Spider through the front doors of Shannon High to find the halls empty. Weird. I thought we had a few extra minutes since we just barely caught the 8:20 bus.

The bell rings, loud and grating in my ears, and I lift my hands to cover them.

Late.

The three of them race down the hall, but I freeze and wait until the bell ends so I don't have to run with my hands up to my ears. The teacher, Mr. Benton, doesn't care if we're five seconds late or thirty seconds late, so why should I? Late is late to him, so late is late to me.

I just wish they'd open the annex tunnel up for more than sports equipment deliveries. It's *way* quicker to come in that way from where the E bus drops off. Practically a straight shot.

We all chose lockers next to each other, all right outside the same first-period class so it's less likely we'll be late.

Yas is the first to reach room 202 and read the sign on the door aloud.

"Period 1 Algebra II has moved to room 603 due to a leaky water pipe in room 202. Please be in your seat by 8:45."

"A whole extra five minutes! Let's go!" hollers Jax, taking off down the hall toward the east stairwell. I backtrack, opting for the west stairwell instead. None of them ask me why I'm not following, or if I'm okay, or where I'm going, or why I'm using a different stairwell. They all know I'll meet them there when I'm ready. The truth is, the west stairwell has less sunlight in the morning, so it doesn't bother my eyes as much, and the east stairwell has this horribly squeaky door that I hate. It may be a longer walk, but it's way quieter.

I like not having to explain all of that.

I reach the stairwell and start the walk up. I don't know when or why I got so interested in mapping infrastructure, or why people think it's weird. So many people walk past unused closets, empty hallways, decommissioned dumpsters, abandoned buildings, and manholes that lead to even more hidden places all over the city. I think it's weird to not care why they're there, where they came from, or how they can be used. There's a whole hidden network right under people's noses, and when it comes to cryptology, the faster you can get to a clue, the greater the advantage.

I get halfway up the second set of stairs when I hear my phone chime, the normally quiet pinging echoing in this empty stairwell. I pull it out and realize the notification is from over a hundred posts I've missed from the Vault master forum thread in the span of five minutes. Some shit is going down.

I stop where I am on the stairs and start scrolling.

I see post after post after post about the new refinery going up in Beacon Hill, and how it just got approved. I think of Jax's parents and their garden and how many times he's brought Baby Bella mushrooms and bell peppers to school for me in exchange for puzzle hints. I know there are laws and rules, and this thing has officially legally been passed, but . . .

. . . I really didn't want it to pass.

Now that the refinery is for sure going up, and that it's just a matter of where, and that Jax's garden is looking like the most likely spot, my dad will probably lose his job.

The pipeline leading to the refinery is supposed to run along the Duwamish Waterway and over to Harbor Island, where my dad works as a kayak instructor. The placement of the pipeline would mean the water wouldn't be safe for kayaking anymore, which means he'd have to either move his business or shut down altogether.

If he loses his job, I go to live with Mom.

And I am *not* going to live with Mom.

As I stare down at my phone, more posts pop up, talking about something called "The Order" and a new puzzle with a first clue that no one can seem to figure out. Finally I see a screenshot of the original post. I brush the hair away from my eyes and zoom in closer.

It's a picture of plain white text against a black background that reads:

WE ARE THE ORDER.
GUARDIANS OF PEACE, AND PROTECTORS OF THE PEOPLE.
YOU'VE SEEN US BEFORE.
WE MAKE THINGS HAPPEN.
WE'RE EVERYWHERE.
WE SEEK ONLY THE MOST ELITE TO JOIN OUR GROUP.
THIS GAME WILL REVEAL THE MOST DESERVING.
THE GAME IS ANARCHY.
THE PRIZE IS POWER.
GOOD LUCK.

What does any of that mean? These people sound like they're threatening us. Weakly. Frankly, they sound like they're full of shit. The original poster's name is "The Order," like the ultra-famous, ultra-elusive crypto-vigilante anarchist group that's been operating in the shadows for almost a decade. Uncreative. Just like that unoriginal eye at the bottom, implying that they're all-seeing or something. And what did they mean by "The game is anarchy. The prize is power"? For a group who wants only the "most elite," they weren't elite enough to remember to post their first clue before wishing us all good luck on a puzzle we can't even start.

But just as I'm about to file "The Order" away as posers, another post catches my eye.

A second picture from the Order that says:

WE BELIEVE KNOWLEDGE IS POWER.
WE BELIEVE INFORMATION SHOULD BE FREE.
WE BELIEVE CENSORSHIP IS UNCONSTITUTIONAL.
WE BELIEVE THOSE WHO ENFORCE CENSORSHIP SHOULD BE
INHIBITED.
AND LIKE WE SAID,
WE MAKE THINGS HAPPEN.

Now I'm a little panicked. These people are promoting civil unrest *and* associating with our forum. Not a good mix. Extremely dangerous. Risky for us.

There's a post shortly after, linking to a news article from ten minutes ago entitled "Fire Alarm Pulled at Downtown Seattle Police Department, Building Evacuated."

No. Way.

Did these people—this "The Order"—send someone into the Seattle PD office just to pull the fire alarm? The picture associated with the article shows several dozen people standing outside the Seattle PD building in downtown, right next to the courthouse on Fifth Avenue. Some are in uniform, some aren't.

I keep scrolling.

GOOD MORNING, SEATTLE PUBLIC SCHOOLS.

I look at the time stamp and realize it was posted only five seconds ago, and I wonder what's coming next. *We're* in a public school. I'm standing in the stairwell . . . Am I safe? I hear the door open several feet above me, on the next flight up, and I hurriedly put away my phone, hop to my feet, and look up, hoping it's not Mr. Benton, coming to hunt me down and drag me off to class. But instead, I see Jax looking down at me with a smile.

"Hey, man, I'm on a bathroom break to check on you. You all right?"

I nod up at him too soon, just as the blaring sirens ring out through this stairwell, and the white flashing lights in front of every bright red fire alarm bell start going haywire, and I crumble to my knees and cover my ears, and all I can do is clench my teeth. But then, through the pain, I hear Jax's footsteps bounding down the stairs toward me, and I feel his arms around my shoulders, pulling me to my feet as we blend into the crowd shuffling down the stairs and outside to the lawn.

And the fresh air.

And the semblance of quiet.

And then, after breathing, and sitting, and squeezing my fists so tight, I've left tiny moon-shaped marks in my palms, I begin to feel okay again.

Spider

At first, even I thought it was an ordinary fire drill.

We shuffled down the stairwell single file like we do with an ordinary fire drill.

We meandered out onto the front lawn like it was an ordinary fire drill.

But while everyone else is now standing around watching fire trucks roll screaming into the parking lot, I'm busy reading the forum and realizing this shit is anything but ordinary.

It's no coincidence that the alarm went off only moments after those guys that call themselves "The Order" posted that last message:

GOOD MORNING, SEATTLE PUBLIC SCHOOLS.

"Wait, wait, wait," says Yas, folding her arms and smacking her gum in thought. "You think these guys are 'The Order' as in *the* Order?"

"I hope so!" says Jax, nervously toying with a purple crystal around his neck that I haven't seen before. Yas rolls her eyes.

"Why would *the* Order be tampering with the Seattle Public Schools system's fire alarms?" she asks.

"Because fuck the system?" offers Jax.

"I agree with Yas, though," I offer. "That's a pretty small system for them to be fucking with."

"Maybe they're going after something more high-profile," returns Jax.

Han looks up from his phone and holds up the screen so we all can see the article he's been reading. The headline reads "Fire Alarm Pulled at Downtown Seattle Police Department, Building Evacuated."

"See? They got the cops, too! Fuck the system!" Jax beams proudly.

"Okay, so they're wasting 12's time," says Yas. "I can get behind that. But why now? Did something happen to set them off? Seems unlike *the* Order to strike randomly. They're usually more . . . precise."

"Hey," says Jax. "Who's the expert on the Order around here? If they've made a move, there's a good reason behind it. These people play six-dimensional chess, nothing less. Maybe Seattle PD has been up to something only the Order knows about. So far."

"You just *really* want the Order to be involved in this—huh, fanboy?" Yas says with a wink in Jax's direction.

"Not nearly as much as you want them *not* to be involved," returns Jax playfully.

"You know, we don't actually know if they're human," says Yas. "Nobody from the Order has ever been identified."

I nod. She's right.

Jax may be the expert on the Order, but I've done some digging on them in the past. Their little "hack" into the US Capitol's records? It got them around *several* blockchain security walls. One alone would be impressive. Next to impossible, honestly.

"She has a point, Jax," I say, folding my arms over my chest. "Seattle PD seems . . . insignificant for them. Could be a sophisticated AI."

Yas raises an eyebrow at me.

"You think a sophisticated AI would be spontaneously setting off fire alarms around the city instead of—oh I don't know—canceling people's student loans or something more useful?"

"Maybe it's the AI's day off," says Jax, lip trembling as he stifles a laugh.

"Hilarious," Yas says flatly.

And just like that, the alarm clips into silence.

We all look at each other with our *Now what?* face.

And then: *Wee-oooh-wee-ooh!*

It's back on.

"What was that?" asks Jax, looking to me, the systems guy.

"Could be a glitch," I say.

Or someone held down the silence button that's on each alarm lever. But then someone—a human—would've had to pull another one to set it off again. And they just evacuated the school, so . . . unlikely.

It *has* to be a hack.

"Okay, Yas," I say, determined to get us back on topic so we can get to the bottom of this. "If it's not *the* Order, and it's not an AI, who do you think it is?"

Jax cuts in before she can answer.

"Listen, I know the Order, okay?" he says. "I've studied every move they've ever made. They've had typos in their social posts. They've made mistakes. Small ones. Inconsequential, but mistakes for sure. Besides, behind every sophisticated AI, there's at least one human anyway, right?"

"I guess," Yas says with a shrug. "So then the question still lingers. Why the fire alarms? Why now?"

Han pushes himself slowly to his feet. Although his wispy brown hair hangs down low over his eyes, I can tell they're still glued to his phone as he scrolls and scrolls. Then an idea hits me.

"Hey, Han, maybe you can help us figure out who might have remote access to the fire alarms. Is it a pretty secure system?"

He looks up at me and nods.

"Is there only one party with access?"

He nods again, and I grin. My heart is beating a little faster, like it always does when I start piecing things together, crawling through the labyrinth of clues in front of us, looking for an out. That's why they call me Spider.

"Which party, Han?" asks Jax. Han glances up from his phone just long enough to zero in on the administration building and point.

There are only a few departments in that building. Administration—of course, admissions, Principal Antony's office, security, and janitorial. I start with the most likely one.

"Principal Antony?"

Han shakes his head.

"Janitorial?" asks Jax.

Han shakes his head again.

And then I'm left with the only department that makes sense anymore.

"Security," I say. Shannon High is notorious for daily incidents, most of which are nonviolent—drugs, truancy, theft, your average run-of-the-mill misdemeanors. But every other month, there's a fight or an assault that lands somebody in the hospital. One kid was pushed down the stairs and ended up in a coma a few years ago. There's enough chaos here to warrant a full-time officer stationed at the front entrance at all times. Armed. Dangerous. Freaks me out every time I walk through those doors.

"You think security has access to the fire alarms, Han?" asks Yas.

"Yas, you've known Han for how long?" asks Jax. "He doesn't *think*. He *knows*."

I spot a few faculty weaving their way through crowds of students closer to the building, so while Jax and Yas continue their debate about whether *the* Order sneaked into Shannon High security's mainframe, I listen in.

"Buses will begin running in twenty minutes. Please board your regular bus number," says one of the teachers I've seen around—I don't know her name. "If you don't ride the bus, you are advised to contact your guardians and seek transportation home. Please wait for them in the library until they get here. I repeat. Buses will begin running in twenty minutes. Either report to the bus roundabout or report to the library, please. Single file, everyone . . ."

"*Hell* yeah!" I say, turning back to the group, whose attention I now have. "Did you hear that? We're all going home!"

Han looks at me blankly from under his wispy hair. Yas raises an eyebrow. Jax lowers both of his skeptically.

"Why?" he asks.

I shrug.

"Maybe they're having trouble turning off the alarms?"

"So they're just going to give us a day off?" asks Yas.

The teacher is closer now—close enough that we can't *not* overhear her.

"Log into your online student portal to finish your day remotely, please."

A collective sucking of teeth, groans, and sighs ripple through our little circle.

"Bold of them to assume all of our parents can just take off work to come get us," says Yas. "Abba has to work, and the school bus route to my place takes so long—by the time I get home, the school day will be over."

"Doesn't the light rail go right to your dad's store?" asks Jax.

"The light rail is an hour and a half between here and the store, and two hours between here and home. It'll be lunchtime by then, I'll be late, and I'll miss my classes and Zuhr prayer. And then I'll have to watch the recordings late into the night, when I should be listening to Billie Eilish and eating garbage in peace."

My stomach grumbles its irritation at having had only a bowl of chicken-and-rice porridge for breakfast. Mom makes the *best* dak juk in the morning, but only for me. The stuff at Seoul Food—our restaurant downstairs from our apartment? It's made with . . . shortcuts. The chicken simmers for only an hour. The rice is ground less finely. The vegetables are chopped coarser. Just enough finesse to satisfy the taste buds of the American students staying in the International District so they can be close to the kinds of Asian food they ate on their summer study-abroad trip to Seoul, and still drive twenty minutes to their parents' houses for their all-American Thanksgiving dinner.

Only my friends get the *real* stuff. The stuff with *love* in it.

"You've all got your laptops, right?" I ask, slinging my messenger bag over my shoulder. "Come to my place! The 21 will take us straight there in ten minutes. You know my mom won't mind. Besides, then we can get to the bottom of this Order business while Mrs. Henry waxes poetic about why some dead white authors were important once upon a time."

Jax, Yas, and Han all exchange a quick glance before silently agreeing, and soon their backpacks are on and we're walking to catch the 21 bus. I'm hungry, I'm tired, and my binder's getting itchy under this shirt.

Besides, I *have* to find out what happened with that alarm situation. As we walk, I can't shake the feeling that some serious shit is about to go down. Whoever these Order people are, if they're messing with the cops and public schools' alarm systems, I'm intrigued.

Here's the thing about my mom's restaurant: It's named Seoul Food—a Korean name with a meaning most Americans understand. Because we're Korean. Living in Chinatown. Selling ramen, tteokbokki, and pad Thai to white people who want a little bit of everything—tech executives with clientele who know their way around some Asian fusion and want "American" service—the smiles, the shameless ass-kissing, the altruism offered up humbly in the hopes that they'll receive a living wage folded between the walls of the receipt wallet.

Shit makes me sick.

I lead the way through the glass front doors with the twin cartoon garlic bulbs smiling under a sign that advertises TONKOTSU RAMEN WITH BLACK GARLIC OIL—$14.99. The prices these people will pay for our food almost make up for the stares I get when I walk in—most people probably wondering what a group of four high school kids is doing walking through the restaurant at this hour in the middle of a school day, some looking at me like I might work here. I silently love when people raise a finger, which I'm sure they think is polite, in my direction and say, "Oh, um, excuse me—" I love walking right on by like I haven't seen them.

Mom *hates* it when I do that.

"You could at least *act* like these people pay our rent," she said once.

We pay our rent with our labor.

And I don't work for free.

Looking these people in the face with a smile is hard enough when I'm *on* shift, let alone on my days off. But at least when I'm washing dishes, or sweeping, or tidying the stockroom—anywhere in the kitchen away from customers—I'm home. Nobody asks me where I'm from, or how to say X or Y in Korean, or whether I'm XX or XY.

Nobody deadnames me.

The minute I told my mom everything, she asked me ten thousand questions. She understood some things, like, I wasn't a girl. I wasn't her daughter. But she didn't understand that it didn't mean I wasn't her *child*.

I heard her say, "It feels like my daughter has died."

But later, I heard her ask, "How do you clean this . . . 'binder'?" and "Do you . . . *need* tampons anymore?"

I smiled, because I do. For now. I was told when I started T that my period might linger for a while.

And eventually, one day, out of the blue, she came into my room with a plateful of sliced Asian pears, told me she'd been watching transgender people on "YouTube"—she says each word separately—asked if I was okay with her telling the staff I was transitioning, and as soon as half a "yes" was out of my mouth, she marched into the kitchen waving a wooden spoon and said she'd better not hear my birth name uttered again in her restaurant or there would be consequences.

It's been Spider, or Daeshim, ever since.

Tae-jin Hyung spots me from his position behind the counter and nods hello with a warm smile and a wave, with his black watch around one wrist and his blue bandanna around the other. He's only a few years older than me, but something about his demeanor—the way nothing seems to really get him down—speaks of someone much, much older.

"Hey, it's Daeshim and the gang, playing hooky from school." He winks. I have to smile as I approach the counter. I've found that the deeper into the restaurant I go, the more deeply I'm understood.

"Guilty," I say, nodding to Jax, Yas, and Han as they shuffle in behind me. "I'm playing hooky and didn't immediately seek out an underground bunker, because I forgot who my mother is."

Tae-jin Hyung nods and sucks his teeth with a smile. "Your mom could sniff out a penny in a river of blood."

"But," I say, "she'd also give her last penny for us. Or her last drop of blood."

He nods, knowing I'm right, and then he looks at the rest of Team JERICHO with a welcoming grin. "Hey, y'all."

They all nod hello and smile.

"Hey, Tae-Jin," Yas says, smiling and leaning on the counter, "I traded Spider here a few secrets for a bowl of that heavenly ramen of yours. Can you spare a bowl before we go upstairs? Veggie broth, please?"

"Ooh, veggie broth for me too, please," says Jax.

Han leans on the counter and nods up at Tae-Jin Hyung in agreement.

"Hey, hey." Yas frowns. "Did *you* all provide some intel? No. So the ramen's mine."

"Is that Yas I hear?" sings a familiar, bubbly voice from around the corner that I'd recognize anywhere. My mom bursts into the room, lighting up the whole place with her ear-to-ear smile. She's as tall as me, and slender like me. Her short, black hair is still as she moves, with one gray streak in the front, the only indication that she's over forty.

"Hello, ma'am," says Jax. Han raises a hand. Yas grins.

"I told you," my mom snaps suddenly, flattening her hands into an X and then yanking them down on either side of her. "*No* 'ma'am.' Please, call me Mom."

"Yes, ma'am," he says, and then quickly corrects himself, "Yes, Mom."

"Good," she coos, her face melting back into a smooth smile.

Everyone calls her "Mom." I'm the only one who calls her "Umma." She's insisted upon it since I was little.

"Hi, Umma." I nod at her. She turns to me and her smile grows threefold.

"Daeshiiiiim, my love," she says, pulling me into a hug. She smells like a blend of her oat lotion and shampoo. "Mind telling me what you're all doing here? School get canceled suddenly? Hmm?"

I know she's playing with me, but actually, *yeah*. I pull away and look up at her.

"They couldn't stop the fire alarms from going off, so we're all going online for the rest of the day."

She looks around at Jax, Yas, and Han, who all nod in turn. She knows I'd never lie, but I guess it's a habit to confirm with the rest of them.

"Ah." She seems to breathe the word out as a sigh of relief, clasping her hands together. "In that case, Tae-Jin, please," she says, motioning elegantly toward the kitchen. Tae-Jin Hyung looks at her with raised eyebrows, waiting for the request. "Ramen for them all. My treat."

Tae-Jin Hyung nods and salutes us before ducking back into the kitchen to get us four bowls of the good stuff.

"I heard *two* eggs this time, Yas?" asks my mom, raising an eyebrow at her.

"Yes, Mom," she says, a hint of unsteadiness in her now-shrunken voice, maybe humility all of a sudden? Yas is cool asking *me* for extra eggs—haggling even, twisting my arm for more info, but bring my mom into this? And she goes as soft as the buttery, soft-boiled yolks.

My mouth waters just thinking about it.

"Must be some *interesting* secrets." My mom grins, raising an eyebrow at me. Oh god, she's at it again, hoping to set me up with anything that moves, especially Yas, who I've known since before everyone knew I was a guy. Except Yas.

That's right. Yas was the first to know. Way back in seventh grade. We'd already been friends for years. We were practically siblings, so it only felt right to tell her. It was around the time she decided to start wearing her hijab.

So many changes happened for both of us that year.

I look over and smile at Yas now, apologetically, and she rolls her eyes back at me in understanding, as if to say *That's just how your mom is*, as if I didn't know. Unfortunately for my mom, I'm just not interested in Yas like that. She's a friend, and she'll probably always be.

Besides, also unbeknownst to my mom, Yas isn't into guys.

"Secrets about a *puzzle*, Mom," Jax cuts in. My mom's eyes get *huge*, and her mouth forms an exaggerated O.

"Ohhhh." The word drags out of her mouth as it sinks in. "A new internet game!"

"*Kind* of," says Jax. "I guess you could call it that."

I've explained to her before how cryptology puzzles work. They're just scavenger hunts, only with digital clues. And they usually cover more area than a traditional scavenger hunt. They're bigger. Sometimes *much* bigger. And if I know anything about this new puzzle from "The Order," it's sure to be the biggest one we've ever seen. The way they phrased the intro made it sound so . . . exclusive. I play the words over in my head.

WE SEEK ONLY THE MOST ELITE TO JOIN OUR GROUP.

THIS GAME WILL REVEAL THE MOST DESERVING.

That sounds intimidating. Not that I'm intimidated. Just that they *meant* to intimidate us. Everyone on the forum knows, JERICHO always wins. The other groups know from the jump that they're competing for second place. But the most fascinating thing I read in the intro was:

THE GAME IS ANARCHY.

THE PRIZE IS POWER.

My thoughts swirl, wondering what kinds of clues they'll have in mind with a prize like that. *Power*—what I'd give to have some of that around here. I'd do away with tips and force all companies registered in the state of Washington to pay their employees a living wage. I'd cap rent prices—Umma refuses to discuss our financial situation with me, but I know what rent prices look like across Puget Sound. Everyone seems to be talking about the cost of living around here *except* my mom, and she's started hiding the mail when she brings it in. I wonder if she's shielding me from it. If she's struggling, I know she'd never let on. But I'll do whatever I gotta do to keep this place afloat. My grandparents lived here. They started this restaurant when my mom was just a baby. What right does the free market have to decide this place can't be ours anymore?

I look at Tae-Jin Hyung again, knowing what it would mean for him if this place closed down. I got him this job, papers or not. Without me, he wouldn't be working here at all.

He still doesn't, not on paper. But the state thinks he does. And that's all that really matters in the end.

A flurry of voices shouting outside grows louder behind me, and we all turn to look out the window, where colorful, bandanna-wearing young people are marching past chanting, *"Fuck your refinery!"* I watch the window, my heart swelling with pride knowing I'm on their side, that what they're doing is helping our cause. Every time I see them, they're even more passionate, this time screaming so loud, their voices are breaking. One even raps on the glass window outside and rallies to all of us in here with an aggressive raising of their hands. But, one by one, customers in business suits with big round designer glasses and fresh haircuts and blue badges turn back to their lunch companions with a snicker or an eye roll that says, *Ugh, sorry for the riffraff interrupting our peace* and maybe even a *This place wasn't always so grimy.*

That pride from earlier sizzles into angry determination.

I'll do whatever I have to. For me. For Umma. For Tae-Jin Hyung.

For so many others in this place who aren't actually on the payroll books, because they can't work in the US. Sure, plenty of places in the International District could "hire" them, but with all the gentrification going on, those places are rapidly dwindling.

This puzzle could mean protection for everyone here, if only for a little longer.

So then my mind turns to wondering what kinds of wild clues we'll have to decode to get to the finish line first.

The first rule of the forum is that there will be *zero* breaking the law. All puzzles must be legal—no reading serial numbers scratched into crack pipes in alleyways.

My mom gasps suddenly as if she's forgotten something. And then, "Tae-*jin*!!!!" she turns and hollers toward the kitchen, startling all of us. I look around the restaurant and clutch my messenger-bag strap a little tighter. It feels like everyone's staring from behind me. I don't dare turn to look.

An indistinguishable yet undeniably questioning yell bounces back from the kitchen at her.

"*Two* eggs for Yas's bowl, please!"

Just as I think the yelling is over, she turns back toward the kitchen and follows up with "*Oh,* and *veggie* broth for Jax and Yas!"

"Got it!" rings out from the kitchen.

"*And,*" she continues one more time, "a fork for Han!"

"Right away!"

I glance at Han, who smiles. A bit of red creeps into his cheeks. Maybe he's as embarrassed at her volume as I am. But as she always says, it's her restaurant, and she controls the volume.

"I'll have Tae-Jin bring it all up to your room." She smiles at me, following it up with two claps of her hands. "You have schoolwork to do! Chop-chop!"

• • •

I've poured every last dime I've ever made downstairs into this PC setup. It doesn't have the flashing rainbow lights like so many others, but the processor *sings* and the graphics card I have was only released last week. Cryptology? Hunting down clues? Making digital connections? It's my life. It's all I want to do. I just wish monetary prizes popped up more often. And exceeded fifty bucks. Then I might be able to upgrade our shitty Wi-Fi.

I'll take power, though, I think, if it keeps me and my family in this city. It's what I'd spend any money I made on anyway. I swing open the door to my room, and my friends and I step into sheer darkness except an orange-and-purple lava lamp in the corner. I flip on the switch for the floor lamp and we all take our places—Jax flops down on the beanbag with a hole worn in the side, Han sits crisscross on the floor with his back against the wall, and Yas curls up at the foot of my bed on her side and stretches her mouth wide open in a yawn.

"Aht! Aht!" says Jax. "*No* time for sleep. We have a puzzle to solve."

"Wait, you're not seriously suggesting we *do* this one," says Yas, rolling onto her stomach and glaring at Jax. It's a statement, not a question. "We don't even know what the prize is. 'Power' is the vaguest reward I've ever seen. What kind of power? Are they rigging the next election? Or bribing people in our favor? Are they shelling out loads of money to get what they—or the prizewinners—want? Highly questionable."

"Aw, Yas," I protest, scooting the stack of milk crates I'm sitting on closer to my desk, which is really a card table that's not quite tall enough to be comfortable but gets the job done. "We can't just turn down a puzzle like this. We're practically royalty on the forum, and the Order are some top-tier vigilantes. Whatever they've got planned, this is some high-stakes shit!"

Jax's eyes begin to sparkle across the circle from me, and he leans forward, twirling that purple crystal between his fingers. Knowing Mama, it's got to mean something. I wonder what message she sent him off to school today with.

"Yas, you're forgetting the most important part of the whole puzzle. Do you realize if we win this," he says, leaning his elbows up onto the edge of the bed so he can talk to her one-on-one, "we could *join* the Order? That was part of their proposal!"

My heart skips as I remember that part. I completely forgot!

WE SEEK ONLY THE MOST ELITE TO JOIN OUR GROUP.
THIS GAME WILL REVEAL THE MOST DESERVING.

"Not necessarily," I cut in. "It says the game will *reveal* the most deserving. What if there's a second or third hoop to jump through? What if these are scammers and they start asking for social security numbers and shit?"

Jax's thick eyebrows lie flat over his eyes. "Just whose side are you on, Spider?"

Han, who's been staring at the floor this whole time, now looks up at my shelf above my computer, studying it carefully. I raise an eyebrow and follow his gaze, trying to figure out what he's piecing together. My soccer trophies are all lined up along the left, with a few small soccer balls next to them—for the basketball hoop on the back of my door. Then a few succulents—miraculously all dead even though they're supposed to be indestructible—and a sticky note reminding me to do a virus scan every once in a while.

Can't remember the last time I did that.

Han pushes himself to his feet, picks up a trophy, and scoops three of the little balls into his arms. Then, just as Yas is saying to Jax, "You're asking me to play a game for a prize I don't want, hosted by a group we can't verify," Han holds out a soccer ball to her.

She seems caught off guard as she glances at Jax for an explanation. She looks back at Han and takes the ball from him with a smile.

"Uh . . . thanks?" She tosses it up and down with one hand as Han holds out a ball to me, and finally, hands Jax the trophy before taking his seat against the wall again.

Yas, Jax, and I all look at each other. Obviously, this means something. Han just *loooves* communicating in riddles, so it makes sense that he's an expert at solving them with us.

"Do you want to play soccer, Han?" asks Jax.

Han doesn't answer. He just tosses the ball between his hands and smiles. Nope. Too basic an answer for a Han puzzle.

I wrinkle my forehead and think. Yas, Han, and I all have soccer balls. Jax has the trophy. Why?

"Han, are you saying Jax should lead us through this puzzle from the Order?" asks Yas. "That maybe since he has the trophy, he's the best of us all?"

Han's eyebrows fall. He looks insulted at that answer, and I have to crack a smile. The idea that any of us would think we're better than the others—*ha*. We all bring something different. That's why we're all part of JERICHO. Four cornerstones, if you will.

So why is Jax holding the trophy?

Then it clicks.

My heart thunders like it always does when I piece something together. There's no better feeling than the warmth that floods your chest when you know the answer to something while everyone else in the room scratches their heads.

"We can all play the game," I say, nodding at Jax. "But Jax can have the prize."

Jax and Yas both look at me as my answer sinks in. Then they look at each other for confirmation. Then we all look at Han, whose mouth has curved into a slight, knowing smile.

"Well, that settles it, I guess." Jax shrugs. "Y'all can play, and I'll join the Order."

"We have to win first," says Yas.

"We're JERICHO," I cut in with a grin. There's not a lot I'm confident about in this world, but JERICHO? My friends? Our ability to murder this puzzle?

I *know* we got this.

"Now, when's the first clue dropping?"

Han holds up his phone to me. I assume he's already been looking into it over there. You can't stay a jump ahead of the other teams if you take forever noticing the first clue is up.

I hold out my hand to let him place his phone in my palm, and when I turn it and look at the screen, I realize I'm staring at the original post. I reach up and run my free hand through my hair and adjust my seat on these crates that are probably leaving a crisscross pattern on the back of my thighs, even through my clothes.

"Han, this is the original post. Where's the clue?"

I know I'm asking myself, and Han knows I'm asking myself, because it's not a yes-or-no question. So, I scroll for the answer. *All* the comments are asking where the Order posted the first clue.

"Maybe they haven't posted it yet," says Jax. "Maybe they're relaxing, reading the comments and letting us all squirm." He folds his arms behind his head and sinks comfortably into the beanbag, pushing a few more beads out of the hole in the side.

"You're poking those back in before you leave," I say with a playful raised eyebrow.

"Always," Jax says with a smirk. "Anyway, *I* won't be squirming. I'll just lounge and wait patiently till the first clue is out."

Yas sighs and folds her arms.

My eyes find the comment at the very top. It's from the Order themselves, and it just says, "May the best win."

"Pretty sure the first clue is out," I say, scrolling through the comments to see if anyone, *anyone's*, found it. My heart's pounding, and I shift my position on the stack of milk crates just as a knock raps at my bedroom door, startling all of our gazes up from our screens.

"Marco!" calls Tae-Jin Hyung's voice from the other side. He must have our ramen. I was so enthralled with this puzzle, I forgot all about our food. Judging from my friends' faces, it looks like we all did.

"Polo!" I say. The door eases open, and Tae-Jin Hyung peeks his radiant face through, pushing the door all the way open with his knee to reveal a steaming tray of four colorful bowls—three with wooden chopsticks laid beside them, and one with a fork for Han.

Tae-Jin Hyung sets the tray down, and we divvy up the deliciousness—an eggless veggie bowl for Jax, a two-egg veggie bowl for Yas, and classic bowls for Han and me, both with extra chashu, extra crispy.

I have to smile up at Tae-Jin Hyung before he leaves.

"Thanks," I say. "Tell Umma I said thanks too?"

"You told her downstairs earlier," he chuckles, "but I'll tell her again." Then he looks at Jax. "Hey, she had me put your mushrooms on the side because she wasn't sure they were vegan." Jax grins, opens his sauce container of mushrooms, and sniffs.

"Mushrooms are vegan," he says with a nod. "And these things smell *good*. I'll take 'em!"

"All riiiiight," says Tae-Jin Hyung with a salute. "She also said to tell all of you 'Good luck with your computer puzzles,' and that she's proud of all of you."

My heart jumps to my throat. Umma has always supported whatever I want to do, even if that means running all over the city looking for clues to inconsequential puzzles online. But what would she say if she knew I was about to compete in one that might mean the difference between us staying in Seattle or losing the restaurant and having to leave? I know what she'd say.

Too dangerous! What if they kill you instead? She's asked me that before about less important puzzles, when zero prizes were on the line. I guess it makes sense. If they set the clues, they generally know where we'll be. Perfect setup to kidnap someone if they wanted to. But that's the thing about cryptology—there are risks. There are *always* risks.

That's what makes this stuff so damn fun.

"I don't see any posts from the Order besides the original," says Yas, scrolling down her phone, seemingly uninterested in her noodles. Then she shrugs, picks up her chopsticks, and slurps up some noodles, bamboo, and chashu. Jax follows suit. I don't.

I reread the original post.

WE SEEK ONLY THE MOST ELITE TO JOIN OUR GROUP.
THIS GAME WILL REVEAL THE MOST DESERVING.

Then it clicks. What if this original post *is* the first clue? I take to my computer and pull up the forum. Han, who immediately notices I'm up to something, pushes himself up and shuffles over to my seat, looking up at my computer screen with both hands on my desk, his fingers tapping as he watches every move I make.

I blow up the picture first—that unassuming black square with the white text—and crank up the brightness for any signs of hidden text. Maybe some words are written in gray? An accessibility nightmare unless you use a . . .

I type in the shortcut for my screen reader to activate, and it begins speaking. It reads, word for word, what I see in white letters and nothing else.

Well, it was worth a try.

By now, Jax and Yas look up from their conversation. I can see them out of the corner of my eye, but I stay focused as they join curiously behind me.

"What is it, Spider?" asks Jax. "Found something?"

"Why you asking me like I'm some kind of basset hound, though?"

Yas nods at Jax. "He's got a point."

"I just wanna know what's up!" says Jax, his voice growing more excited with each word. "Is the first clue out? Did you see it somewhere? Come on, Spider, you can't hold out on us like this!"

"Says he who was just going to 'lounge and wait patiently' five minutes ago," Yas says, smirking.

I ignore Jax and try to focus. I hate having to tune out everything to focus, but it's true, I have to. The team already knows, and they all get quiet around me. I watch the screen and think as the world fades into nothing. The smell of the ramen is gone, my room is gone, and it's just me and my keyboard and this image.

I right-click and open the source code, letting my eyes fly over the HTML for any clues. I see all the usual things: image size and position, pixels, error containers, background color, text color, scroll bar info—all stuff that was predetermined by the host site, not our forum. But then I see a whole bunch of font info. Entirely too much font info—like, my scroll wheel is flying down, down, down, and I'm still looking at goddamn *font info*.

Font family: Helvetica, sans serif; font size: 16.

Font family: Helvetica, sans serif; font size: 15.

And then back to font size 16.

And then back to 15.

Then 16.

15.

16.

15.

Why does it keep alternating like this? This doesn't make any sense. Some of the letters in the ALT text of the photo—the text behind the picture that screen readers pick up on and narrate aloud—are different sizes.

Why?

I practically dive across this card table for the memo pad I borrowed from the school office—hey, if I'm going to waste my time in detention in the office, I might as well get some free school supplies out of it—and start scribbling. My eyes fly from the screen to the pad as I write, isolating which letters of the puzzle are size 16, and which are size 15. The size-16 letters are endless. I've got two lines of them already. The size-15 letters, on the other hand, are few. I overhear Jax behind me.

"Is 'Excalibur' maybe a reference to King Arthur?" he asks, scrolling through his phone. "Looks like King Arthur is the name of a baking school here. Or maybe it's a reference to King County?"

I isolate the size-15 letters, and my heart thunders as I read what I have.

The size-15 letters all spell out:

DEXTERXREPUBLICAN.

Dexter X. Republican.

Who is that?

I think for a minute and lean backward, a little too far, and can't catch myself fast enough. *No, no, no!* I scramble for the card table, which, actually, it's probably a good thing my hands didn't find that or I might've brought my whole computer down with me. I land back-first on the floor, my feet tumbling over my head until I slam into my bookshelves behind me. I'm disoriented, but I hear a wobbling sound from above me, like metal teetering on wood, and then it stops.

Jax gasps. Yas gasps.

I look up to find Han's hand clutched around my biggest soccer trophy, just inches from the tip of my nose.

His mouth is flat, and eyes wide, searching mine as if to ask if I'm okay.

"Thanks, man," I breathe.

That was way too close.

"You okay?" asks Yas, coming over and kneeling in front of me. She rests a hand on my shoulder as I compose myself and catch my breath.

"Yeah, I, um," I say. Then I remember what I found. "I decoded the image! It says 'Dexter X. Republican'!"

"Who's that?" asks Yas.

"Oh, so you *are* in!" says Jax.

"I didn't say that," replies Yas with a sour look.

"I was hoping one of y'all might know," I say, feeling my heart sink a bit lower. "I'll look him up?"

"No need," says Jax. "It's not a person. Those are cross streets. Dexter Avenue and Republican Street."

"Oh my god, you're right!" exclaims Yas. "Jax, you're a genius!"

"Can I get that in writing?" he asks with an eyebrow wiggle.

Han holds out his phone to me, the screen zoomed in on a map of the big tech campus that borders Lake Union, about two miles from here via Fourth Avenue. The 62 bus goes right there. So does the 554. Or we could catch the E line. Or the South Lake Union Trolley— lovingly nicknamed "the SLUT" around here.

Whatever our next move, we'll find Clue 2 in South Lake Union.

But first . . . we've got a school day to finish.

It's like we all realize it at the same time.

We look at the laptop, sink back down into our seats, and I turn up the volume so we can hear the lecture, and pretend to listen, as we hum inside and watch the clock.

Jax

I really thought I was onto something with that Excalibur thing.

But then there Spider go with the hacking again.

Source code? Really?

The Order may have good intentions with posting a puzzle like this, but this will be no cakewalk. If they're bringing source code into this, they're going to want us to *dig*. I bet half the people on the forum don't even realize the first clue is already out. *I* didn't even know! On Mama and Zaza, when we get to South Lake Union, I'ma be the *first* to figure out where Clue 2 is, because I'm getting real tired of coming in second place today. First Han lurking in the shadows like Batman, and now Spider being a cross between MacGyver and Steve Jobs.

I have an idea.

"Yas, why don't we use your place as a home base for the next clue since you live a few minutes outside South Lake Union? We could go after eighth period and—"

"Not as long as Ranya's home," she says abruptly.

"Oh," I say.

Ranya. Her sister. She's home.

Haunting the place.

"She's *still there?*" asks Spider exasperatedly before tossing a couple of potato chips into his mouth. We've long since finished the ramen and moved on to the too-early-for-dinner-but-we're-still-hungry part of the day. "Wasn't she supposed to go back to campus weeks ago?"

Yas shrugs her shoulders, and I sink my teeth into the Fuji apple I'm holding, savoring its sweetness before jumping in.

"Sometimes it takes a while to get over someone."

"Well, yeah, but she broke up with *him*, right?" asks Spider.

Han gives Spider a look like he's wondering how Spider can be so callous.

"*What?*" asks Spider, shrugging at him. "I'm just saying, if you all catch me simping for someone so hard that my whole life shuts down for months if *I* leave *them*, you have my permission to slap me into next week."

"Same," says Yas.

Spider rolls his eyes.

"Please, Yas," he says. "We all know you're tsundere as hell. When you do fall for someone, you'll fall hard. No cap."

"Cap," she says.

Meanwhile, I'm over here pulling up past info about the Order—articles, breaking news, tweets, posts, texts I've accumulated, and most recently, a cryptology forum discussion all about who they might be, and what they might want. The comments are full of *wild* ideas.

"They're probably a lobbying firm," reads one. I have to smile. The Order is many things—a secretive group of hackers, a team of social justice vigilantes, my idols in a way. But a lobbying firm? Nah. They rarely influence politics directly, at least through the regular channels that a lobbying firm might. What kind of lobbying firm pours buckets of red paint down the front steps of a Confederate museum?

Yes, they really did that once.

I love them.

I think back to what Mama told me this morning.

The best way you can help is by voting when you turn eighteen, and by "being the change" in the meantime.

But like Ava said, what does that phrase even mean? "Be the change." Wouldn't competing in a citywide cryptology puzzle hosted by a social justice vigilante group count as "being the change"? Could Mama really be mad at me for something so . . . passive? We're not hurting anyone or disturbing anyone's peace.

It'll probably be like every other puzzle we've done on the forum anyway, except maybe a little harder. In all the puzzles I've built and hosted, I've never made people look through source code to find an answer to a clue. But now I'm thinking maybe I should!

The history teacher on Spider's computer is still lecturing away. Mrs. Brandywine, thank goodness, lets her students keep their cameras off. "Long as you get your homework in," she told us on day one of the school year, "and show that you're understanding the material, the rest is your business."

So here we sit, the four of us, lost in our phones as her voice fills the room with talk of the Clinton administration and all that was done to catapult the "tough on crime" movement into mass incarceration, a.k.a. legalized slavery. Law enforcement ain't sneaky. My people know what's up.

"With regard to the Roundworld refinery going up in Beacon Hill," Mrs. Brandywine continues, "there's much talk about its environmental impact, specifically on air quality in surrounding neighborhoods—"

"And," cuts in Spider, "why that shit would never fly on Mercer Island."

Yas scoffs in agreement, and Han nods without taking his eyes off his phone.

He's right. Ooh, and it makes my heart race with rage when I think about it. The whole system is twisted as hell, and Mama won't let me do a thing about it. I think back to all those crowds of people gathered in downtown, holding signs and chanting in unified conviction that we the citizens of Puget Sound will not stand by while *another* multinational corporation comes in and mucks up our economy.

I reach up and clasp my fingers around that amethyst stone she gave me. One of her precious crystals.

For protection, she had told me.

Like I need protection from anything as long as I do what she says.

I'm surprised at my own rage, and I sigh and try to release some of this steam. I love Mama and Zaza to death. Ava too. But I can't sit by and just let this oil refinery steamroll over everything my family loves, everything we've worked so hard to build. Mama's garden, it's our home. It's where we go for peace and abundance. It's where we meet our friends. I've seen people fall in love there, celebrate babies there, let their children play there.

Maybe I can't march. Maybe I can't be on the front lines swinging signs and chanting "No blood, no soil, only water, no oil" like I want to. But I can still do something.

I can win this puzzle.

I can join the Order.

I can help them take down Roundworld with my new "power."

"Han, you're *brilliant*!" I exclaim, and I look around at my three friends and remember they haven't been in my head for the last few minutes. I clear my throat and try to recover. "Sorry. I, uh, I'm in. Definitely in. In fact, I want to join the Order. Like, even more so now."

Yas blinks in surprise and shrugs. "Suit yourself."

"Wait, you're *actually* not doing this, Yas?" I ask. She *has* to be in. We can't win without her.

"Come on," says Spider, hands held out pleadingly. "How are we going to get to these clues first without our acrobatic makeup guru?"

"Whoa, no," she says, holding up her hand for silence. "Parkour. Not acrobatics. I'm no gymnast."

"You'll have to explain the difference to me one day," says Spider. Han nods in agreement. "Anyway, what if the clues are in weird spots that *don't* include the sewer or creepy alleyways?"

Han nudges Spider's leg.

"What? I'm just saying, you're master of the night, Han. Dark places no one else would ever think to look. Yas is the squirrel, you're the bat. I'm the spider, and Jax is . . ."

He pauses and looks at me blankly. Then smiles sheepishly.

"An octopus," says Yas.

"What the hell?" I ask. "Everyone else gets to be shifty and cunning and sharp, and I'm stuck as a slimy brain with tentacles."

"Precisely," says Spider, apparently agreeing with her. "You're a brain with tentacles. The most strategic brain of all of us. If you're in this to win this puzzle, Jax, we're with you. At least, *I* am."

We *all* look at Yas. Not as a peer pressure thing, but like . . . we need a decision, and we all know it.

She knows it.

"Ugh, fine, I'm in," says Yas.

My heart jumps, and I can feel a smile creeping across my face.

"*That's* it!" says Spider, turning to Han. "You're in too, Han?"

He looks up from his phone with a nod and a grin.

"*Yeah,*" I say. All four pillars of JERICHO are standing. *And* we've figured out the first clue first, from the looks of these comments. "Let's get these oil refinery assholes out of here."

"JERICHO in full effect," says Spider, holding out his fist. We all take turns bumping it, except for Han, who holds out his phone screen instead.

"What's this, Han?" asks Yas, taking it from him and looking at the screen.

Her mouth goes flat. Her eyes go a sliver wider for a second, so quick that I'm pretty sure only I caught it.

"Let me see," I say, just as Spider holds out his hand for the phone. Yas appeases both of our curiosity by holding the phone up so we can both see it. We lean in so fast, we almost bump heads, and I can't read the comments quick enough. Just one that says "On our way."

"That's ROYAL," I say.

Team ROYAL.

Bunch of rich kids from Mercer Island with endless money and time, who can ditch school to chase internet puzzles for shits and giggles. They can probably access the history stream from their phones with unlimited data plans. Meanwhile, Wi-Fi is Team JERICHO's friend. Resources aside, though, these people are *good*. ROYAL's element is fire, like ours is earth, so all of their puzzles have clues on things like bags of charcoal, propane tanks, steam vents in the sides of buildings, bonfire barrels, a "Smoking Area" sign. Once, they even left a clue on a bottle of hot sauce.

A dirty trick, if you ask me. Hot sauce doesn't count as fire any more than a packet of rock candy counts as earth.

"Oh, *hell* no. We need to get there now!" says Spider, muting his computer, cutting off Mrs. Brandywine just as she says, "Neutrality helps—"

We all know the end of that.

The oppressor.

In silent agreement, we all sling our bags over our shoulders and head for the door and down the stairs to the front entryway, where we politely left our shoes earlier. It's not that we're all *okay* with playing hooky, but when an oil refinery is moving into our neighborhood—a refinery that would threaten Spider's apartment, Yas's store, Han's living situation, and my garden—we all agree that missing half a day of virtual school is a small price to pay.

But as we all slide our feet into our sneakers and sprint out the door and down the street, through throngs of businesspeople and colorful folks in protest gear, my eyes begin to notice the vibes around us. Most of these people leave us alone and let us on our way, but a few, almost all of them white, stare us down with raised eyebrows and pursed lips like they think we must be running like this to get away with stealing something.

Because running to catch the bus for any other reason is a totally implausible scenario.

I look up. The sun will be going down by the time we get there in an hour or so.

And we're running to catch a bus to South Lake Union, arguably one of the most upscale spots in all of Seattle. Techies. Fusion restaurants. Grocery stores that feel like a farmers' market with prices double that of Pike Place Market.

And three of us are kids of color.

I wonder if this is a good idea.

But if it's to save our garden, our store, our homes . . .

I'm still in.

Yas

Abba's store has been on the corner of Eighth and Republican for the last forty-nine years, just around the corner from the Space Needle—he always mentions proudly when talking to anyone about it. Prime real estate—he always tells me, as if trying to convince me. He started reminding me more often when property developers first showed up with offers to buy him out of the area. And even more often when construction workers rolled in and built an apartment complex over and all around the store so that it's now nestled into the big shiny silver building like an afterthought, as if the apartments came first.

Grandpa started working at this store when he and Gran had just a few hundred dollars and the clothes on their back. That was when you could support a family with a convenience-store job. He saved and saved until he could buy the place and run it himself.

"My own abba went through so much to keep this place. What kind of son would I be if I sold it off at the sight of a few big bills?"

A smart one, I always want to say but never do. The area is worth so much now. We live only a few blocks away from South Lake Union—in low-income housing at Navigation House, right by Denny Park, where techies go for Yoga in the Park and to walk their Shiba Inus and French bulldogs and feed them organic dog treats from the grocery store across the street that looks more like an Apple store.

Ever since that grocery store went up, traffic at Abba's store has been meager at best. Things in cans are starting to expire. *Cans.* They're called "nonperishables" for a reason. Some pets don't even last that long.

But he says, "It just means nobody wants pickles from a convenience store anymore."

"Or tuna," I say.

"Exactly. Everybody's going vegan now. I'll roll with the punches. A good businessman always rolls with the punches. And he waits."

Abba is waiting for a miracle, and he doesn't even realize it.

I sigh and look out the window of the South Lake Union Trolley as it announces that we're at Westlake and Ninth. We're the next stop.

My heart starts pounding all over again.

I know this puzzle will probably be inconsequential for me. I'm not joining an online vigilante group shrouded in mystery, just personally, even if it does take out those refinery plans. But Jax seems to trust them with his life. And he needs JERICHO to win. So here I am.

And just maybe, if we win, and some of this "power" keeps Abba's delusions from sinking us completely, I'm in.

Besides, JERICHO is a team. What kind of friend would I be if I just dipped because . . . what . . . I didn't *feel* like playing this one?

Plus, prize or not, playing the game is always the best part.

I wonder what we'll find at the corner of Dexter and Republican. A sign? A serial number? Team ROYAL?

I clutch my bag a little tighter at the thought of that. I've seen them post forum puzzles a few times, and they're always tricky. The fire element. Once, when the Discovery Center featured a poster on the outside window about plasma. Which, arguably, is a questionable source of fire. Apparently, someone on the team was under the impression that plasma was closely related to hot lava. That was the day I learned that plasma is actually a state of matter. Fluorescent light is technically plasma. Not even remotely related to fire. Doesn't count as on theme with the fire element.

Jax gave them a strike for that one.

Rule one of the forum: The rules must be followed.

And if ROYAL didn't follow their own rules, they couldn't expect other teams to follow them either. I've never met the three of them in person—yes, there are three of them and four of us—but I mostly know their roles. Purple Suit Guy—the mastermind, Red Cap Guy—the muscle, and the blond girl. She must be new. Not quite sure what she does.

We could run into any of them here, which isn't a problem necessarily. Everyone on the forum is pretty civil in person. That's rule three. Fellow humans must be respected, especially by those in power.

I look up at the sky, fading into a watercolor painting of orange and purple. I'm going to miss Maghrib prayer. I wince. I can hear my mother's voice in my head chiding me to be more mindful of prayer times, something I promised myself to be better at. I'll have to make it up later. Abba will be looking for me at the store unless I text him.

ME: Abba, I'll be home a little late tonight. Studying with Spider, Jax, and Han.

He always takes forever to text back. *When you're at work, you work,* he'd say. I don't bother waiting for a response. The trolley announces we're at the Discovery Center, the doors open, we all pile out onto the street, and the trolley glides off down the rails.

Since it's evening, South Lake Union is growing hazy, lazy, and slow.

The sun has just set over the Olympic Mountains, and all the people who work locally are walking their thousand-dollar dogs back to their four-thousand-dollar-a-month condos—I'm not joking— that's the equivalent of a car paid in full every six months.

I shouldn't generalize, I know. The apartment I live in is provisioned for people like . . . well . . . my parents, and it's just around the corner. But all the tech badges I see hanging on hips and around necks, all the flashy cars I see speeding down Denny toward the Needle and Belltown, where all the bars are bumping on Friday nights, and all the designer clothes I see everywhere . . . I feel some kinda way about my parents' store being boxed out of this area.

I walk down Westlake, leading JERICHO past a fitness center that looks like a space station inside and a sandwich spot that costs eight dollars for *half* an order. We hang a left at the secondhand store that takes donations from the local rich and sells it to the poor and disenfranchised at a profit under the guise of being a charity. I could walk this route in my sleep. That's part of what makes JERICHO such a force around here. We know Seattle. And I mean, we *know* it. We've all got a different zone. I've got South Lake Union. Jax has Beacon Hill. Spider has Capitol Hill, downtown, the Market, and Belltown, and Han has the whole east side where his dad works, and most of Tacoma, since that's where his mom lives.

Oh, and pretty much the whole underground and sewer system.

That's helpful too.

"Do you have to walk so fast, Yas?" asks Jax, the faintest hint of exhaustion in his voice.

"You're welcome to wait at Abba's store until I get back with the second clue," I say. He's like a little brother to me. If our friendship had a contract, there'd definitely be a clause somewhere in there about me teasing him. But Jax is full of surprises.

"You mean the same Abba who gives us gulab jamun and jalebis the second we walk in? Sign me up."

Spider audibly shudders somewhere behind me. I know he's not a fan of sweets, so Abba's generous mithai offerings often go . . .

strategically dodged. With gratitude, of course. But maybe I could convince Abba to give him some biryani instead. After all, Spider's mom did give me a steaming bowl of tonkotsu ramen. With *two* eggs.

We round the corner at Westlake and Thomas, turning left and preparing to walk the last few blocks north to our destination.

Dexter x Republican.

Tricky of the Order to use such a play on words. I wonder how many players immediately googled the phrase as a name, pulling up no matches, and how many thought "Dexter X" might be the name of a Republican politician or billionaire. Not a bad deduction. I guess one has to know Seattle fairly well to excel at this puzzle. Between the four of us, we've got this one.

That "power" they promised might just be enough to run these oil tycoons out of Puget Sound. Might be enough to send their employees packing, away from their provided cafeteria buffet lunches and catered meetings. Abba's preassembled lunch packages cut back into the market a little, but not nearly enough to bounce back from the pull of that glittering eatery. Even though him closing down the store is a long shot, if he's determined to keep it open, running it shouldn't feel like hell.

I look up at the shiny glass building. Now that afternoon is fading into twilight, I can see into one of the cafeterias up there—full of people even though it's almost five p.m. Abba says that's prime snack time—another market he's lost out on with the cafeteria's presence. And he used to get another wave of people around five thirty, leaving for the day and in need of a predinner dinner.

Those folks are gone now too, bellies full of fresh salad and ancient grain bowls with quinoa and hummus and snap peas and endive.

I hate that cafeteria.

If there's no oil refinery, there's no oil. If there's no oil, there's no Roundworld. If Roundworld disappears, so does the cafeteria.

If the Order can get these oil people out of here, then playing their game this one time will be worth it.

I'm in.

I just hope Jax enjoys joining them alone.

I want the refinery out of our backyard like everyone else, but as soon as I've accomplished that, I've got goals to attend to, and they don't include going undercover with a secret organization. How am I supposed to open my own parkour studio while sneaking around on the internet, bringing down multinational corporations and exposing sinister government plots? Parkour wins. Every time.

Just as the light of Abba's shop flickers to life for the night— "Abba's," Grandpa had named it—the blaring sound of a buzzsaw drills straight through my head, and I swear amid the whirring noise I thought I heard a cheery, "Ho, hey!"

I know that voice.

I look to Spider, Jax, and Han for confirmation, but they've already spotted Jeanine, not at her usual spot on the ground outside the espresso place on the corner, but in the doorway of the luxury furniture boutique next door to Abba's. She raises a dusty hand to us with a hello, and my heart melts.

"Sup, lovely?" calls Jax. And I know he means it. Jeanine is a constant bright spot in an ever-evolving tech metropolis.

"Nothing much, lovelier!" she calls back. Han steps out into the road first, and we all seem to collectively decide that whatever happens with this puzzle, we can spare a moment for her company.

"What brings you out to this spot?" asks Spider. "Coffee shop owners being assholes again?"

"On a whole 'nother level," she says, her shoulders falling a bit. She glances back at the espresso shop with the little black-and-white man traced around the word "Southtown," and points toward the door. "Look at the ground."

All our eyes follow her direction, and I spot them. Rows and rows of metal pins poking up through the concrete along the side of the building.

"What *are* those?" asks Jax.

Han steps forward and lays his head down sideways on his hands with his eyes shut. Then he taps one hand with his other thumb over and over, finally opening his eyes again.

Jax's eyes grow wide in realization, and he turns back to Jeanine.

"They put those pins on the ground so you can't sleep there?" he asks, his voice soft with compassion. Han, the infrastructure expert, nods. Spider slides his hands into his pockets.

"Hostile architecture," he says sharply, angrily. "A true injustice. You know how they just replaced those benches in Denny Park? The new ones have those weird bars down the middle."

"I thought those were there to keep strangers separated in case they wanted to share a bench without bumping hips," offers Jax, forever the optimist.

"Nope," says Spider. "They're designed to be unsleepable."

I've encountered a few examples of such architecture in my parkouring. Pins in the ground, park benches with bars down the middle, bus stop seats tilted at a 45-degree angle, which is inconvenient for sitting and impossible for sleeping. Even blaring music during the night if it's far enough away from homes.

By design.

Who does that?

"I'm sorry, Jeanine," I say. "That's awful. Do you know where you're going to sleep tonight?"

"No idea," she says. "S'posed to rain, so maybe up on Fifth Street by the mural?"

"Across from police headquarters?!" exclaims Jax. "Bad idea."

Then I notice the furniture shop behind Jeanine and take a good look at it. There she stands, in the doorway of this place that sells beds for as much as Abba and Mom's rent, next to a café that won't allow their front porch to become a haven for someone who can't afford one overnight. An idea strikes me.

"This place sometimes tosses foam padding from damaged furniture in the dumpster behind the stores."

The same dumpster where Abba tosses his garbage. I've seen them—thick yellow rolls of memory foam from display sofas, old cushions, and sometimes even mattresses.

"You could grab one and lay it over the top of those pins so you can sleep here tonight," I offer.

"Without getting impaled," adds Spider.

"Thanks," says Jeanine, running her hand over her forehead, glancing back at those pins and sighing. "All the money they pour into telling us where we can't sleep. The money they'd save if they gave us a place where we *can*."

Jax, Han, Spider, and I all look at each other as Jeanine turns and walks up the street. Two strangers walk right past her, laughing and engrossed in their conversation. All I catch is:

"Well, yeah, I wouldn't pick an oil company as my first choice either, but the *benefits*. Do you know they sent their employees skiing in the Swiss Alps last year?"

By the time they get to "last year," their voices are trailing off into the distance behind us. None of us have a comment about the conversation, but we all know what it must be about. Roundworld. How are we supposed to fight a force so big and powerful and full of money that people feel like they can't say no to pouring eight-plus hours per day into ensuring that it flourishes?

We walk as a group, and after moments of silence that seem to stretch on forever, we reach Abba's store, and I lead the group right on past it.

"Uh, Yas?" asks Spider. "Aren't we going to stop for a *little* smackerel first?"

I stop to turn around and answer that the store will be here but the chance to win this puzzle might not be, but Jax walks right past me.

"Nah," says Jax. "What if ROYAL's already found—"

He stares past my face and freezes, and I whip around to see what he's looking at, just in time to catch a large white poster being yanked from a wooden telephone pole by a white hand belonging to a white kid in a white T-shirt and a backward red snapback.

The kid in the red hat glances over one shoulder, then the other, in our direction, and we lock eyes.

My heart starts thumping out of control. Did this kid just *steal* the first clue? He lowers the poster as if he's hoping I won't put together what he's doing, and I make my first mistake.

I take a step forward.

He bolts.

I bolt after him.

"Yas!" comes Jax's voice behind me. I hear the pattering of swift footsteps behind me, but they're not as swift as mine. I round the corner at Republican and sprint past the University of Washington Clinic, toward Mercer Avenue—a three-lane highway that bleeds traffic straight from I-5 into bustling South Lake Union.

And it's rush hour.

And the crosswalk is counting down from forty-two seconds.

Which means he's either going to sprint across the street and hope he can dodge traffic fast enough, or—

He darts right.

I dart right, narrowly missing a strikingly tall man talking uncomfortably loudly into his wireless earphone and holding a bag of groceries with the other hand.

"Sorry!" I call behind me.

I hear him growl, probably frustrated at my carelessness, when people go for runs through here all the time. Maybe not at fourteen miles per hour, but still.

I keep my eye on Red Cap as he glances over his shoulder at me. I smirk. Rule number one of parkour: Never look back. I'm gaining on him, closing the gap. I'm so close now that I can make out a symbol on the poster as it flaps in his hand.

An eye.

A cat eye with three lashes. Strange-looking mark. It's not elemental, since all four of the element teams are preoccupied with *playing* the Order's puzzle instead of hosting. Could be one of the anatomy teams since it's an eye. When people play a JERICHO puzzle, they know to look for a hammer.

I guess in the Order's puzzle, we're looking for eyes.

Red Cap is sprinting down this darkening alley so fast, I'm worried a truck will come backing out of one of these loading docks in the covered bays behind the street-facing stores we just sprinted past. We're not supposed to be back here.

That sound of a buzzsaw rings out again, and . . . what the hell? We're making a huge circle! We're heading straight back toward the coffee shop that won't let Jeanine sleep on the public property outside their door anymore. With any luck, maybe I can chase this guy back to where Han, Jax, and Spider are waiting. Han is probably trying to cut him off around a corner somewhere as we speak. I'm still gaining on him.

"Stealing clues, asshole?" I call after him. He glances over his shoulder again as I realize I'm just about close enough to touch him. To grab that poster . . .

A muscular white arm shoots out from the darkness and clamps around my right arm, yanking me into the shadows as I watch Red Cap grow smaller and smaller down the alley.

"Let *go of me!*" I shriek. I yank my arm away and get a good look at my roadblock. A man maybe a foot taller than me in a white T-shirt and yellow construction hat.

"Just what are you doing out here this late at night, sprinting through here? You know this is a construction site, lil' miss?"

Every hair on the back of my neck bristles at that last bit—"lil' miss."

I wonder under what circumstances Red Cap might've been grabbed aside like this and called "lil' mister." But I quell the blood boiling up in my chest and take a deep breath.

"That guy stole something of mine, and *you* let him get away!"

It's not entirely a lie. He *did* steal something. Something that belongs to the forum. He broke a cardinal rule of cryptology—leave clues intact for those behind you. It's the whole fun of the game. Otherwise, it's not a scavenger hunt but a simple race to swipe it first.

And where's the fun in that?

Red Cap has now made it to the end of the alley, where he's hopping another fence with that white poster in hand. *Goddammit.*

"Oh, did he?" asks Discount Bob the Builder, crossing his arms. He's close enough that I can smell the sweat on him. And the aftershave.

"Yes," I hiss. "He did. And I would've caught him if you hadn't interrupted."

He raises a skeptical eyebrow and looks me up and down.

"Why are you out here?"

I prickle at that question. What does he mean by "out here"? Out here in a loading dock behind a building? Out here in the middle of a construction site? Out here in South Lake Union?

"Out here on campus," he says, as if he can hear my thoughts. "You got a badge?"

A badge . . . fuck . . . no. I wish Jax were here. He'd be quick with the retorts. *Who's asking?* he'd say. *Who do you think you are, asking to see my badge? Do* you *have a badge?*

"That's my business and none of yours," I snap. I smile inside in spite of myself. Not bad, Yas. "Now, excuse me. I have to get home."

I step forward to continue down the alley. Maybe there are remnants of the poster on the pole that will give us some clues. Anything at this point.

But Construction Man tightens his folded arms and steps in front of me.

"What if I think security might want to hear about this?"

There's been a shift in his tone that sends my blood cold. Is this guy really trying to *report* me to some authority? For what? Being in a construction area in the early evening on a weekday? So I hopped a fence. Big deal. As far as he knows, Red Cap stole my purse. Who wouldn't hop a fence to get that back?

"Gee, wish I had the time to talk to them," I say, attempting to step around him. But of course, he steps aside to block me. I start surveying my surroundings. There's a dumpster to my left with another fence behind it. No idea what's on the other side of that, but if it gets me away from this man, in this dark alley, who's threatening to report me to the campus authorities, it might be worth it.

Or, Yas, you could take the most efficient route.

Without glancing over my shoulder to give him a clue about my next move, I turn and bolt back down the alley toward Mercer.

"Hey!" he hollers after me. I hear his footsteps, but I don't look back. A man crosses the opening at Mercer, wheeling a stroller nonchalantly and talking on the phone at the same time. I don't have time to slow down. But I do have time to make the jump.

I force all the energy in my body into my arms, dive forward, and push off the ground with a labored grunt, tucking my knees up against my chest as I tumble in a tight little ball through the air. The bottoms of my spotless white sneakers just barely miss the topmost tendrils of the man's coiffed hair, and I kick my feet out, leading with them to propel me as far as I possibly can.

When my feet land, they find the pavement, and my hands follow for stability. But I don't have time to look up and around and explain to all these shocked pedestrians why Black Pakistani Spider-Woman in a hijab just leapt out of an alley and over a man with a stroller.

I have a red-hatted boy to track down and a puzzle to solve.

"Stop right there!" I hear from the alley behind me. But I'm down the street and around the corner so fast, Construction Man's voice fades like a vapor behind me.

A very bothered vapor.

Han

By the time the guy in the red hat climbs over the fence across the street, I'm the only one still standing here outside Abba's store. Once Yas took off, I knew there was no catching her—I have my older brother's text conversation up, and I'm halfway through asking him if he has access to security footage anywhere within a two-block radius of here.

He works for Roundworld. We haven't let it come between us.

He's a big reason why we—him, me, Dad—can still afford our place, so I'm not allowed to be mad at him for selling out and joining the bad side.

And now my restraint is coming in handy.

ME: Do you have footage of anywhere in a two-block radius of Republican and Dexter?

KYLER: . . . mayyyyybe . . .

ME: What does that mean?

I wish he wouldn't talk in riddles like that. Does he mean "mayyyyybe" as in "I'm not sure, but I'll check," or "Yes I do, but I want to see if you'll give me something in advance for my services," or "Maybe, but I'm not going to tell you because I'm mad at you about something"?

Sussing out hidden implications in words is hard enough in person when I can actually *hear* them, let alone doing it via text. Why can't people just say what they mean? He takes forever to text back.

Cars fly past, the whirring sound of their engines swelling and dying as they go by. The beeping of the walk signal rings rhythmically in my ears. Is it . . . is it getting louder? A dog barks behind me, making me jump. My heart pounds as I look over my shoulder at the culprit—a small dog with tight, shiny curls. Looks part poodle. The leash holder is a young woman with earbuds in, a cup of coffee in one hand—why is she drinking coffee so late in the evening?—and bright red lipstick. The dog jerks forward at me and barks again, making every hair on my body go rigid. My hands instinctively slide into my sweatshirt pocket, and my fingers find my phone. I flip it over and over in my hand, sliding it smoothly against my palm with one hand, then the other.

"Sorry about that," says the woman. "Gigi isn't usually like this around people."

I don't talk. I can't talk right now. So I just stare at her. My shoulders are up. Tense. This is all too much. Too much sound. Too bright. My skin feels hot. Feels like the world's on fire. Feels like I need to get out of here.

The dog barks again, and I take steps back.

"Come on, girl," she says. "Stop bothering people." She turns back to me again and says, quieter this time, "I'm so sorry."

I bite my lip and stare at the ground as they leave.

I hear footsteps running up to me, and without looking up, I see Jax's shoes on the ground beside me.

"Hey, man, you okay?" comes the out-of-breath voice of Jax, which makes me jump from the sheer volume. Why is he talking so loud?

I glance up.

The look on his face is one of shock, and then of pity, I think. I nod reflexively, but he shakes his head like he doesn't believe me. Spider runs up behind him, and I keep twirling my phone in my pocket.

Both of their eyes fall to where my hands are and then back up to meet mine.

Jax leans in close and whispers to me, "You're stimming, man. Do you want to go somewhere quiet for a while?"

We're in the middle of chasing down the guy who stole the second clue of a puzzle that's very important to all of us, and Jax and Spider took the time to stop and make sure I'm okay. I . . . don't know how to feel. I want to keep going. The last thing I want to do is slow down our progress. But a bus goes by, the driver leaning on the horn, making the blaring sound rattle through my head like a radioactive blast. My heart skips and I shut my eyes. Too much input. Too much light. Too much everything. My phone buzzes in my hand, and I can't even bring myself to look at the screen.

I pull it out, screen still open to my conversation with Kyler, and hold it out to them, eyes shut tight, hoping they get the message.

I don't want to slow down the puzzle, but . . . I need a minute.

Spider takes the phone from my hand. I know his hands. They're soft and smooth.

Once the phone is out of my hand, and my contribution to getting us past this roadblock has been made, I peek my eyes open and spy a nearby bench, and I realize how good a seat would be right about now. But it would still be too loud. So, I look at the cross-street signs. Eighth and Republican. There's a garage nearby—one with green doors and a keypad. I've seen people come through here and enter numbers on that keypad. I know the code.

I look both ways before crossing the street.

"Hey, take your phone, Han!" calls Jax.

Where I'm going, I won't need it, but they will. I hope they keep talking to Kyler. If anyone can get them intel on what went down with that guy in the red hat, it's him. Maybe it'll lead to some clues about who he is, why he sabotaged the clue for everyone else, and why he wants so badly to win this puzzle from the Order.

I enter the code and slip quietly into the pitch-black garage. The noise of the street—the hum of it all, is muffled as I shut the door quietly behind me. I've never been here before, but I love it. It's dark. It's quiet. It smells faintly like something familiar . . . bread? It smells nice. It feels cold in here, but it smells warm.

I take a minute. I breathe. I try to remember the face of the guy in the red hat and wonder if I've seen it before. He looked our age but muscular, and maybe as athletic as Yas if he's able to scale a six-foot fence like it's nothing, while holding a poster. As I think, I feel my heart rate slowing. The world feels clearer now. I feel less frazzled. You know how when you've been wearing something itchy all day? Or something's been rubbing the wrong way? Maybe a pair of underwear that's too small, or a piece of jewelry or something? And then you come home at the end of the day and take it off?

That's how it feels sitting in here. I feel relief. Some days are bad days, where I can't get out of bed, or where I want to be in a cave where nothing happens. And some days—like today—are good days. Days when I just need a minute. I stand up, fold my arms across my chest, and head for the door, ready to make the jump back into the puzzle.

The sounds of traffic greet me, and it's nearly nighttime now, even though it only felt like I was in there for a few minutes. My eyes find Yas's abba's store, lit up outside, and Abba—we all call him Abba—standing just inside at the counter stretching his back, probably sore from bending and putting labels on things and stocking shelves.

I know that look. My dad comes home with the same one every night.

Tired.

Unappreciated.

I feel bad for both of them.

But I can't think about that now. I have a puzzle to solve. I have a security room to get to. Kyler works in the tiniest room in the quietest corner of South Lake Union, right outside of a Roundworld building, in an alley just around the corner from here. I could walk the four blocks to his "office," or I could take the shortcut through the loading dock behind this garage that's supposed to be impassible due to the padlock on the fence. But it's after six p.m. and before eight p.m., which means the padlock is unlocked. There are so many delivery guys for the Roundworld salad bar and vending machines that they don't even bother locking the fence during those hours. I've sat here and watched them come and go for hours while waiting for Kyler to get off work so he can drive me home, when there was nothing else to do.

Now my spying has proven useful.

I step through the fence and shove my hands in my pockets, walking, walking, walking. I keep my head down and focus on the darkness around me as the sun disappears and takes the brilliant orange sky with it. When I get to the end of the dock, I look around the corner and see the faint glow of the door opening, and Jax, Yas, and Spider stepping inside.

Perfect timing, Han, as usual, I tell myself.

The team's lucky to have me.

I step right up to the door and knock.

No answer.

I knock again.

No answer.

They *have* to know it's me, right?

"Yes?" comes a voice on the other side.

The thing about being nonverbal is that it's not an all-the-time thing. Sometimes I do talk. Sometimes I *can* talk. But other times, I just can't. I don't know why. It's like my brain just . . . decides it won't talk anymore. No signals to the rest of me with the speaking function. I know I *can* at other times. But . . . nope. Nothing. Like right now. How easy would it be to just respond? How easy *should* it be to respond?

I guess I'm still figuring it out.

I just stare at the door, hoping they'll know it's me. And then the knob turns, startling me back a few steps. Jax peers out and a smile spreads across his face.

"Thought you'd never turn up!" he says. "We might have found something."

"How'd you know it was him?" comes Yas's voice from farther into the room.

"Sensed his aura," says Jax with a smile and a wink in my direction. "All . . . *lurky.*"

He ushers me into a dimly lit room bathed in yellow, and Yas and Spider are hovering over a standing computer desk where a super-tall, lanky-as-me guy dressed in a T-shirt and cargo pants is examining the screen with his face resting on his free hand.

"Oh hey, bro," he says, too engrossed in his computer to look at me. I nod up at him anyway. "Dad said to tell you we're ordering out tonight. He'll be home late from work."

A strange chill of disappointment—I don't know what else to call it—flickers up my spine. Dad's been working longer and longer hours lately. "Late" from work means *very* late. Like, two-in-the-morning late. Kayaking lessons all day, accounting all night. That's his life now. And all for nothing if this refinery goes up.

Probably.

Unless I can help it.

Kyler seems unfazed and clicks through black-and-white screenshots from footage of the alley around the corner.

"What even *is* a 'lurky' aura?" asks Spider. "I thought auras were supposed to be different colors. 'Lurky' isn't a color."

"Okay, a *vibe*, I guess? I don't know. Mama's better at this stuff than I am."

"Oh hey, look, bros," says Kyler. "I *did* find something."

We all lean in close to see several shots in rapid succession of Red Cap Guy—although his hat is now dark gray on the footage—sprinting down Mercer before ducking into the alley between Terry and Westlake. Yas follows him with even more speed and finesse. He had planted his left foot firmly on the ground to propel himself to the right into the alley. Yas leaned right and turned her foot to step with only the ball, making for a smoother rotation.

Impressive.

I look over at her and smile, but she's too focused on the screen, brows furrowed. Eyes narrow. Angry-looking, even. I wonder if she's upset that she let him get away.

She shouldn't be.

"There!" cries Jax suddenly, startling me. I wish he wouldn't do that. "QR code! On the poster! Can you zoom in on it, Kyler?"

Kyler does as he was asked, and the picture grows huge on the screen. Jax's phone is out faster than all of ours, and the scanned code goes through, opening a browser window with plain text. We all study the screen like it's second nature to us. And I guess, in a way, it is.

The message says simply:

A CAFÉ AT THE PENTAGON.
FIND A BIN. LOOK AROUND.
ASK NOT FOR WHOM THE BELL TOLLS.
IT TOLLS FOR THE TOWN.

Jax

The Pentagon—the headquarters for the United States Department of Defense—is 2,745 miles away from here, in Arlington, Virginia. The only address I'm seeing in Seattle with a 2745 number is Luna Apartments, with a café next door called Freshy's.

Which is only a bus ride away.

Easy to get to.

We could go right now.

But the bell part.

The bell part is what's making me hesitate.

"I say let's get to that café before ROYAL steals another clue!" says Spider once I've explained all my findings to the team. We're all standing inside Abba's shop where it's warm, since Kyler had to get back to closing up his office down the street. I lean against the counter and scroll, searching for more clues.

"Whoa, whoa," says Yas, holding up a hand for silence. "Team JERICHO does *not* fall. Especially not to manipulation. I won't be rushed through this by some clue-stealing amateur. They should've been booted from the puzzle by now anyway."

When I first started the forum, I decided that each host team should enforce the rules of their own puzzle, since I'm in high school and don't have time to be policing dozens of teams hosting dozens more puzzles. So, if ROYAL is breaking the rules, it's up to the Order to wave the timeout flag and give them a warning. Sure, I still have the authority. I stepped in when ROYAL put that "fire" clue on that hot sauce bottle. But if I step in and get in the way of the Order . . .

"Enforcing the rules of this puzzle is up to the Order," I say.

Yas levels her eyes at me.

"And if they don't? Would you ever boot the Order, Jax? We all know how much you love them."

That sparks a defensive fire in my chest.

If I step in and get in the way of the Order, I lose the opportunity to boot the refinery for *all* of us. It's not just about me here.

"What are you saying, exactly? That just because I want to join them at the end, I won't enforce the rules?"

"All I'm saying is that you'd better," she says, arms folded tightly.

"Hey, hey, hey," booms a voice from behind me. I feel a huge hand clamp down on my shoulder, and I flinch and look up to find Abba staring past me at his daughter. "Jax is your friend," he says. "Your brother. You're on the same team. Now, what's the problem here?"

He unclamps his hand from my arm and steps past me into the big open space in front of the counter, right in front of the heat-and-eat food in the fridges. Then he folds his arms and looks at each of us in turn, finally landing on me.

"Uh . . . ," I begin, glancing at Yas. How do I explain to this man that his daughter just accused me of selling out to a social-justice vigilante organization bent on bringing down the establishment, without telling him that we're solving a puzzle posted by a social-justice vigilante organization bent on bringing down the establishment? "We just disagree about where to go next for a clue," I say. She'd better be grateful I spared her the lecture that would've come from her dad later.

"Oh?" he asks, leaning on the counter and smiling at me. "Where to next?"

I smile. He—all of our parents, actually—may not "get" the whole cryptology thing—how it works, or why we're all so into it, but at least Abba takes interest. And Mama and Zaza. They try to understand, and they let us be free. And if there's one thing I love, it's thinking through my thoughts out loud with someone.

So, I dive in headfirst.

"I'm not sure, but I *think* the phrase 'A café at the Pentagon' means we need to go to Luna Apartments, because the address number matches the distance between here and the Pentagon in DC. But those last two lines: 'Ask not for whom the bell tolls. It tolls for the town.' I just don't know what it means."

"And every part of every clue has to mean something," says Yas. "*Unless* the Order is breaking the rules."

"Which they're *not*," I say, a little too fast. Abba raises an eyebrow at me and then looks at his daughter.

"Rules or no rules, it sounds like the Order is about to come between you two. Never let ambition ruin a friendship."

Han picks up a bag of chips off a nearby rack of snacks and begins turning it over in his hands, crinkling the foil between his palms.

"Okay, so if the clue is leading us to Luna Apartments, *why* aren't we going?" asks Spider, growing increasingly pressed. "I don't understand, Jax—help me out here, please."

"Like I said, it's the bell part for me. Help me figure out the bell, y'all, and then we'll talk about whether we should go to Luna Apartments."

I can't think of a single famous bell in all of Puget Sound. I think there's one on UW's campus? Or maybe one up north in University Village? I take to Google.

"Famous bells in Seattle."

Oh right! The Ballard Centennial Bell Tower. So the "town" in question is . . . Ballard, then? Sounds too simple. I keep scrolling.

Apparently, UW *does* have a carillon with forty-seven bells on their Seattle campus in the U District. But then the "town" . . .

What would the "town" part mean?

"Jax?" asks Spider. "What if 'for whom the bell tolls' is a reference to Hemingway's work of the same name? He died here in Washington, after all—didn't he?"

"That's true," says Yas, also scrolling. I look back down at my phone, reading and rereading the words. It's gotta be simpler than this. Simpler, and obvious to people who know Seattle. Which, we all do in our own way.

For whom the bell tolls.

. . . tolls for the town . . .

My eyes go wide.

Belltown.

My heart is racing. My eyes are flying across the words for the five hundredth time.

"Jax?" asks Yas. I can feel her staring, and the gazes of Spider and Han follow. "What did you find?"

This is my job. Puzzler extraordinaire. Unraveler of clue-filled tapestries, detangler of complicated webs, and sorter of the unsorted. Here I am with a single word—"Belltown." Until I read the first part again.

A CAFÉ AT THE PENTAGON.

Pentagon, pentagon, pentagon.

A five-sided shape.

A café with five sides?

Or . . . five points?

I dive for my backpack, sling it over my shoulder, and dart for the door.

"Jax, wait!" calls Yas behind me, grabbing her own bag and following. "Where are we going?"

No idea what we'll find when we get there, but we're going to the 5 Point Café.

I steal a smirk at Spider before swinging open the front door and turning west, keeping the Space Needle in my sights until I hit Dexter and hang a left. I hear fast footsteps behind me, and I hope we get there first.

Zaza used to take Ava and me to the 5 Point Café every year, the day before Father's Day. Why? Because there's no such thing as "Parent's Day" . . . *yet* . . . so we made our own. And since it was the Saturday before Father's Day, the cafés were *empty*. We usually had the place to ourselves. Now we make breakfast at home, because when you source your ingredients from such a place as Mama's garden, where your own blood, sweat, and tears grow life from the soil, cooking becomes a spiritual experience. Hard for any restaurant to top that.

Apparently, the place opened in 1929, the year of the stock market crash that fueled the start of the Great Depression. In fact, there's a big green neon sign out front that explicitly states: WE CHEAT TOURISTS 'N' DRUNKS, SINCE 1929.

It always makes me laugh.

Here we all stand, staring at the front door in silence.

"Jax," whispers Yas. "Are we really about to do this?"

And I know what she's asking without her having to ask it.

It's dark out here. The streetlights are on. White people walk past us on this sidewalk, holding hands, walking dogs, laughing half drunkenly, texting, carrying grocery bags, and wheeling strollers. We, four kids—three of us people of color—are standing here in the dark, backpacks on, sneaking around a restaurant none of us have any intention of buying anything from that doesn't close until two in the morning, the outside of which is mostly lit by neon signs in the windows. *And* we're looking for clues to a cryptology puzzle posted by a cryptic social vigilante organization that's basically said, in nonspecific terms, fuck the police.

Not a good look.

Not the safest look, at least.

I turn to her and see the neon green lights reflecting in her glossy brown eyes. She's asking me to decide not just as a friend but as our leader. The leader of the Vault forum, and the captain of Team JERICHO.

I think for a moment as Spider's and Han's gazes follow hers, landing on my face.

Is this safe? they ask.

Find a bin. Look around.

I know what this looks like—three kids of color and a white guy creeping through an alley, looking between garbage cans and uglying up these white-owned businesses. Not that I have anything against the owners of the 5 Point. I'm sure they're cool. But *nobody's* immune to bias. Especially at night. Not even me.

That's when I see it go by.

The black-and-white car on the other side of the alley, cruising past at a cool ten miles per hour, the officer in the driver's seat leaning on the window, staring straight at me.

I freeze.

His eyes meet mine, cool and knowing, as if issuing a warning. I'm not even *doing* anything. I'm just a kid standing in front of a restaurant with my friends.

I remember what Mama said earlier.

For protection, she'd said. *Just a feeling. There are a lot of protests going on downtown today—okay, Juju-bean? Be careful.*

I shut my eyes and breathe, suppressing the adrenaline rising in me. I'm more afraid of the cops than I am of protesters. Hell, I want to *be* a protester. I should be more afraid to *not* fight for what I want. Justice. Peace. For Roundworld to get their oily claws the hell up out of my mama's garden. I want them *gone.* And if it means I have to lead my friends through a dark alley hunting through trash to do it, even with cops on patrol, so be it.

"Jax?" Yas asks. And then I remember she's just asked me, *Are we really about to do this?*

"Let's go," I say. A nonanswer. I don't know if this is safe. Depends on how bored the cops are. But we have to do this.

I have to do this.

So, yes. We are.

I step forward first, pulling my hood over my head in case there are cameras. I know hoods are against Mama and Zaza's formula for keeping their little Black boy the safest they possibly can. *Hands on the wheel. Yes sir, no sir. Ask before doing anything.*

No phone.

No music.

No hoods.

I hope this alley is dark enough that it won't matter.

We cross the street and I get a clearer view of this stretch of alley, and my heart sinks. There must be at least a dozen trash bins back here! How many businesses share this one spot? What is this, Belltown's communal dumping ground?

"Which one?" asks Spider. Yas joins me to my left and says, "Maybe they're labeled somehow?"

Han's phone flashlight brightens to life somewhere behind me, startling me. I look back at him, for a moment expecting to see a cop's flashlight in my face. *Okay, be cool, Jax, be cool,* I tell myself. Even though my hands are shaking. No one seems to notice. The flashlight turns to the bins, where we all lean in and see numbers written on the top of each. 410. 415. 445.

"5 Point Café's address is 415 Cedar," says Yas, holding up her phone to me. I grin up at her and nod.

"Thanks," I say.

"Don't mention it," she says flatly.

I feel like I should say something to mend what we both said in Abba's store just now. I hate this. Yas and I have been best friends for years. We *know* not to let a cryptology puzzle come between us, no matter how vital it is for us to win.

"Hey," I say, "I'll always do what's best for our team. You know that, right?"

She purses her lips and stares at the ground in silence as Spider opens the trash can lid and peers inside.

"Let's just find this clue," she says, stepping forward and joining him. Okay, now I'm mad. First, she accuses me of playing favorites with the Order, and now she won't tell me why she's got this chip on her shoulder?

I step in front of her before she can get to the trash bin, and I fold my arms and glare up at her.

"Yas, talk to me," I say. "Who cares which of us is right if our friendship is taking hits?"

"Uh-oh," cuts in a deep, sly voice from somewhere nearby. "Seems we've got trouble in paradise, JERICHO."

Shit. We're not alone. I look around frantically—down the alley each way, and finally up.

Leaping down from the roof of the brick building on the east side of the alley is Red Cap Guy, his white T-shirt gleaming in the light of Han's flashlight as he approaches us. Han, somewhere behind me, begins to step backward, taking his flashlight with him. Yas, still beside me, doesn't move from where she stands. Spider, to my right, glances up at me before deciding to stand his ground too.

"Listen," says Spider, "I don't know how you missed the Vault rules, but clue-stealing assholes aren't tolerated."

The kid presses a palm to his chest in mock suffering.

"You call me an asshole before you even know my name?" He sucks his teeth, and something about his smile sends a chill up my spine. "Damn shame."

"What *is* your name?" asks Yas bitingly.

"That's Lucas," comes another voice from behind me, making me jump. We all whip around to see two people, neither of them our Han, stepping closer. A *super*-tall—seriously, he must be Yao Ming's long-lost Black cousin—kid with a shaved head and a tailored purple blazer is closest, hands casually stuffed into the pockets of his purple pants. Wait . . . are those *velvet*? His whole suit is *velvet*!

"Who are you supposed to be?" asks Yas, probably noticing how weird-as-hell his outfit is.

"Where's your top hat, man?" asks Spider.

"Guys," I say, holding up my hand for a mock request for silence. "Easy on Black Willy Wonka and his clown posse."

That gets a smile out of Yas and a giggle out of Spider. But the girl behind this Dr. Facilier wannabe is unamused. Her mouth is a flat line, her eyes narrowed and scathing. Her blond hair stirs in the slight breeze in this alley, stopping sharply just above her shoulders. Her bangs hang short, only halfway down her forehead, and she's dressed in all black, fists wound tight under her long sleeves.

She levels her eyes at us, folding her arms before saying:

"No need to go easy on *us*, JERICHO."

I glance at Yas, who's sizing her up.

"And your name?"

"Sigge," she says, her voice surprisingly even. "You?"

"Yasmin."

Her *friends* call her Yas, and she apparently doesn't want ROYAL knowing that.

"Splendid," says Dr. Facilier. "Now that we're all acquainted—"

"Hold up," I say, stepping forward and leveling my eyes at the kid who's a monocle away from looking like Mr. Peanut. "You haven't said *your* name."

Sure, this kid has been on the Vault for a while, but that makes hundreds of us.

"My name?" he asks, taking a step forward and lifting his nose ever so slightly higher into the air. He glances past me to give Lucas a knowing smirk. My heart is racing. It feels like these people are closing in on us—on JERICHO. Well, the three members of JERICHO who are still here.

Where the hell did Han go? I can't help but wonder.

"*My* name," continues this weirdo, "is Karim. And *this*"—he gestures around the alley to Lucas and Sigge with his palm upturned like he's holding the world's most delicate teacup—"is Team ROYAL."

Something about the way he says the word "royal" makes me think this guy thinks he's actual royalty. Who shows up to a cryptology puzzle dressed like . . . like *that*?

"We know," says Spider, clearly over the theatrics. "And you're here for the next clue, which you'd better leave alone if you don't want to get kicked out of this puzzle."

"Pardon, but are you the captain of this team?" asks Karim. Spider's eyes go wide. He's clearly affronted, looking to me now for some defense. I don't disappoint him.

"I may be leader of the forum, and I may be the captain, but we are *all* leaders of JERICHO. Based on what your cohort back here was up to, your left hand doesn't know what the right one is doing."

Karim grins a twisted grin that makes my stomach sink like a stone. But I'm careful not to let my face show it.

Lucas steps between Spider and me, knocking his shoulder into mine as he joins Karim and Sigge, sparking a flame of fury in me.

"Watch it," he says, turning to look over his shoulder at me. "Boy."

That word turns that flame in me into a volcano, and I feel Yas's hand on my shoulder. I want to shrug it off and glare at her. How dare she telepathically tell me to calm down right now? Red Cap Guy is a full-blown racist. I *know* that look he just gave me. That wasn't just an "I'm better than you" smile. That was a hard-*R* smile. He didn't have to say it.

It's the three of them facing the three of us who are left.

"Three on three," says Karim, "and you're still intellectually outmatched."

"Imagine," says Sigge flatly.

"Can't relate," says Lucas with a shrug.

"We have resources you all could only dream of," says Karim. "Good luck. You'll need it."

"A team with resources wouldn't need to steal clues," I say. "You're desperate to win this."

"The prize is power," continues Karim, straightening stiffer where he stands. "Something we already have in abundance. But something we don't have is control over *you*. If you win, you're taking down Roundworld. It's not hard to put together. It's just a shame we have to play against people like you who are *actually* desperate. Sad, really."

The nerve of this fucking guy. I try to keep my face even as I wonder how much he knows about us, about me.

About Abba's store.

About Spider's mom's restaurant.

About Han's dad's job.

About Mama's garden.

Wait . . . what the hell? I swear to Black Jesus I'm seeing one of the garbage bins just behind Team ROYAL . . . *move*. Maybe I'm seeing things. Maybe it's too late to be out here looking for clues and my brain is fried and playing tricks on me. Or maybe . . .

Karim raises an eyebrow and follows my gaze to the bin, and I'm hoping it doesn't move again.

Come on, Han, I think, *not when he's looking.*

I know what's happening, and it's taking all the willpower I have not to smile right now. Han didn't desert us—not that I ever think he would—he's found his way into the air vent *under* the bins.

FIND A BIN. LOOK AROUND.

My phone buzzes in my pocket, and I pull it out to check what's happening, ignoring the glances exchanged among Team ROYAL. Yas, Spider, and I all look down at our phones to read Han's text.

HAN: It's a serial number on the bottom of the bin.

I look at Yas. Yas looks at me. I look at Spider. Spider's mouth curves into the slightest of grins.

We *all* know not to look at the bin.

But what *do* we do? I guess as the leader, I'm supposed to know.

And then an idea buds in my mind. They're here for a clue, right? The one under the bin. But . . . they don't know that. So, what if I just made them think . . .

I clear my throat and hope the gang catches on to my plan.

"We're wasting time with these fools, y'all," I scoff, hoping my front is working. "Come on, let's find our—"

I pretend to be interrupted by a thought, and then I pretend to reread the text.

Then I turn around, glancing back at Team ROYAL for only a moment, and take off down the alley as fast as my feet will move me. I soon hear several sets of footsteps behind me.

"Hey!" calls Lucas's biting voice behind me as he closes in like a pit bull. My eyes start darting, looking for a poster. *Any* poster. *Anywhere.* If I can just make them think I have the real clue, maybe it'll lead them off the chase. It's not breaking a rule, as long as I don't steal the actual clue . . .

. . . right?

My arms and legs fly, propelling me through this alley so fast, I can feel the wind under my jacket. Yas pulls up on my right.

"Jax!" she hollers. "What are you doing?"

"I've got it!" is all I have time to say before I reach the end of the alley and realize that I very much *don't* have it. I'm not even sure what *it—my decoy—*will be. Are there really no posters on this whole damn block? I can't stop now, though, or ROYAL will suspect I'm trying to confuse them. I check my phone again for effect and take a quick glance down the street before looking around.

The footsteps shuffle behind me, and I turn back to Team ROYAL.

"Think you can outrun us?" asks Karim, even though I smile at the fact that he's slightly out of breath. I look to Lucas, whose eyes are darting around *so* confused, I feel like I've already won this round.

Karma for stealing the first clue, I think happily to myself.

I notice that Sigge is not only out of breath but keeping her eyes moving. Following the instructions in the clue. *Find a bin. Look around.* A mark of a true cryptologist. I know she's one to watch.

But Karim? Karim don't scare me. And neither does his frat-boy-wannabe sidekick.

Come on, why are there no posters here? Not even a wooden telephone pole that you could staple a poster to if you wanted to. I look around for any scrap of paper that might pass for a clue. But nothing. Nothing at all. Not even a sign or a stray newspaper sticking out of a trash can. But finally, *finally*, I hear what I've been hoping for—the sound of paper crinkling in the wind. I turn to find a single orange envelope tucked under the windshield wiper blade of a dark blue Chevy Malibu, and I don't hesitate. Once more glance at my phone for effect and a look aimed at Karim, who's looking at me like he's gone from mocking us to wanting answers.

Now.

I hear the hiss of the bus I hadn't noticed just behind the navy Malibu. Not the arrival hiss of a bus kneeling to let passengers on, but the hiss of a bus about to take off.

I see my chance.

"I don't need to think I can outrun you," I say to Karim before darting for the car and snatching the orange envelope. "I just need to do it!"

And I sprint to my getaway vehicle, slipping my narrow ass between the doors just as they slam shut. I'm up the steps and to the coin machine just before Lucas's hands land on the glass, slapping the door like a damn child. I raise my middle finger, since I might as well, now that I've got them all fully convinced that I've made off with their precious clue.

"Nah-uh," says the driver behind me suddenly, and to my horror, he lifts his hand to open the door.

"What are you doing?" I ask, more aggression in my voice than even I was prepared for. If this man opens these doors, I might have to fight. For the very first time in my life. "What the hell, man?"

"I won't have you kids roughhousing on my bus, and I won't have vulgarity, either."

"I'm tryna stay *away* from those guys!" I insist, softening my voice. "Please, I'm sorry I flipped them the bird, but . . . you've got to take me away from here. I promise I won't cause trouble."

What the hell kind of activist am I, sitting here apologizing to a white man for flipping someone *else* the bird, begging to be allowed onto his bus in peace? This ain't 1955 and we're nowhere near Montgomery, Alabama.

"Please?" I ask, my eyes welling with tears. Not at the fear of him clicking that *door open* button, but at the fact that I have to beg for my safety like this in the twenty-first century. The point is, I made it onto this bus, and they didn't. I should be safe.

Right?

"Fine," he says, lowering his arm, to my relief, before throwing the bus into drive and turning out.

More of Lucas's hand slaps ring out against the window as he yells for the driver to open the door. As I take my seat in the front row—thank goodness this bus is otherwise completely empty—I can't make out exactly what he says, just muffled whining. Until I hear one distinct phrase hollered, muffled, from outside.

"Fuckin' *thief*!"

The nerve of Lucas calling me that when he's the one who *actually* stole a clue. All I did was grab somebody's parking ticket, which they'll be notified about in the mail later, assuming the owner of the car has a place of residence. But when I look up, the smirk I'm wearing gets wiped clean off.

The bus driver's eyes, icy blue and full of rage, are staring at me in the rearview mirror at the front of the bus. We're stopped at a light, and he's glaring at me like he could kill me where I sit. My hand creeps up to that amethyst around my neck as I realize the full weight of what's just happened.

The driver heard Lucas's words. *Fuckin' thief.* That's all it took.

"I ought to kick you off this bus right now," he spits. "When I was in Iraq, we *shot* motherfuckers like you, you know that?"

"I-I'm not a thief," I say. More tears. Dammit. "This is all a big misunderstan—"

"I ought to take you right to police headquarters."

My throat closes at the idea. Sure, I didn't technically *steal* anything, I don't think. It's not illegal to swipe a parking ticket, is it?

. . . is it? I don't know! Now my hands are all sweaty as I think of a plausible answer to all of this.

"I took this," I admit, holding up the orange envelope. "That was . . . Lucas. We're friends. We got into it. I told him not to park there, but he said it'd be fine. So . . . I took the parking ticket and hopped onto the bus. I was mad . . . I wasn't thinking . . . Please, don't kick me out."

He says nothing. The light turns green.

He moves the bus forward. Rain begins to pelt the window.

I clutch the orange envelope in my fist and send a text despite the blurred vision through my tears.

ME: DID YOU GET THE REAL CLUE, HAN?

Han

Despite being underground, this air vent is still pretty breezy. I saw the grates under bin 415 and knew the clue might be underneath. The last place most people would've looked. And I could've stayed and flipped the bin, but Team ROYAL was watching, and I knew they'd be right behind us if I pointed it out. So, here I am, phone flashlight shining up through the grate at the serial number on the sticker on the bottom, right next to that mysterious eye symbol.

I hear Jax get cut off, and I freeze.

"Come on, gang. Let's find our—"

I peek out from under the garbage can at everyone's feet. I see Jax's red shoes turn and take off full speed down the alley.

"*Hey!*"

Lucas.

And everyone sprints down the alley except me. I don't know what they think they've found, but the clue is right here. I look up at it again just to make sure. The eye symbol. The serial number. Yup, that's the clue.

I open my phone's camera and snap a picture. Then I study what I've got. All numbers. Twelve of them.

934589594853.

I imagine it formatted like a phone number. 93-458-959-4853. Maybe.

Then I imagine doing that thing with Euler's number—the *e* on a calculator, so the number is actually . . . what would that be? . . . I pull up my calculator app.

$e^{27.563}$

Also, maybe.

My phone buzzes in my hand, and I read the text.

JAX: DID YOU GET THE REAL CLUE, HAN?

I think for a moment. Did I get the real clue? Does he mean "Did you get the real clue?" as in "Did you *locate* the real clue after we all ran off after a fake one?" or "Did you take a *picture* of the real clue after we all ran off after a fake one?" or maybe "Did you *take* the real clue after we all ran off after a fake one?"

It could be any of them. And I think back to the boy who called himself Lucas, who tore down that poster in South Lake Union and almost cost us the puzzle, and I wonder if Jax is changing the rules. Maybe the game is changing? Maybe he wants me to take this clue so that we can stay ahead of ROYAL? Maybe he thinks changing the rules like this is the only way to win?

ME: YES

I send the text, peel the sticker off the bottom of the bin, and sink back down into the air vent and off through the dark tunnels toward Westlake Station, where I can catch the Link Light Rail home.

Jax

skipped dinner so I could lie on my bed, stare at my phone, and figure out this sequence of twelve numbers that Han sent me a picture of. A trash bin serial number? Nah, Han already said those don't exist in the downtown area. A phone number? Nah, too easy. Besides, the only country code that starts with a 9 is Afghanistan with the prefix 93, which fits. But it makes the rest of the sequence a ten-digit number, which does-not-an-Afghan-phone-number-make. I tried to call it using a Google Voice number so I wouldn't incur international call fees, but I got a dial tone.

I growl in frustration—I can't tell if it's from this puzzle or from the irritation at that asshole of a bus driver—and run my fingers through my curls as another text comes in from Spider.

SPIDER: Anyone tried plugging it in as a URL?

YAS: YUP. Got porn. Had to explain to Abba.

HAN: HAHA.

I roll my eyes. Funny, sure, but I wish they'd stay focused. Those ROYAL goons weren't there to fool around. It won't take long for them to figure out that the "clue" we led them to was a straight-up decoy, and then what? They'll catch up to us if we don't get our asses in gear. I curl up against the wall behind my pillow, and my fingers fly over the keyboard.

ME: It's not a phone number.

SPIDER: Tried that first. Then I tried translating those numbers into letters, but it just got me . . . hold on . . .

I can't help but hope that there's something in these letters after all, that maybe one of us will see a pattern where Spider saw none, but then the letters come back.

SPIDER: ICDEHIEIDHEC 93-458-959-4853

ME: Maybe they're scrambled? Anyone on desktop and can use a word unscrambler?

YAS: Just tried that. Nothing.

The hell does she mean, "nothing"? You don't unscramble twelve letters and get "nothing"—you get words that don't mean anything to you. But that's why you share them with the group! My neck is getting hot with anger, but instead of jumping in with a "Care to share with the group anyway so we can decide that for ourselves?" I jump up off my bed, log into my computer, and unscramble the letters myself. The longest word available only uses seven of the letters to make the word "deicide," as in "the killing of a god." My heart skips for a moment at the idea that maybe the Order is suggesting that their "power" prize involves murder, specifically the murder of someone already of immense power.

But I wouldn't take advantage of that if given the chance, even if I knew I'd never be found out. Mama says that those who take life are doomed to suffer the rest of theirs, even if they're never caught. The guilt, the paranoia, the bad karma. None of it's worth it.

I couldn't live with it.

I sigh in defeat. The word "deicide" just doesn't make sense, and even if it did, that would leave six letters hanging. HIHICE. Nothing.

ME: I think you're right, Yas. This word unscrambler returned nothing important.

YAS: You looked it up yourself? Then why even ask me??

Oh yeah, she's right. Probably should've just quietly agreed with her. Now she thinks I don't trust her, which isn't exactly helping the situation that is our friendship right now.

ME: Just wanted to double-check. Never hurts to have two people looking at it, right?

YAS: Sure, whatever.

Ugh, I don't have time for this drama.

I look at those numbers again and wonder if it's an amount. Like, dollars maybe?

$934,589,594,853

I search "934 trillion dollars" and find articles like "Hedge Fund Industry Now Worth $934 Billion" and "Student Loan Debt Tops $2 Trillion."

What has a balance of 934 trillion dollars?

SPIDER: Maybe it's a dollar amount?

I grin, loving that my team is thinking the way I am here.

ME: I was just thinking that, but what has a balance that high?

YAS: Maybe something with a balance today could have enough APY over time to get to $934 trillion?

The hell? AP-what?

ME: Explain please, boomer, for the youth in the room.

Sure, Yas is the oldest, but she sometimes sounds *way* older.

YAS: APY? Annual Percentage Yield? Did your parents not teach you about how interest works?

SPIDER: Is that like APR?

YAS: Similar. APY factors in compound interest. When you buy a car, companies looooove saying 0% or 1% APR, but they don't tell you the APY, which is often higher. Predatory, truly.

And *that* is the point at which I check out of the conversation. Yeah, yeah, the white establishment is predatory, especially in the financial department. Why does that mean we have to know every detail of this crap?

ME: I'll call you if I ever need to buy a car, Yas. Now, can we get back to the puzzle, please?

Three knocks ring out from the front door downstairs, and I look at my phone clock to see that it's 10:05 p.m. Who the hell is coming by the house this late? Curious, I push myself to my knees and crawl across my bed to the window, where I look down at the street along our front yard. I guess you could call it a yard. My heart jumps into my throat. Or my throat sinks into my stomach. *Something* inside me gets rearranged at what I see.

A girl my age in a black long-sleeve shirt and tight black pants, with a blond impossible-to-miss straight bob. It's the girl from Team ROYAL!

My mind swims with questions, and panic sets in at each one.

Why is she here?

How did she find my house?

What the hell is she here to do to me?

At this point, I fully expect her to pull a gun out from her back pocket and turn it on whoever answers the door. And then a whole new wave of panic sets in at the realization that Mama, Zaza, and maybe even Ava are downstairs.

"No!" I holler, throwing myself off the bed and scrambling to the door, racing down the stairs so fast, I miss one and lose my footing with just a few steps left. I go down quick, tumbling heels over head, praying to hit the floor soon. When I do land, I'm cheek-first on the tile floor.

I groan and blink my eyes open to see a blurry image of Ava by the front door, which she leaves open to turn and run to me. I see an ocean of black through the door outside, because it's dark, and because that girl—what was her name again?—is dressed in all black, and all I can see is that platinum-blond hair walking over the threshold. I do hear her combat boots on our tile, though—sounding strange and out of place in our tiny, sacred kitchen.

"Jax, are you okay?!" cries Ava. I feel her firm hand on mine. "Can you move?"

"Don't—" I manage to croak out, but I'm interrupted by my own body. *Cough! Cough-cough!* I guess I knocked the wind out of myself on the way down. I instinctively turn on my side until the coughing subsides and I can finally breathe enough to say, "Don't let her in."

Ava looks up at her—Sigge! That's her name. And Sigge, to my surprise, kneels and extends a hand to me.

"I'm not here to fight," she says, her voice quiet but sharp, like the hiss of a soda can when it's pressed open after being only *slightly* tossed around. "If you can move, if you can stand, I'd like to talk to you."

Once I'm off the floor and we're all seated at the kitchen table with cups of Mama's dragonwell tea and agave nectar—I don't know why Ava decided to give this girl Mama's special-occasion tea, but okay—I fold my arms over my chest and look at Sigge without a word.

Now that I can get a good look at her face, I see how smooth and translucent her skin is, like a porcelain doll. Her eyelashes are snow white too. And her eyebrows are the faintest blond because maybe she colors them in—

"See something you like?" she asks me before taking another sip of her tea. I bristle at that, glancing at Ava before a blush creeps into my cheeks and a smirk plays at the corner of Ava's lips.

I clear my throat and move right along, but before I can, Sigge is talking again.

"Relax, kid, I'm not into boys, and you can't look at me without looking ill. I didn't come here to flirt."

"What did you come here for?"

My voice is more biting than even I was expecting, and as she looks up at me mid-sip, I clear my throat again and soften up, remembering Mama's words to me for practically my entire childhood. *Everything you do, do it gently.*

I hope she'd classify taking down Roundworld's stupid refinery as "gentle," because that's exactly what I'm going to do as soon as I win this puzzle and join the Order's ranks.

Sigge sets down the mug she's drinking from—my special Baby Yoda mug that I *only* drink coffee with salted-caramel oat creamer out of. I flash a look at Ava. Doesn't she know I've been through enough today?

"I came to apologize."

That's the last thing I expected to hear in this moment.

"Go on . . . ," I say, turning up the end of the word "on" so it sounds like a question. I take a sip of the crisp tea and let it warm me from the inside out. My muscles already hurt from that tumble down the stairs. I'm just glad we didn't wake Mama and Zaza.

"I'm sorry," she says, leaning back in her chair, which creaks, and crossing one leg over the other. "My teammate Lucas—you met him."

"You could say that."

"He shouldn't have taken that poster," she continues.

I hope she knows it'll take more than that for me to believe her. Why would she take time away from this precious puzzle just to come to my house to apologize?

Oh right, she's in my house! She found my house!

"How'd you find out where I live?" I ask, noticing the gold bracelet around her wrist. The famous Cartier Love bracelet. Saw it on an ad once. The price ranges from $6K to $50K. Assuming this isn't a knock-off, this girl could pay for my future college education with a single bracelet. "You paid somebody on the dark web for my address, didn't you? Just wrote a check, huh? Or did Daddy wire you some money?"

"Jax," snaps Ava. "Come on."

"This ain't even your business, Ava. Why are you still down here?"

Ava's eyes flicker as she holds her mug in midair. She'd been about to take a sip, but now she's setting it down and thinking better of it, pushing back in her chair, standing up.

"I was making sure you weren't concussed after that fall," she says. "Since I'm going into nursing next year. Just wanted to help."

My throat closes up with shame.

What do I even say to that?

She takes her mug to the stairs, turns back to Sigge, and says, "It was nice to meet you," and retreats up to her room, the brush of her slippers against the floor getting softer and softer.

I don't recognize myself.

What the hell have I done? I don't have time to think.

"Your sister seems nice," says Sigge, taking another sip.

I tear my eyes from the stairwell and glare at her.

"Well, you came to apologize, and you've done that," I say, unable to finish the sentence.

So get the hell out, I want to say.

Her mug goes back on the table, her shoulders rise to her ears, and her eyes meet mine.

"I have a little brother myself, actually," she says. "He's very sick."

Silence passes between us. So much that the ticking of the big red apple clock above the kitchen sink is the only sound in the room until I clear my throat and take another sip of my tea.

"I'm . . . I'm sorry to hear that."

"Leukemia," she says flatly. "Of course, we have medical benefits from my father's job at Roundworld to keep us afloat, but if we were to *lose* them . . ."

I let more silence pass by, as I'm still working on absorbing the "Of course" in front of "we have medical benefits." I must be staring at her with eyes glazed over, because her voice cuts through my train of thought.

"It would sink us."

"Can't your dad just . . . I don't know, get another job with medical benefits?"

"No," she says bitterly. "Because the leukemia would then be a preexisting condition. And even with ACA provisions, even if they *did* cover us, it would still cost a fortune."

So wait, this girl, with the six-thousand-dollar bracelet, wants *me*, a Shannon High kid from Ballard who wants more than anything to save his mother's community garden, and barely has money for bus fares, to what? Throw away the game?

"What do you want?" I ask point-blank. "Are you asking me to just *give* you the puzzle?"

"I'm asking you to give up the game so a little boy can get his leukemia treatments without leaving his family destitute."

"It's not my game to give up," I say. "It's everyone's game."

It's my team's game. It's Mama's game, although she doesn't yet know it. I can't just let this refinery demolish Mama's garden.

"I know you'll use your 'power' to take down Roundworld if you win," she says.

Her mouth is pursed, but her eyes are pleading. I know how badly she wants to win this. I can see it in her face. I *know* she's telling the truth.

So I decide to give her some truth back.

"If the refinery goes up . . . ," I begin, hands clasped around my ceramic mug, beige with dark speckles. Ava made it a few years ago at a pottery event hosted at—you guessed it—the garden. "My neighborhood's community garden goes down. For most of the families around here, that's the only grocery store they have. We don't live around much else, and most of the food there is free, all we can afford. You're asking me to choose between your family's medical care and my family's food supply. That's not my decision to make."

A long moment goes by in which she takes a nervous sip of her tea, I take a contemplative sip of my tea, and we both look at each other.

A clear stalemate.

"Fine," she says, her eyebrows going flat. "Then at least give us the garbage-bin clue back so we can have a fair chance."

That takes a long moment to sink in.

"Did someone take the second clue?" I ask.

She reaches down to pick up her black leather backpack—I can smell that it's real leather from here—and reaches in to pull out her phone and starts scrolling. She shows me the screen, where I find our forum, specifically a post from the Order. I take the phone in my hand and examine the words closely.

AMATEURS RESORT TO CHEATING.
TAKE TO HEART THIS REPRIMAND.
THE ORDER HAS EYES EVERYWHERE.
STEALING CLUES WILL GET YOU BANNED.

"But we didn't take anything," I say, unable to mask the alarm in my voice, looking up at Sigge again. Her narrowing eyes says she doesn't believe me. "I swear! JERICHO doesn't cheat. We don't steal clues. For karma's sake, I was there when the damn forum etiquette was written!"

Sigge snatches her phone out of my hand, clearly still doubting me. But I have my own doubts about her.

"How do you know it wasn't your boy Lucas stealing the poster clue?" I ask. "You know he has sticky fingers."

She scrolls, her eyes glued to her phone as she answers, "Lucas learned his lesson."

And that's all she says. Silence.

"Oh, I'm just supposed to *believe* that?" I ask. "He almost got Yas in trouble with South Lake Union security!"

"Yas?" she asks, looking up at me, and then I remember that Yas specifically said *Yasmin*. Dammit.

"Yasmin. My teammate," I concede.

"The girl in white?" she asks, unable to hide the sharpness in her voice. I smile. Does this girl think she can compete with our Yas? Our fearless flyer? Our astonishing acrobat? Our parkour princess?

That stunt Sigge pulled—the jump off the roof back at the bus stop, was pretty incredible. But I've seen Yas do better.

"Yeah. Her."

"Sorry to have gotten her in trouble," she says, a trace of honesty in her voice surprising me. Her eyes return to her phone before she shows me the screen.

On the forum, someone's posted a photo of adhesive stuck to something green and plastic-looking. The photo was taken with flash, indicating that it was probably taken in the dark, outside since there's a streetlight in the far distance, and the adhesive's in the shape of a square.

"You're saying there was a clue on . . . whatever this is?"

"We all know it's a garbage bin, Jax—that was the most obvious part," she says, folding her arms across her chest and leaning back in her chair. "No need to be cryptic. Just tell me where your team hid it, and we can both get on with being professionals here."

"I'm telling you, I have no idea who took it."

And I really don't! JERICHO doesn't steal clues. Han was the only one of us to see it on the bottom of the bin, and he sent us a picture. He wouldn't just . . . *take* it. And then I realize, that's my proof! I've got to give up a photo of the clue. "Just to prove it to you," I say, taking out my own phone out and pulling up Han's picture. "Here's the picture my teammate Han took of the clue. If he took it, *why* would he need a picture of it?"

Sigge takes my phone, blows up the picture, and closes out of the picture to make sure it's really in my messages and really from a contact by the name of "Han."

It all checks out, apparently.

Her face softens into a sad, resigned kind of expression, and she sighs.

"I still don't trust you. Or your team."

I shrug and admit, "You have no reason to, except our word. But I'll send you this picture anyway since the clue is missing."

I want to protect Mama's garden more than anything, but not badly enough to want to cheat my way to the top. I'd better get some *good* karma for this.

Sigge and I exchange numbers, and soon the picture is in her messages, she's standing on my front step, and I'm leaning against the doorframe saying goodbye.

"Thanks for the tea," she says, slinging her backpack more comfortably on her shoulder and turning to leave. "And tell your sister thanks for letting me in."

Oh right. Ava.

Sigge reaches the gate and glances over her shoulder at me and says, "And that you're sorry."

Then she turns the corner and steps off down the sidewalk into the night. I let out a long sigh, knowing I owe my sister a huge apology after treating her the way I did. She was just being hospitable with what we had. Isn't that what Mama's garden is all about after all? Sharing what we have with those who need it?

I turn back inside and shut the door behind me.

"Who was that?" asks a voice from the stairwell, startling me. I look up to see Mama stepping out from the shadows, her orange nightdress sweeping against her ankles as she walks. She reaches up to scratch around the perimeter of the bandage on her forearm.

"Um," I begin, wondering how the hell I'm supposed to explain to my mama that my favorite hobby has evolved from competing in digital scavenger hunts with other teens from all over Seattle to having those strange teenagers over for tea at ten at night. "A friend."

Pretty sure in the silence that passes between us, we both follow the same thought train: I've always let my friends meet my mama and zaza. Why is this friend any different? And then a smile spreads across her face as she looks me up and down, and I realize what's happening.

Oh no.

Oh *no.*

She thinks Sigge is . . .

"Mama, it's nothing like that—"

"Okay, okay," she says, hands up in surrender before she's even said anything. I *knew* it. "Just sayin', if you ever need any positive love energy, I've got plenty of rose quartz and years of advice—"

"Mama, it's not even *like*, let alone *love.*"

I'll never understand the "love at first sight" concept. How do people just *know* they like someone by looking at them? You know nothing about them! Before I like someone, I need to know if they're kind, if they're patient, if they like animals, where they see themselves going in life, what makes their eyes light up.

On the first day of high school, Spider draped an arm around my shoulder and asked if I'd seen anyone I liked, and when I told him I didn't know, the conversation went from *who* I might like to *what* I might like.

"What's your type?" he asked, "Curls? Brown eyes? Long fingernails?"

"Um . . . ," I said, and after giving it some more thought, "Nice eyes, I guess. Eyes that are . . . kind?"

Spider raised an eyebrow.

"What's your favorite body type? Athletic? Slender? Curvy?"

How do you answer "cuddly" without sounding weird?

"Well," says Mama, still smiling knowingly, as if she knows anything about what's going on, "I'll leave you to it. You know my rules. Say them, please."

"Aw, Mama—"

"Come on. Humor me."

I sigh.

"Take protection everywhere. Wrap it up, no matter what. Come to the house before staying somewhere dangerous."

"And?"

"Get tested if something ain't right."

"Very good," she says, turning toward the stairs and resting her hand on the banister. Her eyes warm, and I can tell she's about to have a mama moment. But I have to smile as it happens.

"I love you, Juju-bean."

"Love you too, Mama." I smile.

I hope that however this puzzle goes, whatever happens, she'll be proud of me. New fire flares up in my belly. I *have* to save this garden. Whatever I gotta do—besides cheating—I'll do it.

I feel a buzz in my pocket and pull out my phone, sitting at the kitchen table to look at the text conversation that's been flying by without me, and I see a line that stops me cold.

SPIDER: Jax would never approve of this!

I sit up straighter and scroll up until I see a photo.

From Han.

Of what looks like a crumpled-up, rectangular sticker, white, with the corner of an eye peeking out from a folded corner. The symbol of the Order. And it's sitting in the palm of a white hand peeking out from a worn brown sleeve.

I'd know that brown sleeve anywhere.

Panic sets in as a million questions fly through my mind, least of which being:

What the hell, Han?

and

How could you?

Han

Sometimes it takes me extra time to read emotions, especially in faces.

I'll look for subtleties in faces that everyone else seems to find with ease. Text messages can be just as tricky. But this time? No subtleties needed. I know.

Everyone's angry.

I got us the second clue, and I stopped ROYAL from having access to it, like I thought Jax would want, and everyone's pissed.

At me.

Why?

It all made sense at the time. Made *so* much sense.

Did you get the real clue, Han?

I had a choice. I could've interpreted that so many different ways, and I chose the one that protected the team the most. He asked if I got the real clue, so I *got* the real clue.

I look down at my bowl of macaroni noodles swimming in cheese that's too thin to stick to them, and I raise another spoonful to my mouth and look up at the TV. It's C-SPAN, broadcasting footage of an earlier press conference between the mayor of Seattle and the people. No idea who "the people" are. Which *people* are they talking about exactly?

I keep watching and find out. Diya Mohan, the mayor, stands up and leans into the mic.

"Thank you all for your attendance and your patience as we bring a quite important topic of discussion to the table. As you are likely aware, we are available now to hear your comments, questions, and concerns surrounding the land use approval for the property at 2424 Gilman Road. The property is six acres. Currently, a community garden. First, we will hear from three representatives of the Duwamish tribe, protectors of natural waterways and ecosystems, and advocates of environmental justice. We welcome your words."

And then Diya leads those present in applause, relinquishing the mic to a woman with thick, shoulder-length white hair, a navy blue sweater, and a white-and-red beaded necklace.

I eat another bite of macaroni and lean in closer, interested now.

"Good morning," she says. Disjointed little murmurs of "Good morning" ring out through the room. "My name is Celea Beale, Tribal Council member. The Duwamish people have long advocated for environmental justice. When the Shill Oil Arctic Sea exploration was made public in 2015, we were there to protest. When plastic litter began to affect our waterways and threaten the ecosystems along the Duwamish River, we were there to preserve our ancestral lands. Now our friends and endorsers, the owners and stewards of Love Garden, need our help to protect land that feeds not only communities in Ballard, but eco-communities that nourish Lake Union, Portage Bay, and Union Bay—ecosystems that must be maintained by us—the people. And here we are."

I can barely hear her over the applause of the crowd, and Mayor Mohan raises a hand for respectful silence.

"We, the people of the Duwamish tribe, have been offered an opportunity to speak with the executives of Roundworld about their plans to protect the environments surrounding this land, and to express our deep and intense concerns about their intentions concerning the ecosystems that their land purchase and use will inevitably disrupt."

Groans ring out. Dismissive hands fly up in the audience, waving away the idea.

"There can be no peace without justice," she says, "and there can be no justice without change. There can be no change without action. And the *first* action we are taking, is this discourse."

"Fuck Roundworld!" exclaims someone. The mayor seems to tense up at that.

"Why the hell are we talking to them?" comes another voice.

"They're the enemy!" hollers someone else. My hair stands on end as I realize the audience is angry. All of them. A chorus of voices rises up around the first three into a scrambled mess of sounds. I feel my temperature rising. My hands feel sweaty around my bowl and spoon.

Celea holds up her hand for silence.

"The enemy," she begins, as calm as ever somehow, "is ignorance." The crowd goes silent.

"The enemy is entitlement," she continues, "and the only way those enemies can win is if we. Stay. Silent."

Quiet settles into the room for so long that I wonder if the TV's audio is malfunctioning. But then I hear the shuffling of papers as Celea gathers her speech materials under her arm, leans into the mic one final time, and says, "So we will *not* . . ." And then she stares out at the crowd like a teacher rallying her students who have so far shown that they grossly misunderstood the assignment. "We. Will. Not. Stay silent."

Finally, as calmly as she approached the stand, she leaves.

Another spoonful of macaroni goes into my mouth. I . . . don't know how to feel about this. I mean, I'm glad the Duwamish have a say in all of this. They should. It's their land. But it's *Roundworld* they're up against. What could they possible have to gain by talking with the Duwamish other than to make it look like they actually give a shit about the Duwamish? I feel warm all over, in a bad way. Not in a warm, fuzzy kinda way, but more like a . . . warm salad. I don't know. Every time I see the anti-Roundworld protesters, they seem to get angrier and angrier, like a kettle whistling, like it's needed relief for so long and soon it might explode. I swallow the noodles before muting the TV. It's just a little too loud in here. But now that the TV's muted, I realize why. This whole time, my dad's voice has been on the other side of my door and down the hall, yelling into the phone about something I hadn't bothered to listen to until now.

"If I lose my spot on the waterway, Jerry, I'm *finished*, do you hear me?" he practically hollers. I push myself to my feet and crack the door, peeking down the hallway at him. He's standing with his back turned, in his green flannel shirt and cargo shorts, barefoot, hair a little disheveled like he's been running his hands through it. The clock on the wall behind him says it's 10:02 p.m. The door behind him is an olive green, but it looks like brass in the yellow light of the kitchen.

"Well, where the hell am I supposed to get a permit for Lake Washington? Do you know how expensive that is? You want me to just pack everything up and move bodies of water? You think it's that easy?!"

The hair on my neck prickles. Even though he's not yelling at me, he's yelling so loud, it feels like it's getting warmer and warmer in here. My skin feels uncomfortably hot. The knob on the front door next to him twists and the door swings open, startling me. Kyler steps into the room and sets his backpack down on the kitchen table that's made of cedar and was a gift from Grandma and Grandpa from their second honeymoon when they went to Anchorage, Alaska, on a cruise that cost $647 per person, flights included—

"You know what, Jerry, fuck you," Dad spits before jamming his index finger against the screen and tossing the phone toward the couch.

He misses, apparently.

Clang! Bang! Thump!

It eventually lands on the carpet, but not before sending my senses into overdrive. I want to plug my ears, scream, and take a cold shower all at the same time.

"Sounds like you need one of these bad boys," comes Kyler's voice as I hear the fridge open somewhere outside my vision, hear bottles clinking together, and see an amber bottle fly into my dad's hand. Then I hear Kyler's bottle click and hiss open, and he steps into view, tipping the bottle up almost vertically.

"You know you shouldn't be drinkin' that shit," says Dad, cracking open his own bottle and tipping it up to match him. Unsurprisingly, Kyler downs the whole thing. He's only nineteen, so he shouldn't. But he does.

All the time.

Calls it his "medicine," even. But he knows Dad won't let him touch his beer, so he gives Dad one while he takes one of his own. It's smart, but something about it seems . . . wrong.

Manipulative.

Dad takes a sip and lets out a huge sigh, and enough silence passes that I start thinking about that number again.

934589594853.

Twelve-digit numbers aren't super common, even in obscure places. A standard calculator has twelve digits. Some gift card codes are twelve digits long. Most UPCs—Universal Product Codes—have twelve digits. I dissect the number format in different ways to see if I can think of anything. I can see them all in my head.

93-45-89-59-48-53. No obvious pattern there.

"So seriously, Dad, are we going to be okay?" comes Kyler's voice. Dad sighs again and is silent for such a long time.

Such a long time.

So long that Kyler keeps talking.

"I overheard a little. You thought about that loan?"

I listen even closer. What loan?

I hear Dad sigh again, as if he's thought about it. A *lot.*

Kyler fills in the silence.

"It wouldn't be anything crazy. Just enough to get the business back on its feet. A pick-me-up."

Dad straightens up. I see his hands clamp around his bottle.

"I don't do loans," he mutters. But his words are rattling even as he says them. I don't think he means it. Why don't people say what they mean?

"But there's no interest!" explains Kyler, leaning in, his eyes wide and pleading. "It's an employee benefit, Dad."

"And I certainly don't want no loan from *Roundworld.*"

Dad takes a swig.

I take a deep breath.

A loan. From *Roundworld.* How did the thing attacking my dad's livelihood just become the one thing that might save it?

Is Roundworld really the enemy? For my family, I mean?

They're horrible, I know. They barely pay taxes, push out small businesses, gentrify neighborhoods, and rearrange neighborhoods. But . . . they also have resources.

Which means Kyler has resources.

I used to think I—and JERICHO—could take down Round-world with minimal consequences. Kyler might lose his job, but he could easily get another one anywhere. He's a security wizard. Every company needs one of those.

But . . . not every company gives their employees interest-free loans.

Dad holds up his hand to Kyler.

"You boys just focus on your studies and your work. That's your job. You shouldn't have to worry about mine. I'm a grown man, with grown-man problems."

"But if you lose this business, you lose this place. And if you lose this place . . ." He goes quiet, and Dad rests his hands on the back of his head in thought. "Think of Han. Think of what will happen to him."

"You don't think I think about Han all the time? About what Catherine would do to that boy? She's got the patience and compassion of a rabid hyena. I'm not letting my flesh and blood anywhere near her."

My heart is thudding so fast, I'm afraid I'll have a heart attack right here in this doorway. At the thought of Mom. At all the memories I have of her. All the . . . unkindness.

"There has to be something we can do. Something I can do. I could take up some instructor shifts for free on the weekends and—"

"Kyler," says Dad, sliding into a chair at the kitchen table. He claps his hand on Kyler's shoulder and rocks it back and forth—his idea of affection. "Don't you inherit my problems, okay? You just be a kid. If the numbers don't add up, the numbers don't add up."

The numbers.

I look down at the twelve digits again and wonder if I really want to be doing this.

934-589-594-853.

"You're supposed to be focused on school and fun. That's it. Let me worry about the rest, okay? Please."

I shift my weight in the doorway and bump the door, which makes it creak loudly in my ear, which makes Dad turn around in his chair and look down the hall. We lock eyes.

"Hansel, you're up!" he says with a smile.

I don't talk right now, so I step out into the hallway and prepare to join them, unable to pull my mind away from those numbers. There *has* to be some rhyme to them, some reason. But do I even *want* there to be rhyme or reason to them anymore?

Maybe it's six and six?

934589-594853.

"Sup, lil' bro?" asks Kyler, tipping back the last of his beer and getting up to grab another.

"Hey, slow down," says Dad, but it's relaxed and soft, not commanding. I don't think he really cares if Kyler drinks, but he cares that he's *supposed* to care.

"Fine," he sighs in defeat, shutting the fridge again and stepping through the door of the kitchen to the den, where the TV's playing cartoons.

"Have a seat, son," says Dad, pulling out Kyler's chair for me. I sit and slide my phone into my sweatshirt pocket, flipping it over and over in my palm. I stare at him as he takes another swig. He doesn't drink too much, but he drinks at the wrong times. Happy people drink at special occasions. Dad drinks to feel better.

And that's probably a bad thing.

"What's up with you lately?" he asks me. The emphasis is on the word "you," not "up," and he's smiling, so I'm going to assume he means to ask "What's up with you lately?" as in "Tell me what's going on in your life," and not "What's up with you lately?" as in "Something's weird about you these days."

It matters, because I know to smile back instead of looking confused.

His smile falls a bit, probably because he realizes I'm nonverbal right now.

"Still not talking," he says, drinking again. That hurts. He said it like it's a choice.

I look down at my lap and wish I hadn't come out here.

"Sorry," he says. "I meant . . . well, it doesn't matter what I meant. It matters what I said. I'm sorry."

I say nothing.

9-3-4-5-8-9-5-9-4-8-5-3.

"Listen," he says, suddenly pushing the half-full bottle just a few inches away from him. The sound of the scraping jolts my mind away the numbers and back to the moment. "I'm sure you overheard some of what your brother and I were talking about, and I just wanted to tell you that you have nothing to worry about."

I stare at him, expressionless, intentionally. Dad's business is going under, but I have nothing to worry about? My dad and brother might have a drinking problem, but I have nothing to worry about? I haven't seen or heard from Mom since she left six years ago after she decided Kyler and I weren't worth her freedom, but I have nothing to worry about?

If Dad's business goes under, I have to go live with her, but I have nothing to worry about?

"So, listen," he says. "I know things are tight right now. But just try to be a kid, okay?"

I can't tell my dad that I do cryptology, because of my role in it. If I were logicking out clues like Jax, or hacking into things like Spider, or even swinging across scaffolding like Yas, it might be different.

How do I tell my dad that I'm into creeping around in the shadows of Seattle—the underground—and not the touristy underground? The air vents, the sewers, the subway tunnels, the hidden doorways and abandoned buildings most people don't know about. As if he doesn't have enough to worry about.

"Promise me you'll focus on being a kid, okay?" he asks, resting his warm hand on my forearm. "I want you to watch TV and hang with your friends and eat processed food and play Pokémon Go."

I nod at him, but my mind is elsewhere.

9345-8959-4853.

And then it all clicks, like a beautiful twelve-piece puzzle in my head. Three sets of four numbers. That looks like . . .

No way.

I pull my phone out of my pocket so fast, it almost slips out of my hand. I can't get the app re-downloaded fast enough. My fingers are shaking as I type the twelve-digit number into the Pokémon Go trainer code friend-request box, and a message pops up almost instantly.

ThirtyFoods98004 accepted your Friend Request!

Then a private message that says:

THE NEXT CLUE IS UNSTEALABLE.

THE ORDER SEES.

FIND THE BAR ON THE GOPI.

GET YOUR PHONE AND SAY CHEESE.

My heart is racing. I'm so excited, specifically excited to share it with the team! How many other teams have figured out that the twelve-digit number is a Pokémon Go code? Nobody even plays that game anymore. Nobody my age anyway. Nobody except Spider. Which means I'm probably the only person who's figured this out. Just me so far.

I'm *first*!

"Han, everything okay?" my dad asks, startling me. Honestly, I forgot he was in the room. I nod, not looking up from my phone, and he chuckles, "Whelp, I wanted you and your brother to be regular teenagers. Guess that means being on your phone all the time, huh?"

I can barely concentrate with him talking at the same time, but I fight it, opening my messages to find a few recent ones from the team.

JAX: Han, what the hell?

SPIDER: No idea where he is.

YAS: Leave him alone. We'll just have to share the picture of the clue on the forum to prove we're not here to cheat.

SPIDER: We'll need an explanation for why a member of our team took it.

JAX: He took it because he chose to take it, not because it's what Jericho does.

Rage rips through me. Who does Jax think he is? I took the clue because *he* was unclear. Actually, who do any of these people think they are? Without me, they might never have found the trash bin clue in the first place. Without me tagging Kyler, they never would've gotten ten footage of the first clue. And now, as I'm sitting here with the third clue in my hands, I purse my lips and click off my phone.

The phone goes back into my pocket.

I go back to my room.

And I decide that as soon as school is out tomorrow, I'll be in my Camry on my way to a grocery store for clue number three.

In zip code 98004, like the Pokémon Go username said.

Alone.

Spider

blink my eyes awake, and the first thing I see is the sky outside my window, turning orange with the sunrise. I left the window open, so there's dew on my forehead, or sweat, can't figure out which, but it's hot under all these blankets. Or I've had night sweats. Yup. Yuck. Definitely night sweats. I peel the covers off and roll to my side, thinking about that number again.

I tried everything. I googled it, of course. I called it like a phone number. I called it with several different country codes in front of it. I plugged it into my phone's calculator and looked at it upside down. I even checked it against public library records to see if anyone had that library card number. I checked inmate records. I checked dumpster codes—too easy. I matched up the numbers with the letters of the alphabet and tried to rearrange them.

All turned up empty.

I sigh, pulling out my phone, since I've got nothing else to do this early.

6:23 a.m. Wednesday. I don't have to be up for school for another hour, since I showered last night and don't need to this morning, so I get cozy and listen to the birds chirping outside as I read through the messages I missed last night.

JAX: Has anyone checked if the number is prime?

YAS: Tried already, 934589594853 is divisible by 3.

JAX: Dammit. Wait. What if they want us to divide it by 3? Since this will lead us to clue number 3?

YAS: That's a reach.

JAX: You got a better idea?

YAS: That's 311529864951. Any significance?

YAS: Jax?

JAX: Hold on! Give me a second to think!

Jesus Christ, why is everyone so on edge? Jax and Yas have been at each other's throats since the last clue—I'm *not* getting into the middle of that—and Han is mysteriously missing. Although, I guess we can't really blame him. Who would want to come back to their whole team angry them for a mistake they made? And I *know* it's a misunderstanding. Han wouldn't steal clues. Not intentionally. This shit Jax is spittin' is straight-up character assassination, and I won't hear it.

Just in time, a notification pops up from Pokémon Go that reads *Jumpcutxx accepted your friend request!* A warm, fuzzy feeling sinks into my chest. Jumpcutxx and I have been talking since we met in person at PAX West last year. He only joined Pokémon Go two days ago, so yesterday I gave him my twelve-digit . . .

My heart stops.

There's a lump in my throat.

Is this what a stroke feels like?

I feel like everything I've ever eaten is rushing into my legs.

The twelve-digit code! Could it be . . . ?

No way . . .

I plug it into Pokémon Go.

ThirtyFoods98004 accepted your Friend Request!

And then:

THE NEXT CLUE IS UNSTEALABLE.
THE ORDER SEES.
FIND THE BAR ON THE GOPI.
GET YOUR PHONE AND SAY CHEESE.

Messages fly between Jax and Yas so fast that I only catch a few.

YAS: You're the logic guy on this time, and this puzzle was your idea in the first place! Why are you all pressed now that I'm telling you to move faster?

JAX: Oh, that's what this is all about! You've been against this puzzle from the beginning!

YAS: I want to save Abba's store from Roundworld just as much as you want to save your Mama's garden. I'm just not willing to sell out to ANOTHER multinational power to do it, least of all a secretive, unverified vigilante group!

JAX: You know what? I'm dipping out. I need time away from you. Until you get your shit sorted, don't talk to me.

YAS: FINE.

JAX: FINE.

Between the stress of realizing I'm the first one to this next clue, and being caught between the *Days-of-Our-Lives*-ass drama unfolding in my messages, my adrenal glands don't know what the hell to do. So, I take a deep breath, try to center myself, and unravel what this rhyme might mean.

THE NEXT CLUE IS UNSTEALABLE.

How can a clue be unstealable unless it's locked somehow? It must be locked digitally—online. *My* department. Or there must be multiples of the same clue . . . ? Ooh, maybe they're getting clever on us.

THE ORDER SEES.

Well, of course they do.

FIND THE BAR ON THE GOPI.

Like a *bar* bar? As in a twenty-one-and-older bar? I mean, I'm sure I could cook up a fake ID for one of us. Maybe Yas, since she's the oldest. And maybe the most mature. But on the other hand, after her drama with Jax, *neither* of them are acting more mature than I am. At least I still have my head in the game.

Focus, Spider, focus!

Some quick googling tells me that "Gopi" is both a Sanskrit word referring to one of the wives of Gopa of Braj, and the name of a character from *Saath Nibhaana Saathiya!*—an Indian TV drama series.

Speaking of drama, I get a private text from Jax.

JAX: Yo, man, I'm sorry Yas can't set aside her superstitions enough to focus on this puzzle that's so important to all of us. Did you find anything? I've looked at this number backward and forward, and the logic man has come up empty. :(

Oh god, what do I say? *Yes, I found something?* And then what happens when Yas finds out I told Jax and not her? Before I even have time to think this through, I get another message.

YAS: Spider, Jax is clearly going through some personal things. Can you see if any sequence in the number pulls up online?

Fuck.

They've both made it very clear that they want to work solo with me. I'm now split between a private chat with each of them. They can't possibly expect me to pick a side here. . . .

What if I just . . . announce my findings in the group chat? We're a team, after all! But Han might take that info and run with it on his own. Jax and Yas wouldn't work together under these circumstances, which would mean each of us four would be working alone.

And I'm no puzzler.

The *worst*-possible scenario.

I have to choose.

But then I think of a third option.

ME: Hey, Han, you okay? I know what happened back there—it was a big misunderstanding. Sorry about everything that's going on. Do you want to work together?

Minutes go by, turning into what feel like hours.

No texts.

No read receipt.

Nothing.

I'm back to Jax and Yas, texting me separately.

JAX: Well?

YAS: Spider?

I shut my eyes.

GET YOUR PHONE AND SAY CHEESE.

All I've deduced so far is that we're going to a bar with fake IDs and taking a selfie. No idea which bar. No idea what kind of selfie, or what to do with the picture once we've taken it.

I need help.

From a puzzler. Not a parkourist. My heart hurts. *Everything* hurts. Yas is my best friend. She's been there for me through my worst days, when I felt like no one else understood me. But I need Jax's help to logic all of this out. Which bar? What selfie? What the hell does the clue mean by "Gopi"?

I heave a deep sigh, and with unsteady fingers, I type.

ME: It's a Pokémon Go trainer number

JAX: What?

ME: The number. I sent a friend request to that number in the app, and I got an accepted notice. Told y'all that game is still relevant!

JAX: Bet. You win. Did the Pokémon trainer with that number have a name?

ME: Actually, yeah.

I pull it up.

ME: ThirtyFoods98004.

JAX: Thirty Foods like the grocery store? In zip code 98004?

ME: Any grocery stores you know with a bar?

JAX: A salad bar maybe!

Ooh. See? This is why I need him.

ME: That's in Bellevue! Think we'll find a clue about a "Gopi"?

JAX: That's the part I can't figure out. But at least we know where to look. Meet me there today after school?

I feel a lump form in my throat.

ME: We inviting Yas?

Jax takes a while to reply, those three dots appearing and disappearing over and over and over before I finally get a response.

JAX: She clearly isn't into this puzzle like we are.

I blink in surprise to hear Jax be so cutthroat about it. He's usually . . . I don't know . . . softer. I'm not so sure this puzzle isn't bringing out the worst in him, either. I start typing out "Wow, really?" But before I can:

JAX: I hate to be so harsh, but this puzzle is serious. Only the most deserving, remember? If Yas didn't want to do this, she should've sat this one out. Besides, do we really need a parkourist in a grocery store? Over a logician, a hacker, and a . . . well . . . basically a shape-shifter?

ME: Do we even know if Han will be there?

Another long pause.

JAX: It's a Pokémon Go friend request code. He might have figured it out.

He's probably right. But this still feels wrong. A table needs four legs to stand at its strongest. Keeping Yas out of this makes something in my stomach turn sour. I send the text before I can convince myself this is a bad idea.

ME: **See you at 3:30.**

I flop back on my bed and shut my eyes, thinking.

I hope Yas will understand.

And then a thought flies in from left field and hits me in the face. Something about Pokémon Go. I love the game, still, even though it feels like I'm the only one sometimes. But . . . wouldn't the Order know about its decline in popularity? Hiding a clue in Pokémon Go is like putting clues in an episode of *Lost*. Nobody's going to find that.

Why would a group like *the* Order bury such a thing? Are they really that out of touch?

Just as I pick up my phone to do some research into the popularity of Pokémon Go, how long the Order has been around, and maybe even try one more time to dig up some dirt on the people behind it, I hear a soft voice from the other side of my door.

"Marco."

Tae-Jin Hyung?

"Polo," I say, sitting up in bed as the door swings open.

"Hey," says Tae-Jin Hyung. He steps inside and shuts the door behind him, then leans against it. He sighs, and I study his face. His eyes look a bit red, and his cheeks a bit paler than usual.

"Okay, are you going to make me ask?" I ask. "What's wrong?"

"I didn't want to bother you," he says, "especially so early in the morning."

He's so serious. Way more serious than usual. Did somebody die? Did something happen?

"Is it Umma?" I ask, feeling my body tense up. I throw off the covers and swing my legs over the side of the bed, but before I can hop down and dart out the door, Tae-Jin Hyung raises his hand.

"No no, she's fine! It's my sister."

"Tae-yeon? Is she okay?"

The last time I saw Tae-yeon, she was tiny. Tae-jin Hyung and his mother had just come in from the train station, one suitcase each. Umma called me down from my room and explained that they needed some food, a place to stay, and a job for Tae-jin Hyung while he studied for his computer programming degree.

By the end of the day, Tae-jin Hyung had papers, his mom had a room with another family across the street who worked for us, and little Tae-yeon had new clothes, bottles, and a crib. It wasn't too hard. I'm part of an online no-buy group that gives away baby stuff all the time.

"Is Tae-yeon okay?" I ask, hoping it's nothing dire.

"My umma took her to the hospital last night. Stomach problems. Didn't say a word to the staff. Then she left her there."

"Your mom left Tae-yeon at the hospital? Alone? Why? Which hospital?"

"Rainierview," he says, staring at the floor, shaking his head. Then his voice begins to break. "She said she was afraid they would get reported to immigration if they found out her name. Now I don't know how to get Tae-yeon back. She's a patient without a name or history, as far as the staff are concerned. I tried calling, but they wouldn't give me information over the phone, since I'm just some guy claiming to be her brother. I didn't even know if I could give them *my* name without them reporting us. I . . . I don't know what to do."

He looks up at me.

"I don't know anyone more clued in to immigration laws around here than you. How . . . how easy would it be to forge a birth certificate?"

Before I can jump in with *You absolutely don't want to do that,* Tae-

Jin Hyung holds up his hands to ask me to let him finish.

"I know it's illegal. I'm not asking you to make one—I'd make it myself—just . . . how much time am I looking at if I get caught?"

"Tae-Jin Hyu—"

"Please, Daeshim, just tell me," he says. "I have to get her back."

"You don't have to do that," I say, pulling out my phone and opening the internet app. Some quick searching pulls up an article about Rainierview—specifically, the CEO, Dreeny Finch, explaining Rainierview's resistance against ICE.

"'We work to provide patients care,'" I read out loud. "'Not to enforce immigration laws.'"

Tae-Jin Hyung doesn't look convinced.

"You don't have to worry," I say. "Hospitals everywhere are resisting having to report info to the feds."

"You trust them?" he asks.

"No," I explain, "I trust incentives. Hospitals have no reason to report you. It's extra work they wouldn't get paid for, and it would deter patients from seeking care. I promise you won't have a problem. Besides, you still have that Washington license, right?"

He nods. "I just haven't used it anywhere. Anywhere that would have it recorded anyway. Just to get ID'd at bars and stuff."

"So it's been working," I say with a grin, latching onto that bit of pride. Something I made has been working! I never get tired of that feeling.

"Yeah," he says, smiling. "Should I use a different one at the hospital, though?"

"If it'd give you some peace of mind," I say. "Pick a name. I'll make you one."

He pauses for a moment and then nods at me, but before he can say anything, I cut in.

"Take your time and think about it. Picking a name is important. Even if it's just for an, um . . . interim license."

"Thanks, man," he says.

I nod and smile, and then I sigh and realize he's still shaken from this whole thing. And who wouldn't be? His sister, who's only three or so by now, is alone at a hospital surrounded by strangers, and he doesn't know if he has the right to go pick her up because of our fucked-up immigration laws.

"Hey," I say. "You know Ah-young?"

Nice girl. Washes dishes and keeps to herself, doesn't say much. He nods.

"She came with no papers. I won't tell you much more of her business, but . . . if I can get papers for her, I can get papers for you. And for Tae-yeon. Promise."

He smiles and nods again. I know the kitchen staff talk when I'm not there, and I hope they all know . . .

"You can trust me."

Thirty Foods is like Disneyland but for food. When we step in through the spotless sliding glass doors, there are about two hundred identical yellow shopping carts—also spotless—advertising organic cucumbers for $1.49 each.

Each.

I could get a whole McDonald's cheeseburger for that. A *deluxe* cheeseburger if I wanted. Or I could just get a whole bag of 'em from Jax for a little extra intel.

"Can you believe this shit?" I ask him. "You know, if this all goes under, Mama could always open up her own Thirty Foods. Call it 'Mama's Garden Party.'"

"Because the rich hate it when we party?"

"Exactly," I say, lowering my voice a little as we walk past a woman pushing a cart out through the door in Birkenstocks, harem pants, and a shirt that says *Don't ask me why I'm a vegan, ask yourself why you aren't.* Her curly blond hair is tied into a low ponytail at the nape of her neck, and her huge round glasses look . . . expensive.

Meaning she probably paid hundreds of dollars to look that bohemian.

Her chubby toddler is kicking his legs in the seat at the front of the cart with both fists between slobbery gums and lips, but he's smiling at me as he's wheeled past.

The mom isn't, though.

She's looking at Jax—in his gray hoodie, jeans, and sneakers—like he might be lost. Like he might be in the wrong store. Like he might be here to steal something because, frankly, neither of us are dressed like we can afford anything here anyway. She has no idea she's looking at a fellow vegan, who's just as passionate about animals as she is, if not more so, who volunteers at an animal shelter and is walking into this store to progress further in a game in which the prize is the possible overthrowing of an oil refinery and the salvation of his mother's community garden.

I glare at her as we pass, but she keeps her eyes on Jax before whipping her head back around to walk through the doors and out into the parking lot.

I don't even think Jax noticed.

Thump!

I run into the back of him, bumping the side of my head against the back of his.

"Man, watch where—" I begin.

If he did watch where he's going, he's distracted by something else, stopped in the middle of the aisle, frozen there like a statue. I peer around him, afraid of what I might see, and then anxiety shoots through me like a bolt of lightning.

It's Purple Suit Guy.

Only this time, his suit is forest green. Still velvet. He's taller than I remember him from last night, standing at the salad bar, reading the descriptions of everything carefully.

I don't think Monopoly Man has seen us yet, so I grab Jax and duck into a nearby aisle.

"Spider, what the hell is wrong with you?" whispers Jax, turning around to face me.

"What do we do?" I ask Jax, crawling past him and peering out from around the corner. A white man with a goatee and a buttoned-up flannel shirt goes by with a cart, leering down at us with inspecting eyes, as if we're one misguided eye twitch away from him calling security.

"The hell do you mean, 'What do we do?' We look for the clue! Team ROYAL can know we're here. What are they going to do, attack us? We'd *all* be kicked out of this place and arrested."

Does he *have* to say the word "arrested" so loud around *all* these white people?!

"Jax, listen, we don't even know what we're looking for. Can't we figure *something* out about this clue first before waltzing over and joining Black Gatsby at the salad bar?"

Jax glares up at me with eyes flashing and eyebrows knit together.

"Do you want to win or not?" he asks.

Now that he's so close, I realize the whites of his eyes are a bit redder than usual, his bottom lids the slightest bit darker. He's blinking more, indicating his eyes might be dry.

"Jax," I say, the shock setting in. "Did you . . . did you sleep at all last night?"

"Is sleeping going to get us to the next clue?" he snaps.

I don't know if he sees the pain in my eyes, but . . . that hurts. I realize this is important for him. It's important for all of us. I would give my soul to guarantee that Umma's restaurant gets to stay right where it is in Capitol Hill, techies in suits and all. But he can't miss sleep like this. He can't push himself to the brink. *None* of this is worth his health.

"I'm just . . . concerned about you," I say. "I'm your friend, Jax. Come on, hear me here."

"I can sleep after I win," he spits, pulling out his phone and peering around the corner at—what was his actual name?—Karim, that's right. I look too. He's stopped in front of the hot food, reading every inscription before moving on to the sign above the next dish.

An associate with dark curly hair walks up next to him and asks, "Can I help you find anything, sir?" Karim dons his biggest smile, and in a voice slightly different from the one we heard last night, slightly brighter, slightly crisper, says, "Oh no, thank you, I'm just reading the ingredients. I'm on keto now, you know."

"Oh, nice! Nice!" says the employee, sliding his hands into his pockets.

I have to roll my eyes. Of *course* he is. Jax has his eyes trained on Karim, and I hear him whisper under his breath, "The question is, how do we get to the bar?"

"You don't," says a sharp voice from behind us that sounds strangely familiar, and suddenly Jax's and my skinny asses are being lifted into the air by our shirt collars.

"Hey, what the hell?" I demand, fists swinging before I can think. I open my eyes to realize I'm face-to-face with Lucas, his white, oily forehead glistening under these fluorescent lights, ice-blue eyes smiling devilishly.

"*So*," he says, super loud for no reason, "it's the second-rate clue-stealing wannabes. Just two of you this time?"

I swat his arm away, and he lets go of both our shirts. I straighten out my collar and look to Jax for help. What the hell do we do now?

"We're here looking for the next clue, man, just like you," says Jax—quite diplomatically, I might add.

"Seems you've lost half your comrades," booms Karim from behind us. We're sandwiched between the two of them—Karim at the endcap, and Lucas in the middle of the aisle. Jax and I look back and forth between both of them, and I'm sure we're both thinking the same thing: It'd be *so* nice to have a parkourist with us right now.

I pull out my phone and send a quick text to Yas.

ME: Help. Thirty Foods. Bellevue. Now.

"Speaking of comrades, where's your Russian ballerina?" I have to ask.

"Sigge is on a special mission while we snag this next clue."

"Didn't seem like you were snagging much at the salad bar over there." Jax smirks. "Lazy asses. Couldn't even find the clue before stopping for lunch."

I see exactly what Jax is doing, and I play along.

"Sad," I say. "They don't even know where to look."

Karim's eyes narrow at that, but he straightens his white-and-purple shirt collar under his purple blazer and glances at Lucas before saying:

"Well, who can blame you for not stopping for lunch? If I were a man of your . . . uh . . . class, I might not stop for lunch here either. Overdraft fees these days. *Tsk, tsk, tsk.* It's a shame what the banks are doing really. You have my pity."

Oh, *fuck* this guy.

"I don't need pity from a guy in a Wish suit," spits Jax. A muscle twitches under Karim's eye, and his smile falls so slightly, at first I'm not sure I saw it.

"I wouldn't be caught dead shopping on Wish. I own stock in Wish's parent company, you parasite."

"*Tsk, tsk, tsk,*" I say, hatching an idea and hoping Jax catches on *quick* once we've got an out. "He owns stock in Wish's parent company, and yet never learned to match his socks."

The minute Karim's eyes are down at his feet, we take off, Jax to

Karim's right and me to his left, sprinting for the salad bar like our lives depend on it.

That's how JERICHO gets down!

The salad bar is a food circus, and by that, I mean every food in existence is here, in fancy silver—what do they even call these things? *Bins?* I spot a sign at the very end that says PLEASE USE PROVIDED TONGS. CAUTION: CHAFERS ARE HOT! So, I guess they're called "chafers," then. Whatever. The point is, there's food here from every culture in the world—sushi and saffron rice, biryani and spanakopita, goulash and ratatouille, mahjouba and pastel de nata, and something called "pljeskavica" that looks like a particularly delicious burger patty in a pita pocket. I can't read these labels fast enough. I look around and realize Jax has disappeared, and by the time I spot him on the other side of the buffet, looking at the signs on that side, a voice has appeared in my ear to ask tersely, "Sir, can I help you?"

That same guy that was talking to Karim before like they were old friends is looking at me with unabashed suspicion, and he didn't ask warmly "Can I help you find anything?" But "Can I help you?"

With an implied "out of the store" at the end of that.

All right, time to hack this situation like I hack everything else. I put on my freshest British accent, just to throw him off even further as he stares down at this clearly Asian customer of his.

"Morning, sir. Might you direct me to the spelt flour? I'm making lavender scones for a brunch party this weekend, and a few of my guests require gluten-free refreshments."

His face is absolutely *priceless.*

But I can't bask in that for too long, because I see Lucas, lurking about twenty feet behind him. He knows not to make a scene here so we don't all get kicked out before we figure out this clue.

"Uh, u-um . . . sure! It's in aisle seven," he says, tripping over his words.

"Thank you," I croon. "Your service is most appreciated."

"Yo, man," comes Jax's voice behind me, "over here."

I glance over my shoulder at him, crouched in front of the refrigerated wall of yogurts, milks, and cheeses, but when I look back at the employee, I refuse to break character.

"Ah, there's one of my cohorts now." I grin. "Would you care to show us where on this wall we can find the Roquefort?"

If I can just keep this guy close to us while we look around, I know we can keep Lucas and Karim from hassling us. Speaking of, Karim steps out from the aisle behind Jax and is marching toward him like he's about to put him in a chokehold. I rush forward as loudly and belligerently as I can with an "*Ah, look!* Here's another one now," stepping between them and standing almost nose-to-nose with Karim. "I was just looking for you, actually. How are you with yogurt, Karim? Yogurt is keto, correct?"

And just like that, I've convinced the associate that I both (1) know Karim personally enough to call him by name, and (2) know Karim well enough to know his dietary needs. I'm safe. And since I'm with Jax, *we're* safe. Whatever clout Karim was chasing with the associate earlier is now all of ours to share. The workers think we're all here together.

I narrow my eyes with a grin and tip my head just enough for him to know I'm beaming the word "checkmate" to his brain telekinetically. I hear shuffling behind me, the sound of footsteps walking away as I see the associate leave out of the corner of my eye.

"You think you're so smart," hisses Karim. "But you're flying blind, just like we are, looking for clues in a store that's so far above your parents' class, I'm surprised you can read."

Another associate walks up to the dairy wall, picks up a tub of yogurt, and starts scanning.

"Flying blind, as far as you know," I say. The less they know about where we are in figuring out the clue, the better. I pull out my phone and step away from him, turning back toward the salad bar. Jax, who by now has walked the whole way around it, joins me and gives me a long, blank look before turning to Karim.

Has he found anything?

Would he have told me?

"Why y'all hassling us anyway?" asks Jax, shoving his hands into his pockets. "You here to find clues or give us a hard time?"

"Both," says Karim, smiling triumphantly. Two beeps ring out from his pocket, the ringtone available only on the newest iPhone, and he proudly slides it out of his pocket, holding up the slender platinum device.

"Whelp, gotta go. My colleagues need me."

And he turns to disappear down the aisle of crackers and cookies.

The associate scans another item, inching closer to us, this time a pack of presliced fresh mozzarella cheese.

"So what now?" asks Jax, his voice a whisper. "I have no idea what to look for at the salad bar." He looks down at his phone and reads aloud to me, his voice soft:

THE NEXT CLUE IS UNSTEALABLE.
THE ORDER SEES.
FIND THE BAR ON THE GOPI. . . .

But just as he's about to read the next line, my eyes lock onto the next product under the associate's scanner—another pack of some white dairy product, this one labeled "Gopi Paneer."

GET YOUR PHONE AND SAY CHEESE.

Cheese!

As in paneer cheese!

"It's a barcode!" I shriek, completely forgetting where we are and how important it is that we whisper. The whole store seems to go silent until Jax steps closer and follows my eyes.

"You got a barcode scanner?"

I've already got my phone out and the app open. I grab the pack of cheese and flip it over, my heart racing as I take in the eye symbol of the Order. The scan processes and my phone dings with a new message notification.

THE ORDER:
JUST ONE FINAL CLUE, AND YOU MAY JOIN OUR ALLIANCE.
CRYPTOLOGY IS ART JUST AS MUCH AS IT'S SCIENCE.
WITH SO MUCH TO GAIN, WITHOUT FURTHER ADO,
HERE'S WHAT YOU NEED TO SOLVE THE LAST CLUE.

I blink in frustration. Is that it? What kind of a clue is that?

But then a link pops up and I click it. It takes me to the internet app.

A single explosive *pop!*

A shattering of glass.

A tinkling shower all over the floor ten feet away.

A broken window way up in the rafters.

Lucas peering around the corner of the aisle at us and hurling something hard and gray at Jax's chest.

Jax catches it instinctively, not registering that it's a gun until he's cradling it in his arms.

"He's got a gun!" calls Lucas before disappearing around the corner again.

And then chaos.

Jax

Holding a gun in front of a shattered window in the Thirty Foods specialty cheese aisle was *not* on the cryptology bingo card of this broke, Black, peace-loving vegan boy.

But here I am, setting it down on the floor and raising my hands into the air, backing away from all the scurrying customers looking frantically between me and the door, abandoning carts and hauling screaming babies through the door with zero time for gentleness.

"I didn't do that! It was—"

But when I look back, Lucas is gone. Because of course he is.

Spider is looking at me like I've got leprosy, even though I'm not even holding it anymore and he *knows* I didn't bring it in. But I was still the last one holding a hot potato when it went off and damaged property in a Thirty Foods.

"No, wait!" I yell, more passersby shrieking and shuffling out the door.

Suddenly, *boom!*

My head slams against the floor. My arms are yanked behind my back and wedged up between my shoulder blades, despite my cries.

"Let me go!" I beg. "I didn't do anything!"

"Shut up!" shouts the voice of whoever's pressed their body on top of me. I look up to catch a glimpse of Spider sprinting around the corner, clutching his bag as he makes for the door.

Good, I think. *Whatever happens, win the puzzle.*

I rest my cheek on the cold tile floor just as a tall figure in purple steps lazily from around the corner—sauntering, really—before crouching in front of me.

"Hope the love of the game was worth it for you, Jax."

Rage surges through me, and I struggle against whoever's hands are clamped around my wrists. Who the hell does Karim think he is, walking through here like he owns the place?

"These people," I spit up at him, "don't know you. Don't know how much money you have. You're Black, Karim. You do know that, right?"

I tried to warn him.

But he's on the floor with someone much bigger laying their body weight on top of him.

Someone in blue.

With a gun at their hip.

And shiny, silver handcuffs that clamp around Karim's wrists as if he were as broke and unwelcome here as, well, me.

Yas

I read it again.

SPIDER: Help. Thirty Foods. Bellevue. Now.

No other details. No clues. No context. As I kick my legs up at the front of the 70 bus, I'm left to wonder what the hell is going on. Why is Spider in Bellevue of all places, after school, except to look for clues? Why didn't he include the rest of us in his venture? What kind of emergency could be happening at Thirty Foods that I'd be able to help better than the authorities?

I mean the fire department, of course. Emergency personnel.

No, this *has* to be puzzle related. But why didn't Spider just tell me he was going to investigate the next clue? The last I knew, we were dealing with that twelve-digit number. Had me up till eleven last night researching options, since our lead puzzler wants to sell his soul to have the privilege of kissing the Order's ass. I take a long, slow, deep breath and try to regroup. I know Jax wants to save Mama's garden. We *all* want to save Mama's garden. But I just wish he'd be more careful. Now Spider is in trouble at a Thirty Foods in Bellevue, and if it doesn't have to do with Jax overcommitting to the puzzle, I'll eat my own shoe.

And yet here I am, stepping off the 70 bus and walking past a luxury camping store, a car dealership, and finally under an overpass before seeing the Thirty Foods. And while I expect to see a tranquil scene of rich people walking into the store with designer reusable shopping bags and rolling their carts full of expensive food through the parking lot to their cars, what I'm looking at is a very different scene.

Chaos reigns. People in clothes clearly unfit for running are running. Carts are rolling haphazardly through the parking lot, cars and people dodging them, including me. I dive out of the way of a shrieking man holding the hand of a child who's begging him to slow down. He doesn't. He picks the boy up and keeps running, and I look up at the store.

What the hell is going on in there?

"Shooter! Don't go in!" I hear from somewhere in the lot.

I dive behind a gigantic potted plant, and my heart rate skyrockets into overdrive.

I text Spider frantically.

ME: Where r u?

But I get my answer in the form of what would have been a blur flying out the front doors and past my hiding spot, if not for my reflexes. My hand is gripped around a wad of black sweatshirt and yanking him behind the plant with me before he can register who I am.

"Yas!" he hollers, throwing his arms around me in a big sweaty hug. "You came!"

"Duh," I say, looking back up at the front doors, where I spot Mr. Red Cap—Lucas was his name, I think—waltzing through the doors like nothing happened. "That guy again."

"He threw a gun at Jax!" pants Spider.

Alarm bells go off in my head.

"Wait, Jax is here?" I demand. Then it sinks in that what he just said was hella weird. "And who throws a gun *at* somebody?"

"I'll explain later," he says. "We have to get him—"

An associate with flushed cheeks and dark curly hair is looking at us strangely, like he knows us. But I'm less concerned about him as I am about what I see *behind* him.

Jax, staring at the ground as he walks, hands behind his back, shoved intermittently by a huge boy in blue toward a police SUV with flashing red and blue lights.

"Spider?" I ask, still *so* confused. Why the hell is Jax getting arrested?

But his hand is around my wrist and yanking me backward.

I hear the vroom of a car—a specific vroom with a bit of sputtering mixed in for personality—a Toyota Camry that we all know well.

I turn around to see Han in the driver's seat, wrist resting on the wheel as he waves us over with his other hand. I look back at Jax just as he's being shoved into the SUV, and I'm remembering Freddie Gray, and knowing that the next time I see Jax, he could be . . .

. . . well . . .

I have to do *something*.

"Yas, come *on*!" calls Spider's voice.

Surely he doesn't want me to just *leave* him! Our captain! Spider and Jax are the closest I've had to little brothers. I wouldn't leave *either* of them in the hands of 12, not while I'm alive and breathing and conscious. But as the cop slams the door shut and looks at me, and I hear the store associate yell, "Hey, it's the kid who was with him!" while pointing in my direction—most definitely at Spider—*and* I see the cop level his eyes at me before launching into a sprint, I realize I don't have a choice.

"I'm sorry, Jax," I whisper before turning, running, and throwing myself up on top of Han's car, slipping down through the sunroof and scrambling to buckle up before Spider climbs into the back seat and Han peels out of the parking lot.

The sirens start almost immediately, and Han launches the car out into the street so fast, I swear we go airborne. I hear the screams of two people—one is Spider's and the other I don't recognize as my own until we land.

My organs feel like they've been shaken in a jar, and we're surrounded by honks, but we fly through Bellevue like the road is ours, and I hear Spider's voice in the back seat yell:

"Are we really running from the cops right now?"

Han doesn't answer, but I see him look up into the rearview mirror. I hear the sirens grow louder and turn around to follow his gaze. Blue and red lights flicker far behind us, so far that when we whip around the corner, I'm not even sure they saw us. But we can't outrun the cops. There's just no way.

"Han, stop the car!" I urge.

"You have a better plan?" asks Spider.

I don't, but I know that I've never seen a police chase end in anything except somebody getting arrested, spike stripped, PIT maneuvered, tased, or shot. We have to pull over. *Now.*

"Han, stop the car or I'm jumping out!" I'm hollering now, and Han flinches against my voice before swerving so hard around a corner that the wheels screech against the pavement. The smell of burning rubber fills the air, and I can't believe we're still doing this. I can't believe he hasn't stopped!

I look out the window and down at the pavement zooming by.

Am I really about to jump out of a moving vehicle?

I look at the rearview mirror. No cop lights, for now. If I'm going to do it, now's the time. I reach up, grip the frame of the car left exposed by the open window, and sit on the sill, feeling the wind flutter through my hijab, whip through my hoodie and leggings.

"Yas, what the hell are you doing?" shrieks Spider. But I don't have time to think. As long as Han doesn't turn left—

And suddenly I'm flying backward, out the window, away from the car. I scramble to grab the car frame again, but my fingers find open air, and I realize I'm going to hit the ground. Of all the things that could happen at that moment, Han turned left.

A yelp escapes from somewhere around me before I can realize that I made the sound, and I feel my feet catch something inside the car. I'm upside down, the blood rushing to my head from the centrifugal force of the car turning, and I look up, which for me is down, to see my forehead only inches from the pavement.

But something's holding me to the car as we finish the turn, and I'm pulled up, slowly, legs first, back into the car.

I'm plopped into the passenger seat as Spider's words finally start to register in my ears.

"What the fuck were you thinking, sitting in the window?! We're going sixty-plus in a forty and you want to try 'spinning' for the first time?!"

"I—I—" I begin, but I have no idea what to say now. The car is moving slowly between rows of parked cars, most of them similar, all Camrys or Accords. The sky is getting darker and darker as sunset fades into night. I turn to Han, who's hunched over the wheel, eyes darting back and forth around this place like he's hunting for something. "Han, where the hell are we? We need to turn around and turn ourselves in."

"Are you out of your fucking mind?!" Spider still hasn't calmed down, clearly.

"We are fugitives of the *law*, genius!" I holler back, my temper flaring up inside me like wildfire.

"For what?" he spits, gripping each of the front seats. "For *witnessing* some white guy shoot a window in a Thirty Foods? We didn't do shit! Jax didn't do shit! We need to find out where he went and make sure he's okay!"

My blood is surging. I glare over my shoulder at him and feel the flames gathering at the tip of my tongue.

"They'll have warrants for our arrest, Spider, and then what? We end up in the same place as Jax? Locked up in a jail cell? Is that what you want? Because that's what you get when you run from the cops!"

My heart is thumping in my throat as I stare at Spider and he stares back at me. His eyes are flashing, and I'm sure mine are too, and I wonder what's prompting such a stupid decision. He's not thinking properly, because our friend was arrested. And he doesn't want to be next. But neither do I! How do I make him understand that I don't want to end up dead after being forcefully arrested or shot? I hate 12 just as much as the next person, but I know when to bow down when I need to.

I'll run, I'll climb, I'll jump.

But above all else, I'll survive.

I'm so lost in my thoughts that I haven't even noticed the car has stopped. I glance over my shoulder to look through the rearview window to see a wall of trees. We're parked between two Camrys identical to Han's, only different in color—one white, one green.

"Han," I whisper as he turns the key and the engine hushes into silence, since the darkness makes whispering seem appropriate, I guess. "What are we doing here?"

His eyes are shut tight, and his hands are moving inside his sweatshirt pocket, spinning his phone over and over. His shoulders are hunched up to his ears, and my chest tightens. He's afraid. He's terrified. And why wouldn't he be?

"Han," I say, holding out my hand for support, but careful not to touch him. "I know you don't do hugs, but I want you to know we're here for you, and we're grateful. Thanks for helping us back there. Who knows where we'd be without you?"

Spider leans forward and nods between us.

"Yeah, man," he says. "Thank you."

Without a word, and without even opening his eyes, Han pulls out his phone and hands it to me. I examine the screen, hoping to find some kind of explanation for what the hell the plan is, but instead I find a clue.

THE NEXT CLUE IS UNSTEALABLE.
THE ORDER SEES.
FIND THE BAR ON THE GOPI.
GET YOUR PHONE AND SAY CHEESE.

I read the first part again. Does that mean that the clue is behind glass or something? Or maybe that it's posted too high for anyone to reach? Or behind bars maybe, like Jax?

Focus, Yas, focus.

I read the next line. The Order sees. Of course they do. That's a surprise to exactly no one. The next line is more promising. Find the bar on the gopi.

"Gopi as in gopi cheese and yogurt?"

I hear a clattering behind me and turn to find Spider collapsed dramatically against the back seat, and his phone—still lit up— bounces against his thigh and falls to the floor.

"We could've just asked you the whole time?!" he asks, sitting up again and looking squarely at me. I feel a bit of triumph at that.

"I'm good for more than just parkour, you know," I say before getting back on subject. "So, they wanted you to take a picture of some yogurt?"

"Close," he says, reaching into his messenger bag and pulling out a palm-size cellophane-wrapped white block of paneer.

I raise an eyebrow.

"They sent you on an excursion to Thirty Foods in Bellevue for cheese? Why?"

Spider shrugs.

"Not sure, but we got it."

None of this feels right. It feels like there's a worm weaving its way through my intestines, knotting everything up inside. We've been led to an alley in South Lake Union, a downtown parking lot, an expensive grocery store in Bellevue, and now—

"Wait, back to the subject—where the hell are we?" I demand.

"Isn't it obvious?" asks Spider with a knowing smile, gesturing to Han. "This kid's a genius. Look around! We're camouflaged! They'll never find us here."

I look up at the sign over the tiny building in the corner of this lot to find the name EASTERN PINE AUTO CONNECTIONS. I hear sirens down the street, growing increasingly louder, but before I can react and swing my door open, jump out, and tear across the parking lot like I want to do, a flurry of red and blue lights flies by, sirens blaring and fading into the distance just as quickly as they arrived.

"See?" asks Spider just as I see his Doc Martens fly up between Han and me, landing on the console with a jarring *smack!* Both Han and I jump at the noise and look at each other.

"Han," I start, a smile pulling at the corners of my mouth. "This *is* a brilliant idea."

He grins back at me and gives the slightest nod before reclining his seat, narrowly missing Spider. He folds his arms across his chest and gets comfortable, and that's when everything comes flooding back to me.

"Wait a minute—you can't mean to just *stay* here," I say, although it comes out sounding more like a question. What about Jax?

"I know, I know," says Spider. "You want to keep playing the game—"

"I most certainly do *not* want to keep playing the game!" I thunder. "Don't you think this has gone far enough? These people have us wandering through the *weirdest* places for clues in dangerous spots. Under a trash can? In an expensive store—"

"The first clue was on a pole in broad daylight." Spider's words cut through mine with a finality that demands I shut up, and pain rips through my chest at his tone. But I keep my face even as I stare him down.

"Broad daylight means nothing for us," I say, and his face tells me he knows what I'm talking about. It doesn't matter how much daylight is out. I'm still Black and Pakistani. He's still Korean. Jax is still Black.

And in jail.

If he's not dead.

Tears spring to my eyes, and I decide I won't wait another second.

"I'm going to find him," I say, swinging the passenger door open. "Every second matters when it comes to us being arrested. You know that."

"And how exactly do you plan to find him?" Spider asks, stepping out of his door and folding his arms before leveling his eyes at me. "You just gonna *walk* on up to the front doors of the jail and say 'Hello, yes, my name's Yasmin—yes, the same one wanted for evading several officers earlier today, and I'm here to find my friend Jax, who was seen with a gun at the crime scene—"

"Shut *up!*" I yell at him, feeling my eyes burn. One stubborn tear rolls down my cheek. I have no idea how I'm going to get to Jax, or get him out, but I have to try. And then a thought hits me.

The *game.*

Spider must see something change in my face, because he raises an eyebrow. I can't believe I didn't see it sooner.

The game isn't just the answer to the future of Abba's store. Or Spider's mom's restaurant. Or Han's dad's kayaking business, or even Mama's garden.

This game might just save Jax's life.

Two words bounce around in my head. *Political power.*

Fuck!

WE MAKE THINGS HAPPEN.

They'd said.

I pray they're right and hold out my hand to Spider.

"Give me the cheese."

"What?" he asks in surprise, his eyes darting back to the car. "What for? Now suddenly you're interested in playing?"

"*My* friend is in jail," I hiss. "And I've *always* wanted to play the game, within reason. We've been out of 'reason' for a long while now."

Excuse me for having a healthy amount of apprehension about being strung along all over the city and put in precarious situations, all for an ambiguous prize. All I know is that the "power" promised better be able to bust Jax out of jail.

I didn't even get to reconcile our differences.

I remember the last thing I said to him.

I'm just not willing to sell out to ANOTHER multinational power to do it, least of all a secretive, unverified vigilante group.

I called him a sellout.

I shut my eyes and take a deep breath before wiping away tears.

"Give me the fucking cheese, Spider."

Spider's eyes go back to his car door, and my eyes go to my open window, and just as he dives for the door, I torpedo myself headfirst through the passenger window. My arms are outstretched into the back seat, and my fingertips graze the package of cheese, just as Spider yanks it away with a grunt.

"I can't let you leave right this second. If you get caught out there," he says, pausing in hesitation before motioning to Han, who's staring at both of us from the driver's seat in shock, "we all get caught."

I narrow my eyes at him, and he glances at Han before speaking again.

"It's safer to wait until the cops have called off the search, or at least until morning when this dealership opens."

Han nods, and I realize I'm alone in this.

But if I leave right now, Spider might do something chaotic like follow me, or Han might drive after me, and then I'll *really* have gotten us all caught.

I'll have to go sneakily.

"Fine," I say. I climb back into the passenger seat and fold my arms. My rage is immeasurable. That Spider would just abandon Jax like this. That he would climb back into this car, curl up on the seat, and pull out his phone to text god-knows-who about god-knows-what, while Jax is probably getting his mugshot taken if he's lucky enough to still be alive. . . .

I want to throw up.

But instead, I wait.

I wait for the moon to rise higher and higher into the sky, praying for my friend who's been incarcerated. I wait and pray and make every dua I know for protection, begging for Jax to be safe. I wait for text after text from Abba asking where I am, always giving a cryptic answer that he'll believe but isn't quite a lie.

I'm with Spider and Han.

In car, can't text.

Be home soon.

And I wait till Han's breathing has deepened and lengthened, one arm stretched across his face, and until Spider's snores roll like gravel through my ears. And then, finally, I ease the door open, slip out, and slide it closed again without shutting it completely and causing a ruckus.

And I'm off to catch the last bus to South Lake Union.

Where I'm going, I won't need the Thirty Foods cheese.

Abba's store is closed, but the lights are still on. He's slumped over the counter, his back heaving with snores that I can hear through this locked door. I turn my key and ease it open, holding the bell cord so it won't ring to life and disturb him. I walk past the fridges full of heat-and-eat food, made with love by his hands, probably going to waste, thanks to Roundworld and their cafeterias and on-site gyms and nap rooms and dry cleaners and doctors and yoga teachers and—

I feel the rage rising up again, and I pause before approaching the counter.

This is why I'm playing. *This* is what I'm playing for.

This place.

I reach my hand up, but just before my fingers find his forearm, I hear a familiar voice whisper harshly behind me, "Don't."

It cuts through the silence and makes me jump.

"Don't scare me like that," I say. "What are you doing down here anyway, creeping around in the aisles?"

Ranya steps out from the back of the store and reaches into a crinkly bag.

"Eating Cocomos," she whispers casually. "Want one?"

She tosses one in my direction before I can answer, and I catch it and pop it into my mouth, crushing it between my teeth and letting the crunch and the chocolate wash over my tongue.

"Thanks," I whisper, stepping closer so we can talk without waking Abba.

"So, why are *you* down here so late?" she asks. "Shouldn't you be home by now? It's almost your bedtime."

She's only nineteen—two years older than me. It's not like she didn't have a "bedtime" just last year.

"Shouldn't you be home sulking in your room?" I ask. Her face stays deadly still, but she suddenly loses her taste for Cocomos. She carefully rolls up the bag and slips it into the pocket of her black leather jacket. She leans against a nearby shelf and tilts her head at me. The shimmering silver-and-diamond brooch pinned to her burgundy hijab sparkles in the dim light, and between that and her flawless makeup, she looks like a princess.

"Why are you all dolled up this late at night anyway?" I ask.

"My therapist said doing my makeup might help with my depression," she says curtly. Instantly guilt floods my chest.

"Oh," I say, softening, "I didn't know."

"You didn't ask," she says. I guess I didn't. More guilt. "Anyway," she continues, "in case you care, I wasn't in love with him. Mom and Abba were. You wouldn't know love if it knocked at your front door."

Pretty sure I would, but now isn't the time to press. I don't have time for conversations about love. I have to bail my friend out of jail. Another kind of love.

I step past her toward the fridges where Abba keeps the milk, cheese, and yogurt, and swing open a door once I spot the Gopi paneer, behind a price tag of $4.99. No idea what Spider paid for it at Thirty Foods, but I guarantee it was at least two dollars higher. The money that rich people will fork over, just to be able to shop with other rich people.

"Sudden hankering for a whole block of paneer?" asks Ranya, folding her arms.

I roll my eyes and step past her, back to where I left my phone at the front counter.

FIND THE BAR ON THE GOPI.

It has to be the barcode. I find a barcode scanning app and hit download just as Ranya keeps talking.

"More clues from your little internet puzzles?"

"Shh," I say, glancing at Abba, who stirs and adjusts his arm under his forehead. We really should wake him or he'll wake up sore in a few hours. He works so hard here, pours his very soul into this place, and somehow wakes up with a smile on his face. He deserves a good night's sleep in a nice warm bed next to Mom.

"For your information," I say, "my 'little internet puzzles' are about to pay off."

Power does a lot of things.

Maybe knocks out corporations.

Maybe saves stores.

Maybe saves the lives of best friends.

"What, did somebody finally promise big money as a prize? Thought that was against the rules."

"Thought cryptology didn't interest you," I say.

"Believe it or not, *you* interest me," she says, turning and looking around the store with her back to me. "You're my only sister. I care about what you care about. I mean, I don't quite *get* it. Why would you go leaping all over the city, risking your life for anything but money or career advancement?"

"If I say *love*, will you take back what you said about me not recognizing it if it knocked at my door?"

Suddenly, more poetically than anything else that's happened in my life, a knock comes at the front door. Ranya and I both look from the door to each other. The insignia right smack in the middle of the glass is blocking whoever is there, but I can see slender legs in dark clothes, and a white hand sliding into a dark pocket.

Ranya and I exchange a glance, and she raises a perfectly shaped eyebrow at me as a smile creeps across her face.

"A suitor of yours?" she asks.

"I could ask you the same thing." I grin, looking back at the door. And then a face peeks around the insignia, a face framed by platinum blond hair and icy blue eyes. They cup their hands around their face to shield from the glare of the street lights as they peer in. My blood goes cold as I recognize her. I wonder what the hell a member of Team ROYAL is doing here, right now, at Abba's store. Heat rushes into my forehead, and I swallow a lump in my throat. Ranya must see my face because she says, "But you do *know* her."

It's a statement, not a question, and I decide that if I play it cool, maybe my sister won't realize how freaked out I am by this, or that I'm worried maybe she—what's her name? Starts with an *S*, I think?—isn't here to turn me in to the cops for evading officers in Bellevue earlier tonight.

If Ranya finds out that my "little internet puzzles" have led to such shenanigans, Mom and Abba *will* hear about it, and if Mom and Abba hear about it, I *will* have to quit JERICHO. And given Spider and Han's disappointing nonchalance at Jax's incarceration earlier, if I have to quit JERICHO, he may be doomed.

Ranya *can't* find out.

"I do," I admit. "She's here for this."

I pick up the cheese off the counter and slide it into my back pocket.

"Fine, whatever," says Ranya, pulling out her own phone and stepping up to the counter. "Just as long as you pay for that."

Obviously.

"Hey, Ranya," I ask, looking over my shoulder with one hand on the door handle. "Can you do me a favor and wake Abba? I'm . . . worried he'll be sore if we don't get him up and out of here."

What I'm *really* worried about is this girl seeing two members of my family and possibly threatening their safety if I don't help her win this game. No idea why she's here, but she's from ROYAL, which means it can't be for any good reason. I look at Ranya with what I hope is a poker face, but inside I'm pleading with her to just take Abba somewhere safe.

"Fine," she says, seemingly not suspecting a thing. "But you owe me."

I don't answer as she turns and rests a hand on Abba's.

If I win this puzzle, if I can save Abba's store, if I can at all protect our family, I'll be doing more than paying her back for this favor.

I turn to the door, open it, and find the blond girl looking over her shoulder, startled back into looking at me.

"You stalking us now?" I ask, stepping down the steps to her, and letting the door shut loudly behind me for effect, hoping Abba is awake enough that it didn't scare him. I curse the shaking in my voice and in my hands. I fold them under my armpits to hide them, but her eyes haven't left mine since the door shut. Her eyebrows fall in a determined stare, the wind toying with her bangs as she balls her fists and takes in a big sigh.

As if she herself doesn't want to be here.

"Karim was arrested," she says, her voice pulled into what sounds like a Russian accent. My eyes go wide before I can think to hide what I know, or in this case, what I don't know. Karim was arrested? When? How? At Thirty Foods? If he was there with Jax and Spider earlier, why didn't Spider mention that detail? And then a memory hits me. He *did* mention that Lucas was there, so would it be so far-fetched for Karim to have been there too?

She doesn't wait for me to continue thinking.

"Yasmin," she says, softening her voice and leaning in closer, so close I can smell the faintest hint of shampoo or lotion or . . . *something* perfumed. I hate how she says my name, so formally, like she's here to sell me a time-share instead of . . . whatever she's here to do. "I don't think I need to warn you of the danger that he's in as an incarcerated Black male."

I look her up and down briefly, wondering how much I should tell her about Jax, wondering how much she already *knows* about

Jax, wondering if she's here for Karim's best interest or hers.

"Remind me your name?" I ask.

"Sigge," she says, lingering on the *i* and clipping the second half of the *e*.

Silence settles between us awkwardly, like an unwelcome third guest just walked out here into the cold.

"My mom is Swedish, and my dad's a die-hard fan of Ziggy Stardust, so . . . Sigge it was." That's a cool story, but that's not what was making this moment awkward. It's that I don't know what to say next. I've asked her name, she knows mine—now what? She's on my front doorstep—well, the front doorstep to my father's store—and under normal circumstances, I would've probably invited her inside for a cup of chai. But instead, I tighten my arms around myself, the chill in the air seeping into my bones, and I stand my ground.

"Jax was arrested too," I say, waiting for a reaction.

This girl is hard to read. She stands emotionless before me. A single finger uncurling from one of her clenched fists is the only indication that she heard me.

"At Thirty Foods?" she asks finally.

I nod.

We stand here in silence for what seems like forever, each of us waiting for the other to make the next move.

"Why are you here?" I ask, inviting her to be the one to move first.

"For the next clue, just like you," she says.

My throat closes. So she *does* know about the Gopi cheese.

"This store is the only other place I could find that carries it," she says. "That's open this late anyway."

I feel the weight of the block in my back pocket. There's *no* way I'm giving it to her.

"We're closed," I say, unable to hide the triumph blooming in my voice at the discovery of such a convenient cop-out. "You'll have to come back tomorrow."

"This is *your* store, then," says Sigge.

Well, that triumph was short-lived. As I'm scrambling to figure out what to say next, to my surprise, her lips part into the faintest of smiles.

"It's cute," she says. Does she always talk this sharply? This directly? Why is she still looking at me? Studying me?

I can feel my neck growing hot.

"Thank you," I say, clearing my throat. "But we're still closed."

"Yas," she says, her voice a breathy whisper as she leans in again. I wish she'd stop doing that. That perfumy smell floods my senses again. "The other night, I went to Jax's house."

"You *what*?" I demand, stepping back as if her words have physically burned me. "You looked up his address?"

Sigge glances around, as if she has the *nerve* to be embarrassed at the revelation that she's stalking my best friend.

"No," she snaps, "I didn't. I rideshared after the bus he caught to escape with that bogus parking ticket."

My mouth hangs open. This girl is lucky I'm still having this conversation. I should turn around right this minute and slam the door in her face. Stalking my friend? Creeping around my father's store at night? What, does she still expect me to believe she just *happened* upon this place tonight? She probably stalked me, too!

"I have to go," I say, turning to open the door again. "It's late."

I feel her hand clamp around my wrist, and I bristle, glaring at her. But her touch is gentle and her eyes are pleading, and suddenly I realize the harsh girl who was so confident and rigid before is crying.

"I'm not playing this game for myself," she says. She makes it sound like an admission of something. I wait for her to go on and hope my face is unreadable. "I'm playing so my father can keep his job at Roundworld. So that we can keep our medical benefits. I was so desperate that I went to Jax's house . . ."

Her voice trails off, and she lets go of my hand and stares at the ground like she's contemplating whether she actually wants to finish her sentence. She takes a deep breath, and a tear rolls down her cheek.

"My brother has leukemia."

What?

Is she telling the truth? Who am I to question if she's lying? One doesn't just accuse someone of lying about leukemia. I decide that even with all the fact-checking I do, and as much as I question this girl's motives, I have to believe her.

But that doesn't mean I have to trust her.

"I'm . . . sorry for your family," I say. And it's true, I am. But I'm also sorry for my family. I'm sorry for my abba, who even now is packing up his things and leaving the store that his grandfather opened to survive in this country, who's leaving lovingly cooked boxes of food in the fridges to spoil because the fancy offices in the area can't be bothered to consider the small businesses their free cafeterias are boxing out. As curt and insensitive as she is, I'm sorry for my only sister, Ranya, who's already heartbroken and now having to care for Mom and Abba as they work themselves to the bone.

"My abba . . . ," I say, wondering if sharing this is a good idea. I barely know this girl. Who knows if what she's told me about herself is the truth? But something about the way she's looking at me—the uncharacteristic softness of her eyes, like she has no other options—makes me desperately want to believe her. And so, I continue. ". . . will likely lose his store if I don't win."

Her shoulders fall just a bit, and she glances past me.

"Then," she says, "I guess we're both playing for our families."

"And our friends," I remind her.

"And our friends," Sigge says. She then clears her throat and continues. "So, knowing what I know now, I can't ask you to forfeit the game and live with myself, but . . . can I have a fighting chance?"

She extends a hand in front of her, palm up, other hand dangling at her side. She pauses, blue eyes unblinking, the only movement her hair twitching in the breeze. She's asking me for the cheese again. The cheese that's still in the hand hidden behind my back.

I could easily say no.

I probably *should* say no.

But I think of Jax, and what he would say.

What *did* he say?

"When you went to Jax's house," I start, deciding that her answer to this question will determine my ultimate decision, "what happened?"

"I began by apologizing for what Lucas did," she says, lowering her eyes to the ground in thought.

Wow.

My heart is pounding.

I was expecting *anything* but that. She continues.

"Stealing that poster was wrong."

Hell yeah it was, I think to myself. *That jackass almost got me arrested.*

"I'm desperate to help my father, my brother, and my family. But I'm not a thief." She looks at me again with a face wrought with determination. I know that look. I see it every day when I look in the mirror. Neither of us are giving up this game without a fight. "I'm not a thief," she says again.

I swallow the lump in my throat, and I know what I have to do.

"Thank you for the apology," I say, easing into my decision. Am I really about to hand a clue over to Team ROYAL? Will Jax ever speak to me again after this? Will Spider? Will Han? "Lucas is kind of an asshole."

She looks at me blankly for a moment before letting a chuckle burst from her mouth.

"Yeah, he is," she says. "Actually, I just met him last week. Karim and I go way back, but I only recently joined ROYAL. He said he and Lucas could use some athleticism."

Athleticism?

Okay, now my curiosity is piqued.

"What kind of athleticism?"

"Didn't you see me dive through that golf cart to catch up to Jax in the alley behind the 5 Point Café?"

Her proud grin only grows, as I'm sure she can see my eyes brightening. I can't help it. I can't help my smile. I was hoping for an explanation for that stunt.

"I'd never seen that kind of parkour before," I say with a nod. "It was . . . graceful."

My parkour is like an avalanche—powerful and striking, sharp and quick like a whip. Hers looked more like a wave—bending to her surroundings, ebbing and flowing as needed. I've *never* thought of diving through a golf cart to get where I need to go.

"That's because it's not parkour," she says. "It's gymnastics."

"You could try out for the Olympics with moves like that," I say. I immediately regret it. That smile she gives me, with a bashful glance away, makes me shy too, and I immediately want to crawl into a hole and disappear like Han does all the time.

Why the hell did I say that?

"Could, but then I wouldn't often get to hang with cool puzzly people," she says, letting the silence fill in the blanks for her before finishing with "like you."

Wait.

What?

Why's she looking at me like that?

Is this flirting?

Am I being flirted with, or am I having a heart attack?

"Yeah," I say, my voice cracking. Curse my soft heart. I know what I'm about to do is right, but it's . . . totally illogical. I reach into my back pocket and pull out the thing that could've bought Team JERICHO an extra twelve hours of lead time in this race.

But what is Team JERICHO right now?

Where is Team JERICHO?

Half of us are hiding from the police, and one of us has been *caught* by the police. I'll be lucky if I'm not next. Who am I kidding? We'll be lucky if we all walk free without records after the debacle at Thirty Foods today, let alone win this thing.

So I hand over the block of cheese to someone with a mission as worthy as mine.

"For your brother. For your family. For Karim," I say. It sounded more official in my head. And then I remember who else I'm handing this thing over for. "For Jax."

She takes it and nods gratefully, but I don't let go at first, using the moment to elaborate.

"Whichever of us wins," I say, "whatever this promised 'power' is, and whatever they choose to do about the refinery, winner gets *both* Karim and Jax out of jail."

She smiles warmly and says, "Records expunged."

"Clean slate," I say.

"Wiped clean."

"Like it never happened."

"Done," she says. I loosen my fingers to let go of the cheese, but then something hits me. And I draw back.

"What?" she asks. "What's wrong?"

"Tell me you're not still caping for Lucas."

Her eyes flicker, and she lowers them slightly.

"I didn't like him from day one. But even less when he left you in that alley." She looks up at me again and realizes there's something I'm not telling her. "There's more, isn't there?"

"He put Jax in jail," I say, folding my arms.

Silence lingers between us.

"He . . . what?"

"He shot the window in Thirty Foods. He put the gun in Jax's hands. Jax went to jail."

Her mouth hangs open. "Then he put Karim in there too. What the . . . what the fuck is wrong with him?"

I don't answer.

"I swear, Yas, I'll never talk to him again. He's off the team."

"And if your captain says otherwise?"

"Then I'm off the team," she says sharply enough to disrupt all the silence on our block. Someone down on the far corner looks our direction before turning back to their phone. I hope it's not someone from another team.

I lower my voice and hold out the cheese again.

"You'd better be telling the truth," I say.

"On everyone I love," she says, taking the cheese with a smile. She opens a barcode-scanning app on her phone and holds it up to the packaging. "When I win whatever 'power' this is, I'll even pick Jax up from the jail in a cop car and then help him light it on fire."

A pang of sadness hits me square in the chest. All at once I remember how frayed Jax's and my relationship has gotten lately. The searing things I said to him. The scathing things he said to me. And how now, I'd do *anything* to get him back.

Back. Alive. And well.

Sigge's eyebrows knit together, and her eyes flicker in the light of her phone screen. I can tell she's reading the puzzle, and I step forward and turn to look over her shoulder with her.

YOU'VE PROVEN YOUR WORTH. NOW PROVE YOUR DEDICATION.
TAKE BACK THE TOP. ONE LAST EVALUATION.
COUNTLESS LIVES FOR FORTUNE 5 ON THE STOCK EXCHANGE.
KICK A CAN. BURN A BARREL. BANG A DRUM. BE THE CHANGE.
WELCOME TO THE END. YOUR FINAL DESTINATION.
A KNIFE IN THE HEART OF AN EVIL CORPORATION.

One word, one name, hums through my head.

Holy shit. It's Roundworld.

No.

Maybe.

What would Jax do?

He'd *prove* it, Yas.

So many questions fly through my head at once at the same rate as alarm bells fly in.

Question: *How has participating in this puzzle thus far not proven our dedication?*

Alarm: *Has Roundworld been "evaluating" us? What the hell for?!*

Question: *"Kick a can"? "Burn a barrel"? What the hell does that even mean?*

Question: *The end of what? The game? Is this really the last clue?*

Alarm: *The hell do they mean by "final destination"? I'm not dying tonight!*

Question: *What knife? A literal knife? What heart? A literal heart? Roundworld's heart?*

Alarm: *Are we really going to have to take down Roundworld to win this puzzle?*

"Shit!" exclaims Sigge suddenly, turning and sprinting down the street. She only makes it twenty feet before she stops and turns to look at me. "Yas, I know you know the answer. You know I know the answer. I can't let this happen. I . . . This is so fucked up."

Her voice is breaking.

"Why are they going after us? After my father?"

I step forward, jogging to her.

"Listen," I say. "If you win this 'power,' you won't even *need* Round-world. Right? Maybe you could get your dad a new job with medical benefits. Maybe you could pull some strings to get your brother free treatment. Who knows what the extent of this power is, right?"

Tears are streaming down her cheeks, and she sniffs and holds her arms close to herself.

I know it's not enough.

"If I win," I say, afraid to touch her, but fighting the instinct telling me to hold her hand, "whatever this 'power' entails, I'll do my best to protect your family, okay? *And* wipe Karim's and Jax's records clean, like I promised."

She looks up at me and blinks. Her wet eyelashes are clumped together and more tears fall.

"You'd better be telling the truth." She repeats my words with a sad chuckle, wiping under her eyes with her sleeve.

"I don't lie," I say.

A smile pulls at the corner of her mouth, and she takes a few steps back.

"Let's do this, then!"

Wait . . . what? I can't have heard her right.

I take too long to answer, apparently.

"What's the matter? Afraid I'm faster than the parkour master?"

Too many things run through my head.

Is she . . . inviting me to finish this last clue with her?

Why did "faster than the parkour master" *make for such a delightful rhyme?*

And finally:

"Are we doing this together now?" I ask, pulling my hoodie tighter around me and zipping it up against the chill in the air. I assume yes before she can answer, and I turn to open the door to Abba's store, glancing inside to find the whole place dark and empty. Even the auxiliary lights that he always leaves on are shut off. Ranya must have dragged him out to the car and begged him to take her home for the night. I smile and make a quick dua of gratitude and blessing for her, and then I grab my backpack from the little utility closet just inside the door.

"Better than doing things apart, I feel," says Sigge.

I realize she's wearing only a black long-sleeve shirt that shows a sliver of midriff, and black jeans, and I have to ask.

"Aren't you cold?"

"Where I'm from, we swim in ice water."

I make it a point to ask her where specifically she's from. Her accent sounds Russian, but even if I did guess right, Russia is a big place.

"Belarus," she clarifies, probably seeing the thinking going on behind my eyes. "In Minsk we hold ice-swimming competitions."

"Seriously?" I ask, bewildered.

"Sure! You're welcome to try it if you're ever in Belarus," she says, as if ice swimming is as normal a thing to do as going for a walk.

"In case you haven't realized, I'm Pakistani. I'm not going anywhere near a pool of ice water."

She smiles as I fall into step beside her and marvel at just how strange this whole situation is. Me, walking with this Belarusian girl—a member of Team ROYAL—headed to the last clue in a puzzle I didn't wholly trust at first. Now I have no choice. From the corner of my eye, I see her glance at me expectantly several times before offering some comfort.

"We'll get them out," she assures me.

"How do you know?" I ask, still skeptical. "How do you even know where we're going?"

"Read it again," she says. "I know you'll get it by the time we get there. I won't ruin the love of the game for you, but we also need to get moving if we're going to make it there before Lucas."

Sure, I know pretty confidently it's Roundworld, but . . . *where* at Roundworld?

She hands me her phone, and I read it again. This feels so wrong, puzzling this out without our puzzler. JERICHO is so empty without Jax. But I have to try my best. For him.

YOU'VE PROVEN YOUR WORTH. NOW PROVE YOUR DEDICATION.

Still looks like a pointless line to me. What could possibly come of that?

TAKE BACK THE TOP. ONE LAST EVALUATION.

Take back the top. Does that mean to make it there first? We're not playing for points or anything, so to be in the lead, you have to get to the end of the game first. Right?

WELCOME TO THE END. YOUR FINAL DESTINATION.

We're on the last clue. I get that.

A KNIFE IN THE HEART OF AN EVIL CORPORATION.

There are so many corporations around here, in Puget Sound, many in tech, some in hated industries, like cable providers.

And health insurance.

This could be talking about any one of them.

Think, Yas, think!

"Want a hint?" she asks as we walk farther and farther from Abba's store, the Space Needle rising high into the sky just a few blocks ahead of us.

"Nah," I say.

"I knew you'd enjoy the chase," she says, smiling at me slyly.

Was that more flirting? Is that— Yup. Her eyes are practically glowing. Definitely still flirting. Chest feels tight. Can't breathe. How am I supposed to focus when she's looking at me like that?!

"Um," I say, clearing my throat. She pulls out an ORCA card and holds it up between us, inched between her index and middle finger. So we're taking the bus. Or the Link Light Rail. That doesn't narrow it down at all.

What would Jax do?

He'd work some wild magic and make it all fit together into a way forward.

He'd rearrange some letters and words until something magically clicks.

So I try that.

I already have a jumping-off point—the Fortune 5 list. So, the "evil corporation" they're talking about is somewhere huge. Somewhere *very* significant. Like, Amazon significant. Like Roundworld. I look back at the clue, at the one line in the middle that's bothering me.

KICK A CAN. BURN A BARREL. BANG A DRUM. BE THE CHANGE.

So, kicking a can down the road. Burning a barrel, like for warmth?

Banging a drum, like sounding an alarm? And "Be the change," a phrase Jax has told me he hates viciously, since it's often what people tell you when they want to pass the onus back onto you for enacting the change you want to see, so they don't have to examine their own bias and dismantle the structures in place that uphold their privilege.

I hate it too.

But it can't be that straightforward. It can't just be a throwaway line. This is *The Order* we're talking about. *Everything has to mean something*, Jax said.

"You can do it," says Sigge. "Left here."

We turn left, and I see the bus station just ahead.

Then, when I look back down at the puzzle, I see it.

The words seem to jump off the screen at me.

KICK A CAN.
BURN A BARREL.
BANG A DRUM.
BE THE CHANGE.

I read it again.

CAN.
BARREL.
DRUM.
CHANGE.

Only one word can go before each of those. A word that tells me *exactly* which corporation we're talking about here. *Exactly* the company.

It *has* to be Roundworld.

"I did it, Jax," I whisper softly enough that only I can hear.

Sigge scans her ORCA card against the swiper until it beeps, and then she looks back at me.

"Well?" she asks as I hear the hiss of the bus somewhere behind me.

"Oil."

She nods.

"Did you catch *where* on their campus?"

The heart, of course. The heart of a company. Its headquarters.

I nod.

"Race you to the finish, then."

I pause for a moment before nodding back. I forgot for a moment that we're still in a competition. Sure, Sigge gave me the clue, like I gave her the cheese. But she still has a brother with leukemia, and I still have an abba with a doomed livelihood. We're *both* still in this.

It's her vs. me.

It's gymnastics vs. parkour.

I board the bus and sit next to her, clutching my bag in my lap, having no idea what to expect in about twenty minutes.

Bzzzt.

Bzzzt.

Bzzzt.

In a tiny store tucked away in a corner of South Lake Union, a forgotten phone buzzes on the counter.

Jax

If holding a gun in front of a shattered window in the Thirty Foods specialty cheese aisle wasn't on my cryptology bingo card, I certainly didn't expect to be standing in a jail cell with a phone to my ear and forehead to the wall, *praying* somebody picks up before I have to spend a whole night in this place.

Ring, ring. Ring, ring.

"Come on, Yas, answer," I whisper.

Ring, ring. Ring, ring.

Yas's voice rings out, stringing together a phrase in Urdu that she's told me says, "This is Yas, but if you're not a scammer, you already know that. Leave a message if it's important."

Dammit.

If I leave a message, it counts as the last phone call I'm allowed here for the night. But if I don't, I'm out of call attempts. This is call number three. First was Mama, who didn't answer because she's probably asleep. Then Spider—who knows where he even is right now? This voicemail is my last hope.

"Yas," I whisper, unable to hide the urgency in my voice. "It's me! Listen, I'm at King County Jail. They fingerprinted me, took my mugshot, put me in a jumpsuit, everything." At the word "everything," my voice shatters. I run my hand over the elastic around my waist and pull the navy blue pants they got me in up higher. They're just big enough that they keep sliding down, and they feel like scrubs but thicker.

Itchier.

And I'm so used to Mama's gentle homemade lavender detergent that these things smell like I just walked out of an industrial paint factory.

"Yas, *please* come get me. I'll pay you back for whatever my bail is, I promise, just . . . I've gotta win this puzzle. I have to. And I'm sorry for what I said. You were right. This was a bad idea. I was too invested. I—"

"You have reached the maximum time permitted for recording your message," interrupts the automated voice. My heart stops as another voice joins in, this one right beside me.

"All right, young man, time's up," says the guard, arms folded over his chest, careful not to wrinkle his khaki uniform decorated with a few pins that I'm sure mean something.

"But no one picked up," I say. "Can't I call my aunt or . . . or a cousin? Anyone?"

He shakes his shiny bald head *no* and says robotically, "Sorry, son. Rules are rules. They'll call you in for questioning in a moment. Give me the phone, please."

He holds out a hand as dark as mine, and I look from his hand to his dark eyes. There's a look in them that I can't quite place. Something that's hardened over years, like pearls that once had a single grain of pity at the center. I'm sure this guy's heard all the excuses—*my mom's sick, my dog died, my girlfriend's pregnant,* yada yada.

Whatever I say right now, I doubt he'll care.

I hand him the receiver and turn back toward the center of the room, where I find about a dozen inmates sitting around in blue jumpsuits just like mine. Some are chilling in chairs around a table, three of them with a spread of cards in their hands. Two sit several chairs apart in front of a TV in the corner that's playing old-school cartoons. Most of them are my shade or darker. A few are white, but . . .

. . . yeah, a *few*.

"No *way*," comes a voice to my right. I flinch, cursing my nerves. If there's one thing I know about jail, it's not to let on that you're jumpy as shit . . .

. . . and I'm *clearly* jumpy as shit.

But this guy walking toward me, a tall kid about my shade with loose curls up top and the faintest shadow of peach fuzz under his chin, steps right up to me with shimmering eyes, like he's meeting an old friend.

"Do I know you?" I ask as politely as I can. I don't want anything to do with anyone in here. I don't want to make friends or enemies. I just want to get to whatever this guy wants and get the hell up out of here. I know as soon as Mama answers her phone—even if that's tomorrow—I'm outta here on bail.

He leans in closer, and I take a step back as he examines me excitedly.

"You're *Jax*," he says. "Captain of JERICHO?"

I freeze, staring up at his face. Is this guy . . . from the forum?

"Sorry, but I don't think we've met before," I say. He chuckles and rests a hand on his chest.

"I'm Rodrigo," he says. "Captain of the DUCKLORDS. Wild seeing you here. Did you get canned after looking for one of 'The Order's' clues too?"

This guy *is* from the forum! And he's another captain! Of the one and only water team—the DUCKLORDS, the team that organized the last puzzle. The "chromedome" puzzle, the puzzle that sort of got overshadowed by the Order's dramatic entrance with the fire alarms. But the thing that shocks me most is his use of air quotes when saying that name—*The Order*.

"What do you mean, 'The Order'?" I ask, returning the air quotes.

Some of the brightness leaves his eyes, and his shoulders fall.

"So, no one out there knows yet, do they?" he asks.

"Knows what?"

I *have* to know. Did the Order make a move I hadn't heard about yet? Or my worst fear . . .

Did they choose a winner?

"Did someone . . . win?" I ask, wondering if I really want to know the answer.

"No way to know," he says. "They confiscated all our phones, and all calls in and out are monitored." He tilts his head in the direction of the phone on the wall—the one I was just using. "I hope you didn't say anything about the puzzle while you were making your call."

I swallow the lump in my throat.

"Wh-why, um . . . ," I begin, scratching my neck, afraid to inquire further. "What happens if they . . . you know . . . might have heard something?"

"Jax, there's something you need to know," he says, lowering his voice and clamping his huge, strong hand around my shoulder. "Something you need to post on the forum as soon as possible, and tell your friends if you can, if they're still playing."

I listen closely as he continues, still whispering.

"This whole thing is a setup," he says, his eyes locked onto mine with a gravity that I didn't expect from a guy who was so smiley and cheerful just a few moments ago. "The *whole* thing. They booked me in here a few hours ago, and when they pulled me into that room to interrogate me, they was pulling ultimatums out they *ass*, bruh. I've been to juvey before, and it wasn't this bad. They told me here that I could either help 12 identify people on the front lines of these protests, or I can deal with whatever sentencing comes my way. Snitch, or be a prison bitch. Simple as that for these pigs."

Wait, wait, wait.

What?

"Nah," I say. There's no way the Order would do this. Why would they set up a puzzle just to get us arrested? They're *for* the protesters. They want the refinery taken down like we do! Nah. *Nah.* I know a setup when I see one. And this ain't it.

"I get that you want to win, Rodrigo," I say, narrowing my eyes up at him. "But to be *this* desperate? While we're *both* in here? That's low."

"What?" he says, his thick eyebrows knitting together in shock. "Bruh, I'm telling the truth—"

"The rest of the DUCKLORDS are out there solving clues right now, aren't they? Racing to get through the puzzle while you're trapped in here, and this is all you can do to help them. I get it, I really do, but you're going to have to do better than that."

I turn and walk away, feeling my shoulders trembling with rage. His exasperated sigh booms from behind me, and I hear him turn and walk away too.

The loudspeaker roars to life and startles me so bad, I'm suddenly shaking. Yup. Still jumpy as shit.

"Inmate 3-8-1-26." My number. "Please report to Bay 1."

There's a room along the far wall with a big sign above it labeled "Bay 1," so I walk to it, but not before locking eyes with Rodrigo again, who's now sitting in a chair against the wall with one leg resting on the other, giving me a wide-eyed, raised-eyebrow look that says *You 'bout to find out.*

I hope he's wrong.

But . . . what if he's right?

Han

take a deep breath and my eyes flutter awake. My jaw hurts. I think I was grinding my teeth in my sleep. Where am I? What time is it? I'm staring at the roof of my car, and—

What the hell is that obnoxious snoring behind me?

I look in my rearview mirror to find Spider, sprawled unglamorously over my back seat like a wet blanket. I can smell that cheese, warmed by his body heat—disgusting. I reach behind my seat and tap his leg, and he stirs. The snoring stops, but he goes still again.

I jostle him a little harder this time, and he startles awake.

"Ah, what the hell?! Yas, who—" He locks eyes with me in the rearview mirror. "Oh, Han, don't scare me like that. What . . . what time is it? Where's Yas?"

I glance over at the passenger seat, look back up at him, and shrug before pulling out my phone and texting her. No idea where she went, but I know she knows how to maneuver. How to survive. How to hide.

ME: Hey, you okay?

And then I wait.

Spider rights himself, groggily holding a hand to his head. He reaches under his shirt with his free hand and scratches under the elastic of his binder.

"Hey look," he says with a yawn. "This scanner app finally decided to load."

He leans over my shoulder and holds the phone about a foot from my face. I read it quietly as he reads it aloud.

YOU'VE PROVEN YOUR WORTH. NOW PROVE YOUR DEDICATION.
TAKE BACK THE TOP. ONE LAST EVALUATION.
COUNTLESS LIVES FOR FORTUNE 5 ON THE STOCK EXCHANGE.
KICK A CAN. BURN A BARREL. BANG A DRUM. BE THE CHANGE.
WELCOME TO THE END. YOUR FINAL DESTINATION.
A KNIFE IN THE HEART OF AN EVIL CORPORATION.

"Well, *that's* the most ominous shit I've ever read," he says, retreating into the back seat to pore over the puzzle some more.

I've got it already, though.

Fortune 5? Gotta be somewhere big. Somewhere in the news a lot lately, probably. After all, the Order thrives off publicity.

It's gotta be Roundworld. It's the only place that makes sense. And the heart has to be their headquarters, the epicenter of their . . . well . . . *evil.* Normally, I like to wait for a little more certainty before speeding off to pursue a clue, but these circumstances are *more* than extenuating.

Jax was arrested.

Yas is missing.

Spider and I are fugitives of the law.

And this is the last clue in a puzzle that might win us enough "power" to escape all of the above.

If we don't move now, we might never get the chance.

My mind drifts back to Kyler. To his question for Dad. About that employee loan.

And I wonder if the loan would be safer than whatever we're about to walk into. I wouldn't have to deal with Jax being mad at me anymore, or another police chase—that shit was ridiculous.

But then I think of Yas, where she might have run off to. I have no idea—maybe *she's* been arrested by now. Jax might be dead. Spider hasn't solved the clue yet. I can hear him mumbling to himself back there, piecing things together while our friends' lives are on the line.

I guess I'll need more than just a loan to make sure they're safe.

. . . I'll need power.

I turn the key and throw the car into drive, beckoning Spider to buckle up, which he does.

"Whoa, whoa, whoa, man, where are we going?"

I know it's rhetorical, so I step gently on the gas, easing us around the corner and out of this lot.

"You gotta give me *something*, man. Are we going to Roundworld?" he asks. "Click in Morse code or something!"

I look up at him, confused. There's no way he's serious. Does he think I just *know* Morse code like that? I nod, though. Yes, we're going to Roundworld.

"We're not even sure that's where it's pointing us to. There are five corporations in the Fortune Five, and three of them have headquarters in Puget Sound. How do we know it's Roundworld?"

He's just going to have to trust me.

I follow the signs for 405 South to I-90, which will take us across the water and into Seattle. I just hope that wherever Jax and Yas are, wherever Team ROYAL is, we're not too late.

We stop at a red light and I glance at my phone, where my conversation with Yas is still open.

Still nothing.

I hope she's okay.

I hope after tonight, we *all* make it out of this okay.

Jax

What if they're about to give me the ultimatum of my life?

Once I get to the door labeled "Bay 1," it's not long before the door swings open and that same guy who was monitoring my phone calls appears in the glowing yellow hallway, hand at his hip.

"Oh, they got you doing *all* the exciting stuff, huh?" I ask. His face remains stoic as he pulls out a shiny pair of silver handcuffs and motions for me to turn around. Once the handcuffs are back on, I'm escorted down the hallway to a room that looks *nothing* like an interrogation room—seriously, what kind of interrogation room has potted plants and hideous red-and-blue carpet and . . . is that a damn turtle in that terrarium in the corner?

And what kind of interrogator looks like the guy sitting in the big black armchair across the desk in front of me? He looks more like a Calvin Klein model than a cop, besides the uniform and the badge and the . . . gun.

I see it at his hip before he takes a seat across from me and leans onto the desk with a smile that unsettles every last fiber of calm I had left.

"So," he says with a sweeping tone that ascends into the sky before landing on the ground again, "Jaxon, Jaxon, Jaxon. You're pretty famous around here, from what I gather."

I know better than to give these people any information. Mama and Zaza taught me well.

"I want a lawyer before I say anything," I say.

"Sure, sure," he says, as if he was expecting that. "I should mention, though, that this conversation is *not* being recorded."

He reaches down to his lap and pulls out a phone. Wait. *My* phone! That's *my phone!*

Everything in me is screaming to reach over and take it, to open my messages, to make sure my friends are all okay. But I don't move.

"I'm sure you recognize this, and I'm happy to give it back to you, along with your clothes," he says, pulling up a stack of clothes from somewhere behind his desk—the clothes I was arrested in—my sweats, my hoodie, and my T-shirt in a plastic bag. "Your kicks," he continues, setting my bright red shoes beside the clothes in another plastic bag. "And this," he says, holding up Mama's amethyst pendant in a final bag.

He must see something change in my face, because he smiles like he's won this debate, and I ain't even said a word yet. I think back to Mama, who gave me that amethyst for protection, because she had a feeling I might need it, because she loves me. I feel tears well in my eyes at the thought that she has no idea where I am right now, that it's late at night and she hasn't heard from me.

You better not cry, Jax, I tell myself. *Do not. Not here.*

"So, if you'd like all of . . . *this* back," he says, motioning to my belongings like letting them reside on his desk is an act of charity, "and if you'd like to get out of here tonight, you can help me identify a few of these faces."

He reaches into a drawer and pulls out a small stack of grainy 8½" x 11" photos of crowds of people—people with signs that say BLACK LIVES MATTER and FUCK THE POLICE and HANDS UP DON'T SHOOT and DOWN WITH THE REFINERY. I read sign after sign after sign from these snapshots of different upheavals, most of which look like they're on Pine Street downtown.

THE CLIMATE IS CHANGING. WHY AREN'T WE?

CLEAN POWER TO ALL PEOPLE!

FIGHT TODAY FOR A BETTER TOMORROW!

And finally . . .

IT'S OIL OVER!

They . . . want me to identify protesters? *That's* what they want out of me? Why? What did the protesters ever do to them? I know I'm not supposed to talk, but . . . I gotta know.

"Why?"

"*Why?!*" He chuckles with a smile that makes a chill snake its way up the back of my neck. "Because *these* people make life so much harder. For you and me, really. They cost my precinct time and money, taking up our resources, putting my boys on the front lines of pointless conflicts. Fools' errands. They've trashed private property and small businesses, damaged vehicles and police property, vandalized buildings and littered their picketing signs and spray paint cans and banners all over the city, and *guess* who has to clean all that shit up."

I stare at him, trying to keep my face even, trying to look like I'm not about to shit my pants right now. But this man, with his eyes flashing, his finger still pressed hard against the stack of photos, his other hand somewhere under the desk, where I *know* he keeps at least one firearm—he must, right? I'm terrified.

I clasp my hands together to keep from shaking and decide I can't look at him any longer or I might crack and he'll figure out I'm not as strong as my silence might indicate.

So many faces behind each of these causes, on the same ground. So many people rallying together against tyranny. Against lawlessness committed by law enforcement. Against the inevitable heat death of the planet, at the rate we're going. None that I recognize. Young people in bandannas, some around their heads to catch sweat, some over their mouths to protect them from tear gas and pepper spray. Many hold what look like homemade shields made of wood and scrap metal, probably to repel rubber bullets, which aren't really bullet-size at all. Some rubber bullets are as big as pool balls, and they can kill you if fired at point-blank range.

And then I see her face.

My breath catches in my throat before I can realize that this guy is still talking about something. The face I'm staring down at fully sinks in, and I can feel the tension tightening in the room. He *knows* I recognize someone, and I try to keep my eyes moving fluidly over the pictures as if I hadn't seen anything noteworthy.

As if Ava's eyes hadn't been staring right into the camera.

Her nose and mouth had been covered by a bright orange bandanna, thank the universe and all her treasures, but those eyes. That hair. I'd know them anywhere. That was her determined face, staring at the camera like she was on the front lines in the goddamn US Army.

Ava.

My sister.

I should've known. I had clues.

Nobody knows what "be the change" means. . . . Prove me wrong.

That's what she'd told me a few days ago. She'd stared right at me as I announced to Mama and Zaza that I wanted to join in and protest against Roundworld and their blatant assault on the environment, and said nothing. She's quietly been fighting just as hard as I've been.

Maybe even harder.

"Oh, fantastic," says Officer—what's his name—I check his badge. Hank. Officer Hank. "Charlie to you, as long as you comply," he says, a bit of spunk in his voice as if he just invited me over for coffee with his wife and kids and not threatened me should I choose not to out my own sister.

"No," I say before my voice can crack any further.

He looks at me evenly for the longest time. The clock on his desk ticks away as he removes his glasses in disappointment.

"Oh, Jaxon, I didn't think you'd be *this* stupid," he says. "Listen, you don't even know the terms of the deal yet. You can walk free *right now.*"

I freeze where I am, refusing to move, refusing to give this man *anything* he might use to identify and track down my sister, or any of my friends, or anyone else I love. I don't move a muscle.

"I know you want to get home to your parents, okay? You haven't got so much as a parking ticket on your record, and you're probably scared back there with all the . . . *delinquents* in here who are accused of . . . murder and . . . assault and . . . various other crimes we won't get into. And," he says, resting four tense white fingers over the photo directly in front of me that he caught me lingering on, his index finger right smack over the middle of Ava's face, "I know you've got a game to get back to."

I look up at him now, my blood racing.

He knows about the game?

"You read my texts," I say.

"No," he says, "I never have time to parse out you kiddos' TikTok talk. There's a much easier way."

Have these assholes been following me or something? Following JERICHO? Following the whole forum? I shake my head.

"No," I say. No to whatever the hell this guy has to say to me, no to whatever he's about to ask me to do.

"Just give us three names—"

"No," I cut in, feeling more tears come forth, threatening to overflow.

"Okay, fine. One name—"

"No."

"Name just one person from this spread, and—"

"No!" I say, unable to hide the bite in my voice.

"You can go free right now and get back to your little game—"

"No!" I holler. The tears roll down my face as I glare at him, my wrists shaking in the handcuffs still behind my back.

He leans back in his chair and sucks his teeth before stroking his chin.

"Jaxon," he says forlornly, like asking me to out my family to the people protecting the very corporation that's about to destroy my family's community is killing *him* inside, "I'd hoped you'd make the smart choice here. You see," he continues, scooping up the photos in his hands, the last one being the one with my sister, "without order, there can be no justice. And without us," he says, reaching under his desk to click a button that I can see is blinking red against his palm, "there *is* no order."

It takes me several seconds to realize what he's just told me.

Without us, there is no order.

Without us . . .

The door behind me opens, and hands reach down to gently pull me up by my shoulders.

there is no . . .

They lead me down the hall as I realize how right Ricardo was. About *everything*.

Order.

Yas

I can see the topmost corner of the flag from down here.

It's white, and I can see the corner of the eye symbol we've all grown so familiar with—the symbol of the Order.

"Let's do this," I say, turning to where I expect Sigge to be standing beside me. But she's gone. I look around frantically before spotting her foot disappearing around the corner of the building. I run after her.

"Sigge?" I call as I round the corner to find her sprinting for the scaffolding. I take off after her, wondering why she's running so fast. To get away from me?

She reaches the first step and races up, her shoes softly padding the metal as delicately as if she were running in socks. When she rounds the first corner, she glances down at me. My feet clatter like I'm running in steel-toed boots.

"What, did you forget this is a race?" she asks, sprinting on.

I turn and jump up onto the railing, turn again, and launch myself up to the next level of steps.

"Guess I did," I say, now racing ahead of her. "Must have been your eyes."

I *hope* she takes that as flirting.

Because I meant it to be.

I can hear her behind me, and when I round the next corner, I stop, horrified to see her swinging backward over the next railing like they're uneven bars. Her feet land on the metal, and she turns and leans in close.

"I like you," she says with a smile. "But not enough to let you win."

Then she turns and keeps running with the speed of someone on a mission to save her family.

I look up, realizing we have several stories to go, and as I hurry after her, I think of Jax, where he might be right now, probably without his phone, having no idea where any of us are or what we're doing to get him out. I hope he doesn't think we just continued with the puzzle without him, just to win.

I don't care about winning otherwise. Not at the expense of our safety. Abba can sell his store. I can open a parkour studio with money I've earned the hard way. There are always other cryptology puzzles to be solved.

But *this* one just might save my friend's life. So here I go.

"I'm *going* to win, Jax," I say, stepping forward. "I'm going to win, and I'm going to get you out."

should have listened.

I should have listened to Mama.

I should have listened to Zaza.

And most of all, I should have listened to Yas.

She tried to warn me, and now I've led my precious team, my friends, right into the hands of the cops. I've forced them into creeping around alleyways and through throngs of shopping white women— always risky business—and if they were lucky enough to not get arrested along with me, they're on their way to the next clue, inching closer to wherever these pigs want them to be.

The handcuffs jingle behind me as this guy walks me down this yellow hallway, past windows into a kitchen-type room with lots and lots of silver, boxy equipment, and I wonder how long I'll have to be in here, eating whatever comes out of those big silver boxes, and whether they'd be able to accommodate my vegan diet.

I'm guessing not.

I'm guessing in here, I have to eat what I can get. New tears spring to my eyes at the thought of missing Mama's olive-oil raisin cake, her carrot "bacon" and pulled "pork" sandwiches she makes with jackfruit and homemade barbecue sauce, and—oh my god—her homemade coconut-milk ice cream.

I sigh as we stop in front of the door to the room where I was earlier—the rec room, or more accurately, the holding cell, where I'll be until tomorrow, when I can have another phone call and another attempt to inform my poor parents and sister that I'm not tied up in somebody's basement or ready to be identified at the morgue.

I look to my right through the tiny window to the administration room, where I hope to see Mama or Zaza or Ava or Yas or Spider or Han or *somebody* I love, but all I see is a short-haired Black guy signing something at the desk in a navy jumpsuit and . . . wait . . . I notice the bag he's holding, the clear bag full of the clothes he came here with, the folded purple velvet inside.

My blood runs cold.

"Karim?" I ask before I can realize I've asked it out loud.

He turns to look at me, and the moment seems to drag on forever. I know he was booked right along with me, but I can't believe his bougie ass and I both ended up at the same juvenile detention center. But why's he holding his clothes? I haven't seen my clothes since I got here, until now with Officer Hank using them as a bargaining chip. I remember Mama's amethyst necklace sitting right on the top of that pile, and I shut my eyes in pain at the realization that I probably won't see the crystal she trusted me with—to keep me safe—for days at least.

This is all my fault. Goddamn it, why didn't I listen?

Karim's still looking at me.

The front door of the lobby opens behind him, and a white woman with long black hair and lots of silver jewelry walks in, wrapped in a black fur shawl.

"Oh my god, my baby!" she exclaims, throwing her arms around him and sobbing into his shoulder. He hugs her back tightly and doesn't take his eyes off me.

Wait, this white lady is his mom? We . . . *both* have at least one white parent?

He pulls away from her, takes both her hands in his, and turns to the counter again, where there's a white young man sitting at a computer. He looks over his shoulder at me, and Karim's eyes follow until they land on me too. Then, to my surprise and horror, Karim *smiles* at me. Like, genuinely *smiles*, not in that weird ultra-capitalist *I know something you don't know and that's going to make me money* typa way he was smiling at me earlier in Thirty Foods, but like, he's saying . . . everything's going to be okay?

Finally the officer escorting me has unlocked the door and swung it open, and I'm ushered not *into* the rec room, but *through* the rec room to the administration room!

"What's going on?" I ask the officer. He shrugs like he's just as shocked as I am. "Somebody bailed you out, kid."

I turn to see Karim staring at me, smile gone, face even.

"Don't think this means I like you," he says. "I got you out because we have a clue to find."

The white woman smiles warmly and steps past him toward me.

"I'm Melinda," she says. "Melinda Horrow. I'm Karim's mother. I understand you're one of his, um . . . internet friends?"

Karim rolls his eyes.

"Mom, could we save the pleasantries until after we've won the puzzle?" he asks, turning toward the door and motioning for me to follow. I resist reflexively letting my mouth fall open. If I so much as formed my *mouth* to say something so rude to Mama, she would have words for me. Actually, she'd probably have no words, she'd be so shocked.

I spot my clothes and shoes in a plastic bag on the front counter, and I swipe it up, following Karim, giving Melinda an apologetic smile as I walk past her.

"Melinda will deal with the paperwork while I fill you in on what's about to happen," he says, stepping across the parking lot with the confidence of someone who *knew* he'd never spend a night in jail. Too much money to have to deal with that shit.

"Wait, wait," I say, jogging to catch up to him. "I have some questions, my guy."

"Of course you do," he sighs. "We'll get to that in a moment."

We reach a white Range Rover with huge chrome wheels so clean I can see myself in them, and he holds out his hand to tug at the door handle before grunting in exasperation and yelling back across the parking lot.

"Melinda, the door!"

I hear a beep and a click, and he pulls the door open to reveal a softly lit cabin with striking red leather seats. I've never seen a vehicle so absolutely gorgeous. It looks like a hotel on wheels.

"Whoa, this is nice!" I say as he climbs into the back seat.

"Get in," he says with an air of annoyance to his voice.

"Excuse me for complimenting you," I say frustratedly before hauling myself up into the back seat. How does this kid have friends?

The door closes with the push of a button to Karim's left, and he clears his throat.

"I didn't pay for your bail because I feel sorry for you," he says, looking me up and down. "Although that wouldn't be so unfathomable. I paid for your bail because I knew if you stayed in there, you might die, and if you die, it'll cost my parents months, maybe years, of therapy to help me get over the guilt enough to lead a productive life."

It takes a moment for all of that to sink in, but I have to smile.

"So . . . you *do* feel sorry for me."

"I feel sorry, preemptively, for my parents' wallets," he insists, reaching down and opening his bag of clothes, pulling out his precious purple suit. He smooths out some of the wrinkles and refolds them along the crease down the front. "The police are the real degenerates, if you ask me," he mutters. "Can't even fold a suit correctly."

He has *no* idea just how degenerate-like they are.

And then I realize, I have to tell him what I know.

"Karim, did they ask you anything when they interrogated you in there?"

"Interrogated? No, I told them I would have no conversations with anyone until I'd consulted with a lawyer."

"So they didn't take you back? To anyone's office?"

He looks at me questioningly now.

"No," he says. "Did they take you back? *Please* tell me you didn't talk."

"I didn't talk," I say. "But . . . they wanted me to."

"Of course they did."

"No, no, they wanted me to take a plea bargain."

"Of course they did."

"They wanted me to identify protesters," I finally blurt out. "And the officer said, *without us, there is no order.*"

He stops folding and looks at me. Then he reels his head back in the ugliest laughter I've ever heard.

"Are you saying the police are behind the Order, Jax? You can't be serious—"

"They are! And doesn't it make sense? They sought *us* out. The forum. Kids with skills, man. Think about it—we forum kids know how to solve clues. How to hack into things, some of us. How to track down dirt. They want us in jail so they can force us into plea bargains—identify protesters, and we'll let you go. Maybe. If we feel like it."

Karim's face betrays his skepticism, and my heart sinks.

"Come on, man, you *have* to believe me."

"Why would I trust you when you've been working against my team all this time?"

"If you won't believe me, believe the captain of the DUCK-LORDS! He was in there too!" I snap, turning toward him now, clenching my fists in my lap at the realization that I'm now in the exact same position Rodrigo was in, trying to convince this guy that the whole thing was a setup. And then, as karma would have it, Karim follows the same logic I took with Rodrigo.

"Very clever, Jax," he says, setting the delicately folded suit on the seat between us. "Convince me that the whole puzzle is a trap so that I pull my team out before we fall right in the hands of the police? I have to admit I underestimated you—"

What can I do?

What can I say to convince him?

I pick up the plastic bag full of my things—my clothes, my shoes, my phone, and Mama's crystal. I pull the necklace down over my head before I do *anything* else, and then I click the home button on my phone and open my messaging app.

ME: Hey everyone, I'm okay. I'm sorry for everything. Yas, you were right. Pull out now. This whole game has been a setup. The Order isn't what they say they are. I'll explain later. Go home!

I hand the phone to Karim, and he glances at it like this is some new trick of mine, but I jab it closer to him and he takes it skeptically, reading quietly as silence settles into the car.

The driver's door swings open, and Melinda climbs in with a sigh.

"Oh, the release paperwork they made me fill out in there," she seethes. "This all has to be a huge misunderstanding, one they'll pay for. The money we donated to that police memorial can go *right* back into our bank account, if you ask me."

The money they . . . *what*?

Karim, a Black kid, has at least one white parent who *donated money to a police memorial*? In *this* city?!

He looks up at me and hands the phone back.

"Well?" I ask, pity for him settling into my chest at the realization that his parents are funding a group that's potentially about to ruin our lives and the lives of our friends.

He clears his throat and leans back in his seat, fingers resting on his lips in thought before he says brokenly:

"Here."

He hands me his phone, where I find the next clue lit up across the screen.

YOU'VE PROVEN YOUR WORTH. NOW PROVE YOUR DEDICATION.
TAKE BACK THE TOP. ONE LAST EVALUATION.
COUNTLESS LIVES FOR FORTUNE 5 ON THE STOCK EXCHANGE.
KICK A CAN. BURN A BARREL. BANG A DRUM. BE THE CHANGE.
WELCOME TO THE END. YOUR FINAL DESTINATION.
A KNIFE IN THE HEART OF AN EVIL CORPORATION.

"You know where it leads?" he says.

"Can? Barrel? Drum? Change? That line means oil," I say.

"There's only one oil corporation on the Fortune Five list," he says. "And that's Roundworld."

I nod.

I believe him.

And I know *exactly* why this puzzle would be taking us to the top of the Wells Porter building. That's the heart of Roundworld's operations. Their headquarters. It's high-profile, the perfect excuse for the police to arrest us all.

If creeping around alleys and hopping onto buses and scanning products in Thirty Foods wasn't enough, sending us to the top of a building where one of the most heavily scrutinized anti-planet corporations lives is sure to be.

"Let's go," I say, pulling my seat belt and clicking it into place.

"Before they're arrested."

"Or worse."

"Step on it, Mom, we haven't got all night!"

Han

old up, Han," comes Spider's voice from behind me as I creep the car along the block, bringing it to rest along the curb on Fairview Avenue. I can see Roundworld's headquarters just a few blocks ahead, an unassuming brick building with spotless windows and the word "MANTLE" written sideways in huge all-caps letters along the door. All the buildings Roundworld owns are named after things like this—elements or pieces of the planet or endangered species. Performative, all of it, if they continue doing what they do.

I turn the key to shut the car off and look over my shoulder at Spider, who's still engrossed in his phone.

"Just got a message from Jax," he says, handing me the phone. I read it in silence.

JAX: Hey everyone, I'm okay. I'm sorry for everything. Yas, you were right. Pull out now. This whole game has been a setup. The Order isn't what they say they are. I'll explain later. Go home!

I can feel the anxiety swelling up in my neck like an allergic reaction.

"Well, I guess we're pulling out now, then," says Spider in frustration. "Goddammit."

I look up through my windshield, wondering if this is really Jax texting us this, and from where. What if it's the cops? What if they've read our message history for context, and now they're hoping one of us texts back so they can trace our phones and find me and Spider?

And then I look up and see a sea of black. Black everything. Black cars, black suits, black cameras, black microphones with flashing lights everywhere, flickering like popcorn as a woman in a white sweater with shoulder-length white hair exits one of the cars.

Everything around me seems to stop. I can't believe what I'm seeing. She's walking up the front steps to the glass doors, bombarded on all sides by flashing lights and cameras and microphones. Is that . . . It can't be.

"Whoa," comes Spider's voice again. "Is that Celea Beale?"

Of the Duwamish tribe.

I'm surprised he knows who she is. But I guess it's Spider's job to know *all* the prominent people in Puget Sound. A creeping, cold feeling snakes its way through my body as the dread sets in.

The meeting is *tonight*.

"Aren't they supposed to be meeting with Roundworld soon? Is that what they're here for?" asks Spider rhetorically.

This can't be coincidence. The final clue found on the evening of the high-profile meeting between Roundworld and the Duwamish? I refuse to believe it.

But before I can let that sink in, something else catches my eye. It takes several seconds before I can process that I'm watching Yas and Sigge, flipping through scaffolding and leaping up onto railings after each other, leapfrogging up the side of the Roundworld building.

Without a word, I get out of the car.

"Han?" comes Spider's voice. "Where the hell are you going? Didn't you read what Jax said?" But I don't have time to explain. Either Yas is here to solve the puzzle and in danger, like Jax said, or Yas is here to solve the puzzle and needs our help to make it there first.

Either way, I have to get to that building, and I have to get in, past all those lights and mics, without anybody seeing me.

Since I'm on the run from the cops now.

I know South Lake Union well, down to a few padlock combinations on some gates behind the café we're next to. There's absolutely no way into the building named "MANTLE" without walking through the front door and scanning a badge.

A person wheels a big orange trash bin up from a ramp leading down to a loading dock behind MANTLE, and I crouch behind a tree, grateful that it's night and my brown sweater makes for perfect camouflage.

"Fine—go, then," says Spider. "I'll just be figuring out what Jax meant and looking into this before you walk straight into a trap." And I hear the car door shut behind me. I'm sure he's confused and frustrated, but it's almost better that he stays here while I get into the building.

The janitor parks the trash bin in front of the shallow steps leading up to the glass front door, where I see a spacious lobby with a thirty-foot wall that's cascading with running water. In front of that is a security counter, where I see a guy in a bright red hat.

Fear creeps through me, fastening me where I am behind this tree, as I realize there will be no walking through the front door of this place if he's here. Lucas was the same guy who shot a gun through a window in the middle of a crowded grocery store to frame Jax and Spider, over a cryptology puzzle.

There's no way I'm going near him.

But I look back at the janitor, who's now wheeling the orange trash bin farther down the way. He turns around and sweeps some leaves into his dustpan before walking even farther away. I look about twenty feet ahead of him at an empty chip bag sitting under a tree, and I know he's likely going to sweep it up, so this is my chance.

As quietly as the wind, and as sneakily as a rat, I slink forward close to the building, keeping to the shadows until I can safely make it across the street.

The janitor sweeps up the chip bag, and I hope the noise of the crinkling masks the sound of me putting both hands on the edge of the big orange bin, lifting my knees to my chest, jumping inside, and replacing the lid over my head. I quickly cover my mouth with my hood, and I wait.

It's pitch-black in here, and so dusty, but I take out my phone and watch it light up with a text from Spider.

SPIDER: What the absolute fuck was that stunt?? What if that guy wheels you out back and tries to pour you into a dumpster?

I smile.

ME: He won't.

The janitors with orange bins store them inside the Roundworld buildings. They're not emptied into dumpsters until the following morning when the daytime janitors arrive. It pays to pay attention. One of the things I love most about myself.

SPIDER: And what the hell am I supposed to do here while you go creeping around?

ME: What you do best.

SPIDER: I mean, duh, I'm already doing that. Finding plenty on the members of the Duwamish, but coming up empty on this meeting. No livestream, no minutes, nothing.

I wish I had time to help, but it's in Spider's hands now.

ME: Good luck. g2g.

And we're moving.

I can hear the wheels rumbling over the pavement and the door swing open as I'm wheeled into the lobby. The sound of the wheels grows soft, as I'm sure we're rolling over finished concrete, or marble or granite—something smooth and glossy. I can hear shoes squeaking against the floor, and I hear Lucas's voice now, tense with suppressed rage.

"Listen, asshole," he growls. "I'm offering you four hundred dollars and no more. I'm being more than generous, and you're lucky I have that much cash on me."

"I told you, I cannot be bought," says the security guard. "Now, you'll have to leave, or I'm going to have to call someone to escort you."

I stifle a giggle. Is Lucas really trying to *buy* his way into this place? He'll be lucky if that guard isn't working *for* the Order.

But just as I hear the elevator ding, I hear a sound I've heard before, late at night walking past bars and during the day when people get into skirmishes on the bus. The hollow thud of a fist against a face, and the rustling of clothing.

"Hey!" comes the security guard's voice. Those squeaky shoes ring out closer and closer, and I hear Lucas's voice *way* too close.

"Shut the door, *shut the door!*" he hollers. I can hear that he's shoved the janitor out of the way and is frantically clicking elevator buttons, but the security guard's voice booms again, also close.

"Young man, please exit the elevator. The authorities are on their way."

"*Fuck* you, man!" shouts Lucas before I hear his shoes squeak through the elevator doors and down the hallway. He's sprinting, but he probably won't get far.

I breathe a sigh of relief and stifle a cough, hoping this ride will be over soon.

It's not long before my hopes are answered, and the elevator dings open again. I hear an accordion door squeak open and I'm rolled inside, where I hear plastic clicking against plastic, and I feel the reverberation of the bin making contact with its brother bins. Once the door squeaks closed again and I hear the janitor's now-familiar footsteps shuffle away, I know it's safe to unlid this thing and hop out.

Way too easy.

ME: I'm in.

Not sure where I am, though. I look around in the darkness before leaning out the closet to make sure there's no one around.

SPIDER: Thank the universe.

"What the *fuck* are you doing here?!" bellows a voice from down the dark, dimly lit hallway. I look over my shoulder, feeling that trembling creeping into my hands as I clutch my phone close. That yell echoes through this place like the adrenaline you feel after being shocked by an electrical outlet. My chest hurts.

But I don't have time to breathe all of this away.

Because Lucas is running.

Straight at me.

Jax

Melinda drives like she's tryna star in *The Fast and the Furious: Seattle Drift* in these South Lake Union streets. It took us five minutes to get here, and I know from riding around with Han that it's supposed to take at *least* ten minutes with no traffic.

But we've got a puzzle to crash, so I don't say anything.

I just check my phone again for a message from literally anyone.

ME: I'm on my way to SLU to make sure you're all ok. I hope none of y'all are there.

I glance over at Karim, who a while back told me to look the other way so he could change back into his purple suit because he "wouldn't be caught dead in that thing," referring to the jumpsuit I'm still wearing because I'm too busy telling my friends not to die.

But now he's glued to his phone too, and pity floods me as I realize he's in the same boat as I am, and that anxiety is the same, even when wrapped in purple velvet.

"Anything from your crew?" I ask. He shakes his head without looking at me, fingers still flying.

"Sigge won't text me back, and Lucas . . . I never know what that buffoon is doing."

A snort escapes before I can cover my mouth.

"What's so funny?" he asks. *Now* he looks at me.

"I've just never met someone who uses the word 'buffoon' unironically."

"What's wrong with the word 'buffoon'?" he asks, genuinely confused.

"Nothing!" I assure him with a smile. "Nothing at all."

His eyes narrow like he doesn't believe me, but after a shrug he turns back to his phone and shuts it off before slipping it into his pocket with a sigh.

"We're not friends, you know," he says.

Yeah. Uh. I guessed that when he tried to run and leave me at the site of a fucking shooting.

"I mean, me and Lucas."

. . . Oh.

"Well, that's good, I guess." The hell else am I supposed to say? *Sorry you lost a friend?* He didn't. He lost a mentally unstable racist who happens to know him.

"I . . . can't believe he just left me there."

That pings something awake in my throat—half of me can't believe Karim really trusted that guy. And half of me can't believe Karim's parents let him trust him.

"He has to know what it meant for me to be there, right?" he asks. "I mean, because I'm . . ."

I smile.

"You ain't gotta say it, man," I reply, glancing up at Karim's mom out of habit. She may be his mom, but something buried deep in the back of my brain says if they're not my zaza, I have to be careful how I phrase things. "You and me. It means more for us to be places, you know?"

His eyes linger on me for half a second too long, and when he blinks and swallows, I realize he's holding back tears.

"Thanks," he says. "I . . . I think you're right."

And thus, the day came when Karim woke and realized, no matter how much money you got, how close-shaven your head, how purple your suit, how well versed you are in fancy-ass cheeses, you're still Black.

"So," I say, seizing the opportunity to change the subject, "Sigge mentioned she's new to ROYAL. Is that true?"

"I asked her to join ROYAL because we needed an athlete. She's the agility, Lucas is—was—the muscle, and yours truly is the brains."

Wow, that sounds conceited as hell. Isn't the whole team supposed to be "the brains"? That's how JERICHO works anyway. I may be the official "puzzler" of the group, since I started the forum, and hashing out clues is my favorite thing, but I couldn't do what I do without Yas's athleticism, or Spider's hacking skills, or Han's passion for, uh . . . secret infrastructure navigation.

We're *all* the brains.

"I just mean we all have a role to play," he says, pinching his purple collar and smiling at me. "Imagine me jumping from building to building in *this*."

Speaking of buildings, ours is coming up. I stare out the window as we round the corner, and my heart sinks. Simultaneously I hear Karim say behind me, "Oh no," while I say, "Oh shit."

Cars line the street in front of the building labeled "MANTLE"— no idea why Roundworld called it that. Maybe because the hearth is often the heart of the home? Nah, but that's spelled m-a-n-t-e-l. Maybe like its headquarters is to the company? Whatever the reason behind the name, the flag flying at the top is unmistakable. This really does have to be the last piece of the puzzle, as huge and sharp as that big white flag is with the red eye stamped on each side. The wind is surging through here tonight, sending the flag flapping angrily. And suddenly, to the left of the building, I catch a flash of white, and then another, and I realize it's Yas and . . . is that—

"Sigge!" exclaims Karim. "Mom, stop here! We've got it the rest of the way."

He swings open the Range Rover door and leaps out, taking off down the street faster than I ever knew anybody could run in a suit. Melinda looks over her shoulder at me apologetically, as if she wishes he hadn't left me so rudely. "He does track, you know," she says, looking through the windshield at him as he sprints down the sidewalk. "That's my baby."

My heart breaks for her, and I recognize in her tone that she just wants him to be safe. Which reminds me. I reach down into that plastic bag full of my clothes from the detention center until I find that familiar twine string and pull out Mama's amethyst crystal.

For protection.

I drape it around my neck and step out the door.

"I'll keep an eye on him, Melinda," I promise. "Thanks for the ride."

She smiles back at me and nods gratefully, and I shut the door and take off after Karim. *Damn* this kid can *move!* He's flying so fast, I can hardly keep up. I doubt even *Yas* could keep up, and I don't say that about just anyone. After barely glancing each way before darting into the road, I sprint out after him, startled at a blaring *HOOOOONK* that shoots through my ears and rattles my brain.

"Hey, what the hell, man?" comes an exasperated voice from the driver's seat.

"Sorry, sorry!" I say to the poor cab driver, whose headlights are bright enough to beam straight through my soul. But my attention is still across the street, where I see Yas and Sigge reaching the top of the building. I *have* to get up there before either of them can get to that flag!

"Yas!" I holler. But she keeps sprinting up the stairs ahead of

Sigge, her white hijab fluttering at her neck as she goes. I hurry after Karim as he grabs the scaffolding arm rail and hurls himself up the first row of steps.

"Sigge!" he yells after her. "Sigge, stop!"

"What?" she asks, stopping where she is to look down at us. "Karim?" Her face spreads into a smile! Sigge! Smiling! I had no idea it was possible! "Karim, you're okay! How did you get—"

"No time!" he snaps, pointing past Sigge to where Yas has just disappeared over the top of the roof. "Stop her!"

"Don't let her get that flag!" I scream as Karim begins running again, and I follow. When I glance up, Sigge looks *so* confused. I can only guess what questions are running through her head. She's probably wondering why Karim and I are working together, how we're both miraculously out of jail, and why we're both screaming at her to stop Yas before she can grab that flag and win this game.

Just yesterday, I wouldn't believe I'd be saying this, but I *cannot* let Yas win this game.

I hear a strange rustling from somewhere below me, and I glance down to where we just were on the ground, where a small crowd is gathering—only a few people standing there watching us all race up the side of the building. One guy toward the front yells:

"Hell yeah, they're taking over Roundworld!"

"They're attacking the building!" screams someone else.

"Down with the fucking establishment!" chants another.

Shit.

As much as I appreciate the passion from these folks, the last thing we need right now is an audience. I want to grab Yas, get back down those stairs, and go home quietly and without incident. Karim and I are already out on bail, and Yas is about to fall right into the hands of the cops. If she pulls that flag, I have no idea what might happen, but

I know the Order—the *real* Order—well enough to know it can't be good.

"Yas!" I say, turning my attention back to running after Karim, who's now disappearing over the side after Sigge. When I finally reach the top, I pull myself up onto the rooftop, where I see the worst thing I could've hoped to see.

Yas, standing there, pulling the flag from its stand in the middle of the roof as her eyes lock onto mine.

"Jax?"

Yas

I t all happens so fast.

One second, I'm elated, yanking this flag from its stand.

The next, I'm questioning the *pop* that I just heard from the now-empty holder.

Then I'm looking up at Jax and Karim, who are supposed to be in jail.

And Sigge is looking just as confused as I am.

And . . . is that . . . do I smell . . . *smoke*?

Han

It's dark in here.

And Lucas is sprinting at me.

"I'm gonna fucking kill you!" he shrieks.

There are a few things I can do at this point. Option 1: I can fight him. No, I can't. Not only am I a pacifist, but this kid is chaos personified, and I'm not about to take on a boy who fired a gun in a Thirty Foods to create a diversion. Option 2: I can run. No, I can't. Lucas is coming at me like a freight train. I can't run that fast in actual track clothes, let alone my jeans and sweatshirt. Option 3—

Before I can think of an option 3, my worst nightmare flares up again, like a raging flood of lava washing over me, covering my body in this awful tingly feeling, seeping into my ears and frying my brain. The blaring sound of a fire alarm.

Another one.

I resist the urge to collapse inward, to retreat. To crumple up into a little ball until this goes away. Lights flash angrily all the way down the hall, gluing me to the floor, but I know I have only seconds until Lucas reaches me, so I command force into my feet and hurry my screaming body the opposite way. I fly down the hall as fast as I can, past utility closet after utility closet, wondering how the hell I'm going to escape this kid.

"How'd you even get in here?" he bellows. "There's no way you paid the guard enough!"

Something inside me smirks at hearing that. You don't need to bribe people to get out of bad situations when you've had to be scrappy your whole life. I know so many Seattle buildings inside and out. I turn another corner, hearing Lucas's footsteps gaining behind me, and the light of the open elevator dwindles from the other side now that we've rounded the hallway in a U shape around the elevator shaft. And now, suddenly, I know what I have to do.

I go against every responsible piece of fire safety I've ever been taught.

I dart into the elevator.

The elevator that opens on both sides.

I hear Lucas jump in behind me just as I press the emergency lock button and hop through the opposite door. I turn just in time to see his tomato-red face hollering at me to "open this thing the fuck up" before the doors seal his screaming ass inside and begin to lower him safely to the ground floor.

But just as I'm able to smile and breathe a sigh of relief, I breathe in something else . . .

. . . smoke?

Jax

'm too late.

Yas is holding the flag.

The crowd below has erupted in cheering, and she and Sigge are both looking at Karim and me like they want an explanation. *Now.* So, I do the honors.

"Okay," I say, "I'm sure you're both confused about why this is bad."

"I'll say," says Sigge, folding her arms across her chest. "What are you both doing out of jail?"

"Money can get you out of almost anything," says Karim, beaming, as if it was his money and not Melinda's that got us out.

"You're out on bail?" asks Yas, just as a series of *pop pop pop*s ring out from somewhere below us. Gunshots?

"The hell was that?" I ask, knowing nobody here knows any more than I do. Whatever it is, I'm sure the Order knows, and it can't be good. Four different phone alert chimes ring out among us, and we all reach into our pockets to find a new post from the Order.

WE HAVE A WINNER. TEAM JERICHO.
STAY WHERE YOU ARE AND CLAIM YOUR PRIZE.
YOUR DEDICATION HAS PAID OFF.
TO JOIN OUR RANKS, LOOK TO THE SKIES.

I look at Yas, Sigge, and Karim in confusion at everything that's happening right now. The crowd growing at the base of the building has begun to chant, "Down with Roundworld! Down with Round-world! Down with Roundworld!"

"Jax? What's going on?" asks Yas, lowering the flag to her side.

Karim looks over at me like, *Better tell them now*, and I take a deep breath and—is that smoke I smell?

I look around at first but see no flames. The hell is going on?

"Jax!" demands Yas.

"You were right!" I blurt out. Even the words sear my tongue on the way out. I *still* don't want to believe it. "Yas, you were right. You were right about everything. The Order isn't who they say they are—"

"Jax, what are you saying?" she asks as little wisps of dark smoke rise up behind her. That smoke smell is getting serious now, and I realize those little wisps have turned to clouds, and they're all around us now, rising up from all sides, turning blacker and blacker, growing and growing. Karim lets out a cough, and Sigge covers her face and grunts, "The building's on fire! We have to get down!"

What? What the hell? How did the building catch fire?

The Order . . . They *wouldn't*. They *didn't*.

Did they?

"Come on," urges Yas, stepping forward and gripping me by my elbow. "You can explain later. Right now, we have to get down from here!"

A long, angry *CREEEEEAK* gives way somewhere beneath us, and Sigge stops where she is on the scaffolding steps, looking up at us through the bars.

"Guys?" she begins before the whole metal structure starts, ever so slowly, to buckle. "Guys!"

"Sigge!" shrieks Yas, throwing herself stomach-first to the edge of the roof. She reaches down to Sigge, and I instinctively dive forward and grab her ankle with all the strength I have. The smoke is thickening around us, and a cough grips my chest. Sparks are flying now, and I wonder how much longer we have before the whole building gives way.

"Do you have her?" I scream, hoping to the universe for a yes. I feel a set of strong arms grip my left ankle, and I look back to see Karim, stomach down, looking up at me, eyes narrow.

"Just saving my parents from more therapy costs."

This guy.

"I can't reach her!" hollers Yas, yanking her foot out of my grasp and pushing herself to her feet. "I'm going down to get her."

"What?!" Karim and I yell simultaneously.

This girl wants to jump down a metal staircase that's warping from the heat of the fire blazing in the building *we're standing on*? To save a girl from Team ROYAL?

"You're better off helping her from the ground," says Karim, and I nod in agreement. We're *all* better off on the ground. An explosive *boom! crack! pop!* rings out from behind us, and I jump and see a flurry of sparks fly up from an air vent on the other side of the roof.

"We're going to die up here, aren't we?" asks Karim. I look over and see tears glistening in his eyes as he kneels and clamps the side of the building overlooking the crowd at the bottom. People have backed away into the street and across the street on the opposite sidewalk. And now, to my horror, red and blue cop lights have lit up the whole road and sidewalk below us. One officer raises a bullhorn to his mouth and has the nerve to announce:

"We're here to help you. Please cooperate and no one has to get hurt. Help is on the way."

And right on cue, I hear chopper blades descending from out of the night sky.

LOOK TO THE SKIES.

A spotlight flashes on like somebody turned on their high beams after a long, sleepless night, and I shield my eyes and cover my nose and mouth with my sweatshirt sleeve. The chopper blades are blowing down on us so strongly, I have to brace against the ground just to avoid getting blown off.

"We're saved!" I hear Karim's voice over the *whip-whip-whip* of the thunderous blades.

"Don't!" I holler. "It's a trap, remember? They're going to arrest us for arson!"

"Why would they do that?" he asks.

"Don't you get it, Karim?" I scream, half to make sure I'm heard, and half from sheer rage. Sadness. Terror. I've been duped. We all have. And then I notice it. "The flag! Look at the holder!"

He follows my finger to the gaping hole where the flag used to be, where a single wire pokes out, spitting an occasional spark.

"They set all of this up to frame us!" I say as it all sinks in for me, too. "The police want any reason to put us back in jail. We're standing on top of Roundworld headquarters after waving around a resistance flag, as the building burns down around us. How the hell do you think this looks? They had us set up from the jump!"

A *clang!* cuts through the noise of the chopper blades and the crackling building as orange flames creep up and begin to lick the sides of the roof, and I turn around and realize Yas is no longer there.

"Yas!" I yell, hurrying to the side and peering over the edge. "Yas, have you lost your mind?!"

She's really climbing down. She's *really* climbing down there to save Sigge. The flames are licking the windows right next to her. She'll be lucky if her clothes don't catch fire before she even reaches her.

"Yas!!!!!" I scream until my voice breaks. My eyes are burning from tears and smoke, and I have to recoil from the edge before the flames reach my hands. I feel fingers on my shoulders, and Karim looks down at me in a full panic.

"We gotta go, man—there's no other way out of this," he says, although I can barely hear him over the chopper blades. He looks back to the middle of the roof, where there's now a man hanging from a ladder that extends all the way up to a huge black helicopter hovering about thirty feet up.

Shit.

The man is holding his hand out and yelling at us, his voice amplified by a mic.

"I'm here to help!" he insists.

But he has a badge.

He's in uniform, the word "SWAT" written across his lapel. And I know exactly where I'm going after climbing up that ladder and sitting down inside that helicopter.

Back to jail.

And eventually to prison.

But I have a plan. And my heart races as I step toward the man in the SWAT uniform.

"What are you doing?" hollers Karim over the noise. His purple suit is flapping in the harsh wind, and he's looking at me like I'm betraying him. All I can do is give him a wink and hope he can keep up. Then, when I know I'm about fifteen feet from the edge of the building where Yas and Sigge disappeared down the scaffolding, I turn and bolt.

I lock my eyes onto the gap between the buildings. Flames licking up the side of the building I'm standing on, coming for my shoes if I don't make it. The scaffolding creaks and lurches downward just before I reach the edge.

Just before I plant my shoe on the black beam, then the other.

"Jax!" hollers Karim from behind me.

But I barely hear him.

I'm flying through the air, feet-first like Yas taught me, arms outstretched, Mama's amethyst necklace going airborne in front of me, rising up in front of my eyes as either a nod of good luck or goodbye, depending on where my feet land.

I see the brick wall in front of me rising too fast. My feet sail down, down. My hands reach out as far as they'll go.

My fingers find the rough brick edge, and my feet find the wall, and just like Yas taught me, I bounce myself against the wall and launch myself up and over, rolling to cool, dusty safety on the other side.

I find myself looking up at the clouds, such a dark hazy gray against the navy sky that I almost can't see them. Black plumes of smoke billow up from Roundworld's headquarters to my right, and I take a deep breath of cool, clean-ish air. But a sharp, shrill screech cuts through the moment like a serrated knife.

"Jax! Help!" I hear Karim shriek. I look over to see his knuckles clamped over the edge of the building, and I push myself up and dive for him.

"I'm right here!" I yell, clamping my hands around his wrists. He's looking up at me with eyes wide, full of tears, the orange glow of the flames behind him burning my eyes. Cinders are flying through the air, singeing my face, and I shut my eyes against them.

"Please don't let me die!" He cries up at me, *"Please!"*

I remember how Melinda looked at me before I got out of that Range Rover, and I grit my teeth and *pull* with all the strength I have in me. He comes up slowly, painfully. Every muscle in my arms and back are screaming, but I don't let go. I can't.

I promised.

He's up and over, and we both collapse backward.

"Oh my god!" he screams. "We made it!" And then his huge eyes narrow and his face darkens with rage. "You're insane, you know that?! Leaping off buildings like you're Miles Morales, what the hell's wrong witchoo?"

I caught that last blending of "with" and "you" at the end there. Even the bougiest of us start blending words when we're mad, huh? I smile.

"But we made it, didn't we?"

The helicopter spotlight is trained on us in an instant, now that we're both over here, and that bullhorn guy is at it again.

"Surrender now, and no one has to get hurt!"

Oh, before it was *I'm here to help*, and now all of a sudden it's *Surrender*?

"You realize we're both getting arrested tonight, right?" asks Karim as his shoulders fall in defeat.

"Not up here we're not," I say, lifting my hands in the air. "If I'm getting arrested or killed tonight, it's gonna happen in front of *all* those phone cameras," I say, nodding down to the crowd, then glancing at the rooftop stairwell in the corner. I keep my eyes moving, across the way and along the ground, hoping to see a trace of white amid the smoke. But it's all too thick. I look up at Karim, who catches my drift, nods, and we both race, hands still in the air, to the stairwell before scampering down and preparing to meet whatever fate is about to befall us.

I reach up and clutch the amethyst.

Yas

can almost reach you!" I scream, barely recognizing my own voice. A fit of coughs overtakes my throat, and I cover my mouth and nose with my graying sleeve. All I smell is the bitter stench of burning plaster. Black smoke is all around us. I reach my free hand down toward Sigge, whose hands are clamped around the bottom rung of the ladder. Her legs dangle under her, a sheer drop of about forty feet below her.

Below both of us.

I ease my body farther forward until my fingertips touch hers. Something heaves below us both, creaking and screaming as the metal buckles. Sigge's eyes double in size, and she snatches away her hand that just touched mine and grips the scaffolding with both hands again.

This structure won't hold much longer.

"Sigge, listen to me!" I scream, feeling a strategy bloom in my head. We're up much too high to make such a jump. Forty feet? That means broken ankles, broken pelvises, and maybe even worse. But if we wait . . . if we time this just perfectly . . . "Sigge, when I say jump, you have to jump, okay? Not before!"

"You want me to *what*?!" she shrieks. I've never heard her sound so panicked before.

"Please, trust me!"

Creeeeeeak!

I'm thrown forward, and even I have to use both hands to hang on to the scaffolding. I feel my feet being thrown up into the air and over my head, and instead of gripping the bar so tightly to keep myself latched onto it, I loosen my grip, and fall into gravity.

I roll forward, letting the bar rotate in my fists until I'm dangling off the structure, my feet feeling nothing beneath them. And I wait.

I look down, where Sigge is still hanging on to her own bar, looking up at me, scared to death.

"Didn't they teach you anything about timing in gymnastics?" I smirk, trying to find a scrap of humor in this moment, since it might be either of our last. Her mouth tugs at one corner and her eyes warm just barely.

"Of course," she huffs, descending into another fit of coughs.

"You can do this," I urge.

Another lurch from the metal, and then I realize we're still moving. Slowly.

This thing is still creaking.

And we're *still* moving.

I look over my shoulder and . . . what the hell? The building is moving away from us! The scaffolding is bending behind me! It kneels and buckles so smoothly, I would never have noticed if I hadn't looked.

"Yas?" asks Sigge.

"Not yet," I say, almost a whisper. I concentrate, and I calculate. If I calculate this wrong, we could both lose our lives.

"Yas??" she asks again.

Twenty feet.

"Not yet!"

Ten feet.

"Yas!!" Sigge screams.

"Now!!" I holler, swinging my feet forward and uncurling my fingers from the bar. I'm flying through the air in slow motion. This has to be one of the most chaotic moments of my parkour career. Leaping from a moving base that's falling apart due to flames from the building it's attached to, jumping toward a ground I can barely see through black smoke, with another person somewhere else in the smoke, jumping from the same structure, hoping I don't run into her or land on her.

But guess what.

I'm Yasmin Emami.

And Yasmin Emami *always* makes the jump.

My feet connect with the pavement, and I tuck and roll into it four or five times before finding my footing again, however shakily, and stumbling back against the building across the alleyway, struggling to catch my breath. I cover my nose and mouth with part of my hijab, unable to contain my coughs.

"Sigge?" I scream through the smoke. My eyes are burning, and so is my throat, but I look through this alley for any flashes of platinum blond hair. The scaffolding, even as it clings to the side of the Roundworld building, is empty. Sigge is gone.

She's got to be somewhere on the ground.

"Sigge!" I yell again, just as I hear it.

A cough so faint, at first I think I've imagined it.

"Sigge?" I ask.

And then that almost-white hair, now dingy with soot and dust from the smoke. Her black sleeve is covering her nose and mouth as she stumbles forward, and I rush to grab her and hold her as she crumples to her knees.

"Sigge, this way! The scaffolding is coming down!"

She looks up at me, her face tired, her whole body wanting to go limp in my arms. But she nods weakly and pushes herself to her feet, and follows me.

Trusts me.

I sling her arm over my shoulder and push all my energy into my legs, which are throbbing with pain now that they've had time to absorb the shock of jumping from such a height. But I have to keep going, for both of us now. I feel Sigge's fingers wrap around mine and squeeze.

"Yasmin?" she asks.

"Yeah?"

The crash behind us comes suddenly—we don't have time to say more. I glance up at the mess of black metal barreling down on us, and I grip her arm and dive forward to the ground. I roll out of the way, and our hands are ripped apart as a whoosh of black dust and soot rushes straight at my face.

I cough and rub my eyes.

"Sigge?" I call out, my voice an unrecognizable croak. I sit up halfway, sideways and awkwardly, and I try to fan away the smoke and look for her hair again. Her face. Any trace of her.

"Sigge!"

And then I hear more coughing. And then I see her hair. And then she looks up at me.

She crawls closer.

"Yas?" she asks, dragging her sleeve across her mouth. Her eyebrow is marked with a red gash, a trickle of blood beginning down past her eye.

"You're bleeding," I say, reaching forward instinctively.

"Yas," she says again. She reaches me, but she doesn't stop. She climbs over my feet first, then my legs, until her legs are over my hips, warm against me. I feel a different kind of heat flood my face, my cheeks, my whole body. I feel something trickle from my hairline down my cheek, and I wonder if it's blood or sweat or both, and she leans down close to me and whispers, like she almost can't believe it herself.

"We're alive."

She's *so* close to me. Her ice-blue eyes. Her soft pink lips. Her cheeks, flushed from the heat of this place, of *us*.

"Yeah . . . we are," I say, marveling at all of this myself.

We really made it.

She brushes her fingers against my cheek.

I reach up and loop my arms around her, pulling her down into an embrace and enjoying the warmth of her. And suddenly, somehow, although I have no idea what I'm doing, I feel free.

"There's two of them!" yells a voice I recognize. I look up, and the rush is gone. I can feel the blood draining from my face as my eyes lock in on two cops darting straight at us. That voice. I know it.

As the cops descend on us, ripping Sigge from me, even as our eyes lock onto each other's, I hope she understands what I want to say right now: *It's going to be okay.*

And then the voice, closer this time, appears again, with a "Thought you could run forever, huh?" I'm lying on my stomach, hands pressed against my back, cold handcuffs snapped over my wrists, and I see red shoes, inches from my face. I crane my neck to look up, the smoke burning my lungs with every breath. And I see a red hat.

"You're all so goddamn stupid," he says. "Thought you could out-smart the law. Good luck taking down Roundworld when you're *under* the jail."

Horror sinks into me as I hear him snorting in dramatically, and I shut my eyes, prepared to feel the spit on my face, but it never comes.

"Son!" exclaims the cop who's still straddling my back. "Don't.

That's assault. She'll get her consequences. Both of them will."

Son, he'd said.

So, Lucas was in on this the whole time. A mole. I wonder if Karim knew his "speed" was secretly ratting all of us out. Or if Sigge knew, for that matter. I look over at her, lying next to me with her face pressed to the pavement. She glances up at Lucas and rolls her eyes before looking back over at me.

"I should've seen that coming," she says.

Spider

This car is getting toasty.

My eyes are glued to my phone. Sweat is running down my forehead as my thumbs fly. I am *deep* into correspondence I shouldn't be reading. Emails. Text records. Encrypted areas of the forum most people can't access. My eyes fly over usernames I've seen floating around on posts from the Order.

PLUTO: Hey how's Clue 2?

SAMSHUNG: Great, no way to get out.

PLUTO: Brilliant with the alarm at the precinct.

SAMSHUNG: Thx

PLUTO: They'd never expect cops to attack their own.

My eyes narrow. That fire drill at Shannon High, and the one at police HQ. No wonder "The Order" was able to set off both alarms. The police have access to *both* systems.

PLUTO: Got confirmation letter.

SAMSHUNG: Got it.

I find an email sent just a few hours prior entitled "Pacific Insurance Inc. confirmation of coverage" and read.

"Officer Hank, please find enclosed a detailed record of general liability insurance for Roundworld Inc. If you have any questions, I'm only an email away. Godspeed."

I open the letter to find *way* too much insurance talk, and then I find a reply to this email that just says, "So they're in?" and a reply to *that* email with a winking emoji.

So wait . . .

Why is Roundworld sending the cops their insurance information? And why the hell are the cops acting all smug about it? I've already pieced together that the cops are behind "The Order." I can only hope *someone* out there on the Vault reads this post. I hit submit.

THE ORDER IS 12, ABORT MISSION, GO HOME

I have a feeling that's what Jax had meant when he told JERICHO to steer clear of SLU.

A fire truck blares past, flying down the street past where Han parked, startling me back into reality, and that's when I see it.

The flames.

The flames that are flying out the glass windows of that refurbished brick MANTLE building, which is now probably as hot as the earth's mantle. The flames that might have . . . consumed my friends.

My heart is racing.

What the hell do I do? What the hell do I do? What the hell do I do?!

Shit, the *building's on fire*! Do I go over there? Do I stay? I send another frantic text.

ME: WHERE ARE Y'ALL?!

Please be okay.

My eyes are welling with tears at the realization that I have no idea how long the building's even been on fire. I've been so engrossed in . . .

And then everything clicks.

The cops set up this game to catch us—a bunch of kids who have committed to taking down Roundworld—putting us in alleys and stores and dumpsters and golf carts and other places we have no business being in, hoping to arrest us. Now they've put us at the top of Roundworld's headquarters, and the Duwamish representatives are inside Roundworld's headquarters, and the cops set it on fire to make it look like we did it.

And Roundworld agreed.

For publicity. And as a bonus, insurance money.

So they're in?

Oh, they're in all right.

They're in *deep*.

I'm still staring up at the building, the black smoke billowing from the roof, flames licking the wall outside above the windows. *Please* let them be okay.

Let them all be okay.

I look down at my phone and read the words again.

So they're in?

What can I do?

Here I am, stuck in Han's car without a key, a wanted fugitive by now, I'm pretty sure, with evidence in my hands that could ruin people's lives if it gets into the *wrong* hands.

Or . . . the *right* ones. Jax's words come back to me.

Think I won't enforce the rules?

And the first rule of the forum: *The rules must be followed.*

Would leaking personal conversations between Roundworld and 12 count as breaking the rules? Or . . . would I be shining a light on the rule-breakers? Would breaking the rules be justified if I'm outing the original rule-breakers?

Tae-Jin Hyung's face pops up into my head. I remember his words about lying low and keeping our heads down and—

What would this do to us? To Umma's restaurant and everyone who works there? They're my family! They've all worked so hard to be there, living in peace, working in peace in a safe place. Am I willing to put their lives on the line for this?

For what I'm about to do.

I make my choice.

And then I open up every single social media platform I can think of.

LEAKED ROUNDWORLD EMAILS REVEAL ALL

ANONYMOUS WHISTLEBLOWER SOUNDS ALARM

ROUNDWORLD AT CENTER OF INSURANCE FRAUD?

ALLEGATIONS OF INSURANCE FRAUD HIT ROUNDWORLD

COMMUNITY GARDEN DEMOLITION HALTED AMID ROUNDWORLD ALLEGATIONS

ROUNDWORLD FACES ALLEGATIONS OF INSURANCE FRAUD—LAND REPURPOSE DEAL ON HOLD

Yas

t's been a week since Roundworld HQ was reduced to a black shell of a building.

Since we were all arrested.

Since Spider leaked the emails, and the documents, and the text conversations.

And I'm walking down the sidewalk just a few blocks away from where it all happened, out on bail, walking free, for now.

No more parkour for at least a few weeks, though. Jumping down melting scaffolding will put a girl off that for a while. I'm doing some good old-fashioned walking, to Abba's store. The sun is out, surprisingly, since it's April in Seattle. But the breeze rolling in off Lake Union ripples through my clothes and reminds me to breathe deeply.

And there it is.

The store that I might have saved, inadvertently. With Roundworld HQ gone, with that cafeteria gone, Abba's customers have picked up. Mostly people who live locally and used to eat his biryanis and kormas and mithais before the cafeteria opened. Even now, a woman walks out holding one of his lovingly boxed-up heat-and-eat lunches, and as she walks past me, she smiles. I doubt she knows I'm related to him, or that I'm one of the "rebels" who "burned down the refinery headquarters," but I smile back, knowing she's helping a small business thrive—a small business that's very, very dear to me.

I turn and walk up the steps to the glass door and swing it open to find several people milling around looking at products. One guy who seems to be in a huge hurry opens a fridge, grabs a box, and raises it so my father can see from the counter.

"Put it on my tab, sir!" exclaims the man before rushing past me and flying out the door. Abba waves in the guy's direction with the biggest smile I've seen on him in a while. Then he notices me.

"Ah, my Yasmin," he says, arms outstretched as he makes his way around the counter to me. I step into his warm embrace and press my cheek against his chest.

"Salaam, Abba," I say. He smells like delicious food and patchouli, black pepper and cardboard boxes, probably from unboxing inventory in the back before he opened the store this morning. "Looks like business is booming again," I say, stepping behind the counter as two customers step up to the register, each with two meals in hand.

"Would you like a bag?" asks Abba. They nod, and soon he's rung up and bagged forty-eight dollars' worth of product. I marvel at those who spend twelve dollars on a meal I eat every week or so with my family. It's nothing so special, but as Abba says, *If they'll pay nine dollars for a boxed salad, they'll pay twelve dollars for homemade meals.*

He takes the broom off the wall around the corner and begins sweeping dust from under the counter back here.

"You know, dear," he says softly, "I have you to thank."

"For burning down a building?" comes Ranya's voice from behind me. She bites into a crisp apple and leans on the counter. Then, seeing Abba's face, she winks. "Kidding."

"No," says Abba, quite seriously. He rests the broom against the counter, crouches so he can look me in the eye, and takes both my hands in his. "That *weed* of a company was killing everything around it. Poisoning the neighborhood. You and your friends uprooted it. You exposed its twisted network for what it was, and now we have some hope. This place has its customers back."

"Most of them," says Ranya. Abba narrows his eyes at her. "What?" she asks, taking another bite. "I'm just being realistic here. Anyway, yeah, sis—you, uh . . . you really did take them down from the inside. Well done."

I roll my eyes and have to smile, knowing that's as close to a compliment as I'm going to get from her.

"Thanks, Ranya," I say, turning to Abba. "Thank you, Abba."

To my surprise, his eyes are glistening, and he cups my face and smiles.

"I'm honored to have you for a daughter," he says, looking up at Ranya. "You too."

"Gee, thanks," she says with a smirk. He extends his arm out to her, she joins us behind the counter, and soon we're all wrapped in one big cardboard-pepper-patchouli-perfume bear hug, Ranya and me encircled in Abba's arms.

My phone beeps with a tone I know well—a special tone I've reserved for *her*—and the minute the hug is over, I can't pull out my phone and read it fast enough.

SIGGE: Hey, it's nice out. Meet me at the sculpture park for some partner yoga?

Partner yoga?

A million feelings swirl through my head, none of which I'm ready to process. It's been a lot. Roundworld. My parkour aspirations. Sigge, of course. I feel my face warming at the thought her and the word "partner."

Abba raises an arm above his head and leans backward, sending a flurry of crackles up his spine. I shudder at the sound, but he looks relieved.

"Ah," he says. "Time to flip the sign."

Ranya doesn't take *half* a second to jump into my business.

"Is that *her*," she whispers.

"Shh," I urge, as Abba doesn't know yet and I'm not ready to tell him.

"You can't hide it from me," says Ranya, resting a hand on my shoulder. "But . . . when you're ready, I'll be here for you." I smile at her, grateful, and nod. But my thoughts are swirling, orbiting around that one word: *partner*.

ME: Will there be snacks?

SIGGE: Partner snacks? Coming on a little strong, don't you think? ;)

ME: Regular snacks, between partners.

SIGGE: So that's a yes, then?

ME: Depends what the question is.

There's a long pause where that ellipsis springs to life and vanishes, and my heart is thundering.

SIGGE: Will you be my partner?

Oh my god. What do I even say? I can't text back fast enough.

ME: Still playing games, I see?

SIGGE: We'll see.

I do something I've *never* done. I send a heart emoji. She sends one back. And I make up an excuse to leave the store, sprinting through the city to the sculpture park to join . . .

. . . *her.*

Han

The kitchen is quiet except for the sound of a bird chirping just outside in the tree by our front door. It's pleasant. And grounding. The sun is brilliant outside, summer peeking its face around the corner to tell me it's on its way. My phone dings with a text notification.

SPIDER: Hey, man. My attorney is dope. Here's her info.

Then he sends a link to Annette Coleman and Associates.

ME: Thanks.

SPIDER: Also, wanna come over later for some food and meditation?

ME: What kind of food? Also, yes.

SPIDER: Any kind of food! Let's order something and go over our legal shit together.

That lifts a weight off my chest. There's been so much paperwork to go through, and it's hard to make sense of it all alone. I haven't found an attorney yet—well, until the reference Spider just sent me.

ME: Yes, please.

SPIDER: Sweet! My place around 7?

ME: Ready your food-ordering fingers.

The kitchen door unlocks and swings open. Dad steps through and looks at me with a smile.

"Hey, man, where's your brother?" he asks. I shrug.

Haven't seen him since he left for the store about an hour ago. Dad nods and opens the fridge. Maybe drinking beer reminds him of his older son, who talks to him whenever he feels like talking. Dad hasn't said much to me since the fire, and I wonder if he's disappointed, if he believes what they're saying on some news stations, that we're a bunch of degenerates and hoodlums wreaking havoc on the workplaces of innocent people, or other news stations that say we're standing up for what's right and taking down a company behind one of the biggest insurance fraud claims in the history of corporate America.

I wonder which ones he believes.

He sits down and cracks open the beer, the hiss of the can filling the room where silence was.

"Hey, so, listen," he says. "Son."

He glances down at my hand and holds out his own, inviting me to take it. I smile at him and do so, feeling the warmth of his fingers close around mine.

"I, um . . . I just wanted you to know that I'm proud of you, okay?"

It warms me inside, makes me feel like I've done something right. Proud of me? For what? He swallows and stares down at my hand. "Whatever happens to the kayaking business, I'm not going to let anything happen to you, okay? You're *not* going to live with Mom. I don't care what I have to do. It's like I've always said—Mom left because of Mom, and not because of you, okay?"

Sure. He says that, but I know it's just to make me feel better. But what he says next? With tears in his eyes? He looks me straight in the face and says with a passion I haven't heard from him, ever, "Mom doesn't know what she's missing. Everywhere you go, things seem to get better. I'm proud, *so* proud, to be your father."

There's a long pause where I don't know what to do or say. I mean, I'm happy. I'm *really* happy. I want to jump up and run around and scream in elation at hearing this. My dad? Proud of me? His younger son who he had to remeet all over again after my diagnosis? His son who is too young to drink a beer with him? Well, technically, *both* of us are too young, but . . . I guess his son who's *way* too young to drink a beer with him.

I smile, and I realize I . . . I want to hug him? I want to hold him? I stand up and reach down to him, and amid his shock and surprise at my gesture, he jumps to his feet and pulls me into the coziest hug I've gotten in a while. He's warm, and he smells like pine and freshly cut grass. I close my eyes and rest my chin on his soft flannel-covered shoulder.

"I love you, son," he whispers.

I sigh and let my eyes close, basking in the warmth of this closeness, and I nod. And I know he knows I love him too.

Spider

This paperwork is bullshit.

The amount of forms I've gotta fill out, dates I've gotta remember, receipts I've gotta produce, and names I've gotta drag is exhausting. All I did was expose possibly the whole Seattle police force and a Fortune 5 company based in one of the most densely populated neighborhoods in the state, for insurance fraud and corruption. I already did the work. Now I just want to rest on my laurels, eat my imported shrimp-flavored potato chips, and focus on moving on with my life.

But I know that's not possible.

Even though I'm a minor and my attorney, Annette, is trying to protect my identity as best as she can, I know I'll have a target on my forehead for a while, if not the rest of my life. If there's one thing I know about 12, it's that they don't play. Annette told me they're saying "The Order" was actually two rogue retired cops, not the whole force. Fine, I'll buy that. Maybe. But I'm still off social media and using my heavily protected burner phone.

I hear a knock at my door and look up from where I'm lounging on my beanbag.

"Come in," I say, but before I can even say the word "in," the door is easing open and Umma is peering through the crack.

"Daeshiiiiim, my love," she coos, stepping inside holding a small ceramic bowl of something with steam rising from it. "I made dak juk.

The onions are from Jax's mama's garden! So fresh and fragrant."

I smile as I take the bowl and lift it under my nose. She's right. The veggies from Mama's garden are just—chef's kiss—otherworldly. My phone dings with a text, but I leave it alone, because Umma is lowering herself to her knees in front of me. She reaches out and guides the bowl in my hands to the table beside my bed, and takes both my hands in hers.

"My Daeshim," she says, kissing my fingers, "I must tell you something."

Oh god. This is it. The moment she tells me the business is going under, the moment she tells me Seoul Food will be a thing of the past, the moment she tells me we have to leave the Pacific Northwest for cheaper pastures.

But she doesn't.

Instead, she squeezes my hand and says, "When you were born, I was *so* happy to be a mother. And then, when you told me the news, that I have a *son* . . . well, it took me a while. Lots of questions. But I learned to be happy all over again."

I swallow, my jaw burning, threatening tears.

"Thanks, Umma," I say.

"*And,*" she says, "when you told me *new* news, that my son found criminal information and took down a company that ruins so many lives"—her face is twisted into a grimace now—"I was more proud of you than I thought I could be."

No way.

Umma? The one who's all about rules and order and bending her menu to meet the needs of the masses?

"I am *so* proud," she continues, "to have a son who fights for what is right, even when it's hard."

She kisses my fingers again, and before I can think to say more, I throw my arms around her neck and hold her close. She nuzzles her face into my neck and plants kisses all over it.

"I love you, Umma," I croak, my voice breaking.

"And I love you," she says.

I sigh. Whatever happens with the lawyers and the paperwork and the inevitable courtrooms and appearances, right now, in this moment, in Umma's arms, I'm okay.

"Oh!" she exclaims suddenly, pulling back and looking me up and down. "You haven't eaten today!"

Have I really not eaten a single thing?

I woke up.

I opened my laptop.

I read new emails from . . . well . . . everyone I know, about Roundworld, about my friends, about what happens now. And I've been here ever since.

I guess I really haven't eaten anything.

I shrug sheepishly, without explanation.

"Eat your dak juk. I'll go cut up some oranges and pears."

"Umma, please, this is plenty—"

"They're fresh from Pike Place Market!" she says, standing up. "You can't power your brain without fuel. Oh, and I forgot to tell you. About Tae-Jin."

My ears perk up at the mention of his name. He hasn't been to the restaurant since he left to pick up his sister from the hospital. I've feared the worst. Maybe somebody . . . I don't know . . . is torturing him in a back room somewhere for info about me, related to the forum. My chest tightens at the thought that something might have happened to him . . . happened to his whole family. Because of me.

I muster the courage to ask.

"What about Tae-Jin Hyung?"

Jax

My bingo card is completely shot. A week ago, it was missing so many things.

The incident at Thirty Foods.

Getting arrested.

Getting bailed out by the captain of Team ROYAL.

Racing to stop my teammates from "winning" the game I would've given my life to win just days before.

Busting a police-corruption-and-insurance-fraud scandal *wide* open.

Eating Mama's pulled "pork" sandwiches made with jackfruit, with coleslaw from carrots and cabbage from the garden. The garden that gets to stand for so much longer, hopefully, now that Roundworld is busy explaining to the public why emails between their executives and two rogue cops seem to depict them enticing teens into compromising situations in the hopes of arresting them, in exchange for facilitating a wildly high-profile insurance fraud scheme that endangered the lives of several Duwamish committee members. As a shock to no one, Lucas's dad was one of the cops involved, and he was in on it the whole time. Sigge turned out to be pretty cool. Yas certainly thinks so. I'm just glad they're happy. And Karim?

Karim is sitting right across from me, leaning against a raised garden bed, lifting a jackfruit sandwich to his lips and taking a big bite. Another event that wasn't on my card: Karim finding out his dad was arrested as one of the executives at Roundworld and having to go into hiding at the request of his mother, Melinda, since she'll be busy answering questions for the next few weeks at least, and their house isn't safe for Karim anymore.

Karim is now sitting with me and my family in the very garden his dad tried to destroy.

"You know," he says, "this is actually incredible!"

"You sound surprised." Ava smiles, taking bite and crossing her feet one over the other in the dirt.

Two small children sprint down the path between us, laughing and chasing each other, the one in the lead carrying a basket of mushrooms and the one behind carrying a watering can.

"No, no!" says Karim, holding up his hand apologetically. "I only meant that I'm not used to vegan food tasting so . . . you know . . ."

"Good?" I ask.

"I was going to say *flavorful*, but have it your way," says Karim, taking another bite. "I mean, this is so moist and just—"

"All right, man, cool it or it'll go to Zaza's head." I smirk, watching Zaza turn their attention from the greenhouses to us.

"Hey, I can take a compliment, or two, or three, or fifty-seven. Keep 'em coming."

Mama walks up behind Karim with a basketful of carrots.

"Look at what's come up!" she says before leaning down and planting a kiss on Zaza's lips. A kiss that just . . . keeps going.

"Jesus, Mom, *must* you?" I ask.

"Since you're the *teenager*," she says, setting the basket down on the counter and putting her hand on their shoulder as she looks at me, "aren't I supposed to be ruining your fun?"

"You already let Constable Killjoy stay with us," I say, sending a playful smile at Karim.

"Don't you think things might get a little confusing between you calling me Constable and me calling—"

"Don't even say it again."

"Say what?" Zaza just *has* to ask. Karim turns around to look at them and says:

"Themperor."

Oh god, the cheese on this guy.

"What?" Karim asks as Mama starts to chuckle.

Ava rolls her eyes and asks, "Yeah, actually, what's up with that word? 'Themperor'?"

"Listen, if Mama gets to be the queen of this house, and you get to be the princess, and Jax gets to be the prince, then Zaza gets to be the 'themperor.' I don't make the rules. That is, if they're okay with it?"

Zaza nods from the couch.

"I like it!" they say. "'Themperor' has a ring to it. But you can just call me Jesse, as decreed by the themperor."

"Jesse it is," says Karim, standing up with his now-empty plate. "Excellent meal. Is there more?"

"Right up there in the white Crock-Pot," says Mama, nodding toward the gazebo where several people are milling around with plates full of food made from things grown right here, all around us.

I look over at Ava, who's scrolling through something on her phone, taking advantage of Mama's leniency about phones at the table when guests are over. And when we're not technically at a "table."

"Hey," I say quietly. So quietly, she doesn't hear me. *"Hey."*

She looks up at me, startled, and I lean in.

"I'm sorry for how I treated you when we were doing the puzzle," I say. "It was wrong. I snapped at you, and you didn't deserve it. And . . . after talking to the cops at the detention center, I, um . . ."

What do I say to her? I can't get into how the cops have pictures of her on the front lines of protests, and how she's probably okay since only her closest friends and family would be able to identify her from that picture of her eyes alone, without taking up the whole lunch conversation. Plus, Mama and Zaza and Karim don't need to know about her activism until she *wants* to tell them.

"After talking to the cops at the detention center, I think we should grab lunch somewhere sometime, and, I don't know . . . talk?"

She raises an eyebrow at me, but a smile curves her mouth.

"Sure, little bro," she says, "and apology accepted."

I nod. *God*, I misunderstood her. My sister. My sister who's always journaling and looking inward and retreating into her room, on the front lines of protests, I assume without Mama and Zaza knowing a thing.

I'm so proud to be her brother.

"All right, so," says Mama as she and Karim return and take their seats on the logs behind us, nestled into the dirt, framing the path. Zaza soon follows with a plate of their own. My phone beeps with a message.

HAN: Thanks, everyone.

ME: For what?

SPIDER: For being awesome, of course.

HAN: For being my friends.

YAS: Course, Han! Pleasure's all ours. And thanks, everyone, for sticking together through all of this.

SPIDER: We may not have won the puzzle, but we damn sure got some power.

I have to smile at that.

ME: Yeah, I guess we did.

HAN: So, Jax . . . are you still going to try to track down the real Order and join them?

JAX: Pretty sure I'm done with the Order for now, real or not.

And I mean it. Sure, the *real* Order is super glamorous and all, but after all of this, they haven't taken interest in what's happened here, in what the people of Seattle—the *kids* of Seattle—have done to protect what we love, so maybe my time is better spent here, in the Vault, with the people I love.

SIGGE: So . . . what now? . . . Are we still going to be two teams? Karim and I don't exactly make a whole unit by ourselves.

ME: I think a 6-person team would be pretty dope.

YAS: What would we call ourselves?

HAN: A blend of JERICHO and ROYAL?

SPIDER: Royalicho? Jeroyal?

SIGGE: Jeroyal sounds like something that'll have you unconscious under a table after a few sips too many.

ME: Something to commemorate all of this, everything we just went through.

We've come so far together in just a few days. It has to be something *good.*

My phone dings with another message.

KARIM: How about the Jump?

I look up at Karim as he looks up at me, his smile warm and eyebrows raised in anticipation. The Jump. To commemorate *the* jump that almost got Karim and me killed last week? Or that jump that Han took through the elevator to escape Lucas? Or the jump that Yas took to save Sigge on the scaffolding? Or the jump that Spider took when he leaked everything? Or the fact that this whole thing was rigged from the jump? Or "The Jump" to mean the beginning of something new?

We'll go with the last one, I decide. I nod up at Karim.

ME: I like it.

Spider

Umma shuts the door, and I open the letter with trembling hands. It's written entirely in Korean. And it mentions no names.

> Hey, man.
> Thanks so much. For everything. I can't say much,
> because, you know, the situation at hand. But I'm
> doing well. I'm safe. And so is my sister.
> I get my degree in two months.
> And I have a new employer.
> They're the real deal.
> They make things happen.
> Call me if you're interested.

I read it again and again.
No way.
The real deal?
They make things happen?
Tae-Jin Hyung . . . who exactly . . .

ACKNOWLEDGMENTS

When I dedicated this book to everyone who is sick and tired, I meant it. We are the arbiters of change. And when I said we're going to make it, I meant it. None of us are alone in wanting better for this world.

The inspiration for *The Jump* started when I read about the events of the Cicada 3301 puzzle (it's quite an interesting story if you enjoy mystery and intrigue), and I realized that if a group of teens got into cryptology and encountered such a puzzle, I'd want to read about it.

So, I wrote about it.

Thank you to everyone who continues to give my chaotic ideas credence, starting with my agent, Quressa, for always seeking the absolute best for me and my work.

Thanks to my editor, Deeba, who (I don't know how you do it) handled so much in so little time. Thank you infinitely for keeping these characters three-dimensional and root-able (root-for-able?)—I'm sure you know the best way to phrase that.

Thank you to all three sensitivity readers who made Han, Yas, and Spider come to life. They are real characters because of your emotional labor, honesty, and detailed critiques. Thank you for helping me to write responsibly.

Thank you to my closest friends—Becca Boddy, Jackie Mak, Sydney Clark, Annastasia Nuñez, Ari Bloom, Alexandra Keister, Christopher Mikkelson, Eric Smith, Roseanne Brown, Laurie Halse Anderson, Grayson Toliver, Aaron Oaks, and James Stoner. I love you all.

To my love—my husband—Steven, who has overcome so much to be as incredible as you are. Thank you for taking care of me and you. I wouldn't have anyone else. And to my son, who already takes on the world with more curiosity than I could have hoped for, never stop learning. Never stop asking questions. Explore all you want, not-so-little one, and the world will meet you.